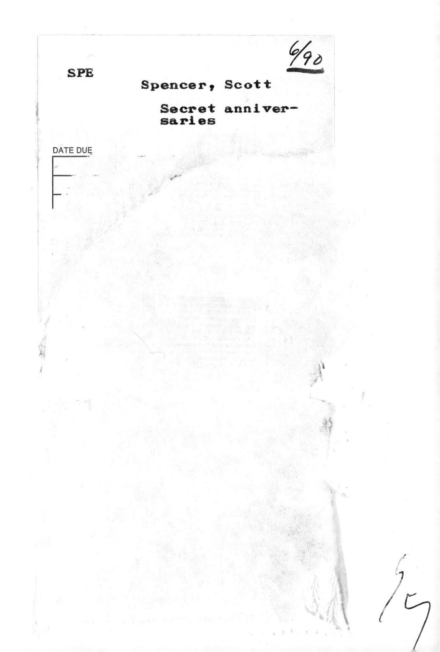

SECRET ANNIVERSARIES

SECRET
ANNIVERSARIES

Scott Spencer

Alfred A. Knopf   New York   1990

THIS IS A BORZOI BOOK
PUBLISHED BY ALFRED A. KNOPF, INC.

6/90 Brodart # 19.95

Grateful acknowledgment is made to the following for permission to
reprint previously published material:

The Estate of Spencer Williams: Excerpts from "Ticket Agent, Ease Your
Window Down" by Spencer Williams. Used by permission.

The Songwriters Guild of America: Excerpts from "Empty Bed Blues" by
J. C. Johnson. Copyright 1928, renewed 1956 by Record Music
Publishing Company. All rights administered by The Songwriters
Guild of America. Used by permission.

Library of Congress Cataloging-in-Publication Data

Spencer, Scott.
    Secret anniversaries / Scott Spencer. — 1st ed.
        p.   cm.
    ISBN 0-394-57817-1
    I. Title.
    PS3569.P455S4   1990
    813'.54—dc20   89-43361   CIP

Manufactured in the United States of America

FIRST EDITION

For Esther and Hougan,
Charles and Jean

ACKNOWLEDGMENTS

In researching the historical dimensions of this fiction, I found several books immensely informative. In particular, I am grateful for *Sabotage*, by Michael Sayers and Albert E. Kahn (Harper and Brothers, 1942); *Under Cover*, by John Roy Carlson (Dutton, 1943); and *Wunderlich's Salute*, by Marvin D. Miller (Malamud-Rose, 1983). And to Terence Boylan, George Budabin, Coco Dupuy, Tom McDonnough, Alice Quinn, and Victoria Wilson, who read and encouraged along the way: thank you.

The holiest of all holidays are those
Kept by ourselves in silence and apart;
The secret anniversaries of the heart.

—HENRY WADSWORTH LONGFELLOW

SECRET
ANNIVERSARIES

ONE

She knew and she knew it well that there was nothing but shame waiting for a girl of her class who even thought about romance with one of the river people. But loneliness and frustration with the narrowness of her life engendered in Caitlin a kind of emotional adventurism, and it wasn't as difficult as perhaps it ought to have been for her to turn a blind eye to all the wisdom and all the advice that girls of her station were born knowing: there were two kinds of people in Windsor County—the rich in their mansions and then everybody else.

Jamey Fleming was home from college. Caitlin had known him all her life. Not only were his parents river people but they owned the estate on which she was raised.

Jamey was going to school in Princeton and he was having a difficult time of it. He was not studious; no Fleming ever had been. Their money came from import and export, and their social position, though it was for rather obscure reasons insecure, seemed lofty to Caitlin and her family.

"You are the most beautiful girl I have ever known," Jamey said to Caitlin the day after Christmas. Caitlin was helping her father remove the Flemings' empty gift boxes to the rubbish heap. And he told her as much again a couple of days later, as he skied past her house at the bottom of the hill. "More beautiful than any movie star," he added, having noted that his first fling at flattery had fallen short of its mark: she was used to people remarking on her looks and it irritated her as much as it pleased her.

Jamey was a tall boy with reddish-brown hair and pompous, defensive eyes. He dressed like his father in tweed suits and heavy workman's shoes. There was a neediness in him that did not exactly touch Caitlin's heart but that set her at ease. Today was the last night of his holiday break, and though asking Caitlin to dinner was out of the question, he did ask her to the house for what he called "a couple of drinks and some boring conversation."

"You can come to my house, then," she told him. "After dinner, and we'll walk up together."

"I'll be there at eight-thirty," he said.

And he was as good as his word about that. Caitlin was in her small, slanted room. She wore a dark brown woolen dress with a blue cardigan the color of her eyes.

She lay on the bed, beneath several quilts, reading *Wuthering Heights*. She could hear Jamey as he made his way down the long, curving road that led from the top of the hill into the snowy hollow where the tenant houses were scattered. There were high, moonbright drifts of snow on the ground, but Caitlin's father had shoveled the driveways and there was just enough powder to crunch beneath Jamey's footsteps.

Though it was eight-thirty at night, Caitlin's parents were already in bed; they stayed up past nine only in the summer, when the glow hovering above the river and the shreds of light caught in the branches of the willow trees goaded them into wakefulness with memories of youth. But now it had been dark for hours and the noises of their repose came through the wooden plank door to their bedroom: Peter's adenoidal snore and Annie's oh-oh-oh, as if the suffering of a child had been bred with the ticking of a clock.

Caitlin let Jamey in and let him stand there while she buttoned her coat. She was nervous; she seriously doubted she was doing the right thing. No Van Fleet had ever spent a social evening in the Flemings' house; when someone from her family was there it was to fix, lift, or serve something. She fastened the large buttons of her coat slowly. Jamey was stomping the snow off his shoes in the kitchen, near the wood burner. The dark pine floor was unswept; the painted chairs around the table were pushed in at odd angles. The sink was full of dishes; the cookstove was splattered with grease. A kerosene-soaked wick spluttered within the blackness of its glass chimney. All Annie's impulse toward tidiness was spent in the main house, and Caitlin wondered why she herself hadn't bothered to make the place proper, knowing she was going to have a visitor.

"Ready?" Jamey said. His voice sounded enormous in the silence of her house.

Caitlin put a finger against her lips, furrowed her brow. "My parents are sleeping," she whispered.

Caitlin opened the door, and because there was no wind the cold air did not rush into the kitchen but just waited for them, patiently. There were so many stars in the sky it seemed as if some of them would be forced out and fall to earth.

"Did you have a nice dinner?" she asked Jamey, as they made their way up the road. A trail of smoke rose from the chimney of her house; at night her father burned unseasoned locust, so there would be chunks of it still smoldering to start the fire up again in the freezing half-light of morning.

"It was good," said Jamey. "The Honorable Elias J. Stowe is visiting us, so naturally Mother wanted everything perfect. My parents want to impress Stowe, not because they like him but because he is a congressman and it kills them that the really important families around here still sort of snub them."

"I thought Mr. Stowe was a good friend of your family."

"Stowe has to like them. He's a politician; he can't stick his nose up in the air like some of the others." They were at a steep part of the road and Jamey casually linked his arm through Caitlin's. He wore no gloves and his breath made visible by the night streamed behind him like a plume. For all the small flirtations, this was the first time he had touched her with anything like gentleness in the gesture—until now it had been playful pushes, pokes for attention, flicking snow off her collar, that sort of thing.

She was still young enough to register the significance of every time she was touched. She was two years out of high school, graduated at the top of her class, and now worked at the George Washington Inn, at the center of Leyden, New York, where the road to New York City crossed the road to Connecticut. Caitlin worked behind the main desk, and if she worked nights there was a room where she could spend the night. She made it a point to get rid of her virginity, as if it were a provincial accent she wanted to overcome. A fellow who worked as an assistant manager, named George Pelkhart, a round-faced young man with a nervous laugh and argyle socks, sometimes rapped on the door to Room 111, if he knew Caitlin was spending the night, and twice Caitlin let him in. He had a large red birthmark right above his pubic hair. He pounded himself into her quickly, with short, powerful thrusts, and when he ejaculated into his condom he kept on going so she wouldn't know he had come, but she knew, she could feel him withering inside of her. It made her think of lights going out in a grand house, one at a time, until all the windows are dark.

"Let's stop here for a minute," Jamey said. Even when he tried to be winsome, the habits of command shaped his voice. Caitlin didn't mind; it was who he was, a part of what made him exotic. There was always something to decode in what Jamey said, but that was what made him interesting to her. Right now, he was the only person she knew who commanded her full attention. The others she could get without trying.

"What for?" she asked. She knew if she continued to walk he would pull her back, maybe even put his arm around her to keep her in place, and he didn't disappoint her.

"I think this is the most beautiful spot on the farm," he said. (All the Flemings called Twin Ponds a farm, though really it was a country estate, a summer and holiday and weekend place.) "You can't see our house, or your house, or any of the other buildings. No wires or poles, no lights, road, nothing. Just trees and fields and the river. Nothing to spoil it."

"I like seeing signs of human life," Caitlin said.

"Empty," Jamey said, letting go of her and mounting a bluish snowdrift. "Just like it was, pure and clean. Life is so debased, Caitlin. The human race." He shook his head. "I don't believe God made us in His image, not at all. Darwin was right, we all come from the ape. But now it's even worse. We live in the age of the ape in a suit, the ape with spectacles on his nose and a briefcase full of utility bonds." He slid down the drift and put his arm through hers again. "Did you know they're going to pave River Road?"

"The apes? The apes in steamrollers?"

Jamey frowned. "The most beautiful road around here. There's dirt on that road that George Washington's troops marched over."

"Well, you're not here that much, Jamey," Caitlin said. They were walking again; the main house loomed suddenly at the top of the hill, an apparition with its tall bright windows and its smoking chimneys. "You don't know what it's like in April and May when that road's mud. It's murder. Anyhow, I think it's about time things got modern around here."

"There are no heroes anymore," said Jamey. He looked

pained, as if he were also admitting that he himself was no hero. "There's no one to pull the sword out of the stone. And if you think the future's going to be so great you should go down to the city and look around. Money grubbers, filth. The little weak men who suck you dry. If you want to see the future."

"Then take me down there, why don't you?" Caitlin said, disguising how much she longed for just that by shoving him playfully.

He slipped momentarily on the icy road. The main house was close now; a silhouette passed by an uncurtained window. "You would hate New York, Catey, you really would."

"We could go to a Broadway show, and the top of the Empire State Building, and a French restaurant."

"I guess if Mr. Hitler succeeds they'll be serving Wiener schnitzel in most of the French restaurants," Jamey said, laughing.

"I've only been there once my whole life," Caitlin said. "A hundred miles away and I've only been once."

"I'd rather take you to India," said Jamey. "There are ancient things there, mysteries. There's magic in India, not everybody going for the dollar. Even the goddamned English bastards haven't been able to ruin that. Do you ever notice how the snobs around here like to brown up to the British? God, that makes me sick."

Case closed, plan canceled, over. Caitlin could as soon see herself attending Vassar as imagine herself in front of the Taj Mahal. She knew Jamey introduced this far-flung fantasy as a way of avoiding her reasonable request. But he would rather have it complicated, with visions of passports, visas, inoculations, lengthy crossings. He had taken a simple wish and turned it into a pipe dream.

They mounted the broad stone steps to the main house. There were pine needles embedded in the snow: only that afternoon Caitlin's father had dragged the Flemings' Christmas fir out of the entrance hall. Several sets of snowshoes rested against the outside wall, looking like the petrified footprints of a giant. The porch lights hung from spears borne by unclad maiden warriors carved from stone and standing guard on either side of the huge black mahogany door.

Jamey took her coat and draped it carelessly over a Teutonically carved chest in the front hall, and then he let his own overcoat simply slip to the floor. Caitlin had heard all her life about the messiness of the Flemings.

It was gloomy in the hall. The flame-shaped bulbs in the wall sconces seemed distant, cold. The door was closed to the library to preserve the heat thrown off by the fireplace, and there was a voice, muffled, yet still somehow loud, full of booming, truculent energy, coming from behind the door.

"Uncle Roscoe won't go home," said Jamey, touching Caitlin's elbow, guiding her across the hall, toward the library.

She looked up at the carved teak ceiling. She wanted to stop, to preserve the moment. The first Van Fleet to be in the main house without a hammer in hand, or a basketful of apples.

"He was on his way to Europe three weeks ago and he's still here," Jamey whispered, moving his mouth close to Caitlin, letting her feel the warmth of his breath. "Mother is mortified in front of Stowe."

Jamey opened the door to the library. It was painted dark green, with Persian carpets on the floor, fussy uncomfortable furniture, portraits of relatives about whom nobody had a good word to say, and shelves full of books that were for the most part unread—books in Latin, German, books about phrenology, hygiene, Egypt. They were books suitable for a stage play about a certain kind of family.

Jamey had already announced that he was bringing Caitlin up for drinks after dinner, and it was his parents' method of discipline to "refuse to dignify with a response" what they did not approve of. He knew full well that they did not think it wise to socialize with staff. Not enough time, money, or prestige separated the Flemings from their own somewhat clamorous beginnings. More-established families along the river—Delanos, Roosevelts, Astors, Vanderbilts— might be able with impunity to bed the help. For them it would be a dalliance, but for a Fleming it might be construed as a regression.

Neither Fulton nor Mary Fleming turned to greet Jamey when he came into the library with Caitlin. Caitlin felt with a lurch in her stomach that she had made a mistake, but she did not altogether regret it. Where is your defiance? she asked herself. Where is your pride? She meant it as an incantation and, as it happened, something like defiance and pride did rise up within her, a wisp of it, as if from a very small fire.

Congressman Stowe looked at her as Jamey led her to a small sofa beneath a set of Goethe. Stowe was small, compact, with carved yet smooth features, like a puppet. He sat with his feet propped on an ottoman, his legs covered by a blanket. He had a piece of medicine-soaked cotton in his right ear. He made a brief, bright smile at Caitlin, as if he might know her; his friendliness poked itself out at her like a cuckoo as the clock struck the hour, and then it was gone again and he slumped back in his chair.

Mary Fleming sat in a pale green armchair, her slender legs curled beneath her. She held a brandy snifter in front of her face and looked at the room through it. Her hair was cut short, just as it was when she and her husband courted. She still had clothes from that happy time and she took care to wear them from time to time. It was part of what made her brave and unreasonable; she would not take no for an answer, even if it was given by her own body. Fulton Fleming stood behind her, staring into his highball glass, frowning, as if to accuse the ice of drinking the four fingers of blended whiskey he had poured a few minutes ago. He wore a tweed suit thick as oatmeal and he needed a shave. Caitlin fought back the impulse to stare at Mr. Fleming. Seeing him at home, with no orders to give, no walking stick with which to point at the part of the stone wall that needed shoring or the roof that needed flashing or the elm that needed pruning, was like seeing an actor outside of his role, and Caitlin felt fascinated and disappointed, too. Without authority he had no glamour.

Mary's brother Roscoe stood in front of the enormous fieldstone hearth. He dominated the conversation; it was his way of singing for his supper. He was a sturdy, florid man, with a fondness for full, flowing suits, floppy bow ties, and theatrical asides, which he would deliver in his basso profundo.

"I don't know why you want to get mixed up with going to Europe," Stowe said to Roscoe. His voice was thin, querulous, somewhat piercing. "It's a madhouse now. War, you know."

"There's a fellow over there I want to see," Roscoe said. "Chap named Biro, Lazlo Biro. He's one of those whizbang Hungarians who can do anything. Marvelous character. Worked as a hypnotist—half Gypsy for all anyone knows."

"My brother is an adventurer," Mary announced to Stowe, trying, it seemed, to encourage Stowe's tolerance. "A mad, daring adventurer."

"I see," said Stowe. Then, to Roscoe: "What business do you have with this Hungarian, then?"

"He's invented a new sort of pen. Rather than a nib it writes with a sort of rolling ball. It doesn't leak or smear and you never have to fill it with ink. I'm absolutely dead keen to get my hands on it, take out a patent, bring it over here, and I'll be rich." He laughed happily at the idea, as if he might be hearing it for the first time.

"Oh, Roscoe," said Mary. "You and your wild schemes." She stole a glance across the room at Stowe.

"Oh, but it's not a wild scheme, my dear. It's the pen of the future and I think I'd better hurry."

"Yes," said Fulton Fleming. "Hurrying would be good."

If Roscoe heard that, he ignored it. "Sooner or later," he said, "according to my sources, Hungary will be joining the Reich and then old Biro might be in for some rough sailing."

There was a draft circulating near the floor. Caitlin felt it against her legs like the breath of a dog. She looked up and saw Mary Fleming glancing at her and then turning away.

"I'm sick and tired," Congressman Stowe was saying, "of people just assuming the worst about Germany. What gives you the idea that Hitler wants to meddle in Hungarian affairs? People just have to realize that Herr Hitler is a transitional figure, a figurehead, nothing more, a leader to help reorganize Germany and bring about a decent balance of power in Europe. Strikes me as a hell of a lot better idea than letting Mr. Stalin organize things over there." Stowe leaned forward, reached for his drink on the little inlaid Oriental table next to his chair. It was just an inch out of reach and his fingers waved like underwater plants as he strained to touch it.

Then he gave up and sank back into his chair. To Caitlin, he looked like an invalid, defeated, gray. He had a reputation as a ladies' man and she wondered how that could be.

She had an image of him striking a woman with a cane.

"Perhaps Hitler will go after Hungary to get his hands on this miracle pen," Fulton suggested. Mary laughed at his joke and he reached over the chair and touched her on the collarbone.

"I don't give a hang for politics," said Roscoe. He made an apologetic little bow in Stowe's direction.

Stowe nodded back, as if to say, That's perfectly all right, I'll look after those things.

"But I just don't want Biro going underground like a weasel, that's all," said Roscoe. He sounded genuinely worried.

"Is your Gypsy a Communist as well?" Mary asked. "Oh, Roscoe, you're just much too trusting. All that California sunshine has made you . . . oh, I don't know."

"He's not a Communist."

"A Jew then?" suggested Fulton Fleming.

Jamey put his hand over Caitlin's. When she looked at him, he winked.

"No, no, no, and no," said Roscoe. When he smiled he looked serene. "He's no Red and he's no Jew. But I think the Nazis will be keeping an eye out for Mr. Biro because, if what I hear is correct, he happens to be as queer as Dick's hatband."

Caitlin felt her own heart thumping. She was a spirit, a spy. One of those chambermaids before whom the masters went naked.

She turned to whisper something to Jamey and saw he was no longer beside her. Had she been in a trance?

Without him, she had no legitimacy in that room. A sudden hollowness within, like a dream of falling.

She turned and saw him stalking out of the library into what had once been the conservatory but was now merely a room, with sofas, a globe, a hutch filled with flowery china. Jamey gestured for her to follow.

"Roscoe, you're spilling," Mary was saying, as Caitlin got up and slipped out of the room.

"Are you crazy, leaving me there?" Caitlin said, grabbing Jamey's wrist.

It was dark in that shabby, infrequently used room. The others, sitting in the library, were bathed in the gold the lamps breathed out through their umber-fringed shades.

Jamey was wearing a ring, from college. It was gold with a dark sapphire in the center.

His mother had already spoken to her mother. Casually, drifting through while Annie plumped the cushions on that sofa right over there, the one with the green-and-silver stripes. "Jamey's so restless," she had said. "I only hope he doesn't get anyone else in trouble because of it." Annie was no fool: she knew it was a warning; she knew who was meant by anyone else.

"Let's go upstairs," Jamey said. "I want to show you my room."

"I've already seen your room."

"But not with me in it."

He led her through the room that used to be the conservatory, through the dining room, then the pantry, and up the pantry staircase. Caitlin was no stranger to this part of the house. She had often helped Annie clean, and two summers ago when Mary's sister came to the house, Caitlin was hired to look after the sister's baby, an ill-tempered child who scowled at Caitlin like an old woman who thinks you are trying to cheat her. Little Joan was fat, her stomach gurgled with milk and graham crackers and red grapes, which she ate seeds and all. When Caitlin lifted the child's legs to change a diaper, the pressure against the hard pink belly caused the baby to break wind.

He led her down the hall, past the bedrooms. Each door was closed, as if the place were a hotel. Their way was lit by small wall sconces, with bulbs the size of pigeons' eggs and little heat-stained lamp shades tilted like hats on drunken playboys.

"Your parents know we're up here," Caitlin said.

He clutched his chest as if he were having a heart attack and then smiled, held out his hand for her.

She took it. She felt she deserved a little fun.

The walls owed her that much, and the floor, the closed doors, the whole house.

Jamey's room was small, rather cold. There was a Princeton pennant on the wall, a shelf of trophies he'd won years ago at horse shows—before his horse threw and almost crushed him. There were scuff marks along the woodwork, left by tantrums, a long time ago. How long has it been since this room's been painted? Caitlin wondered.

His bed was stern, cast iron, with a black blanket so coarse it made Caitlin shudder to look at it.

Jamey closed the door. He leaned against it and looked at her.

She looked right back at him. He didn't frighten her. If he wanted to make her nervous he should have kept her down in the library, but in this room she was his equal.

He strolled past her and sat on the bed. He reached behind and took out a bottle of Old Grand-dad bourbon.

"Do you know the story of this room?" Jamey asked. He put the bottle on his lap and tapped his fingernails on it. "Charles Dickens stayed in this room," Jamey said. He unscrewed the cap of the Old Grand-dad, took a swallow, and held the bottle out to Caitlin.

Caitlin felt something turn in her stomach. That Dickens had slept in this room seemed both wondrous and profoundly unjust—how could a man whose work exposed heartlessness and hypocrisy have spent the night beneath any Fleming's roof? She tilted the bourbon bottle back and let the warm liquor touch her lips, searing them, and then she let a trickle of it into her mouth.

"My father read *Great Expectations* to me when I was nine years old," she said. She was about to hand the bottle to Jamey but she stopped herself and took another swallow, this time letting it go into her with more abandon.

Jamey smiled. He had a look on him: a hunter watching a doe nose up to the salt lick.

He's got another guess coming, thought Caitlin.

"Next to Tolstoy, Charles Dickens is my favorite writer in the world," she said to Jamey.

"He was on some kind of lecture tour," Jamey said, "and making piles of money. And when he came to this area he was my great-grandfather's guest and he was put right in this room. He stole a soup spoon, sterling silver, made by Paul Revere. God, I hate the English. I hope Hitler eats them alive."

"How long did he stay here?"

"The people around here practically think they *are* British, Oxford, Eton, all that crap." Jamey took a long drink and passed the bottle to Caitlin, who was still standing in the middle of the room. Jamey's eyes sparked feverishly.

He was on his way to an adventure and Caitlin felt he was leaving her behind. She took the bottle from him.

"I think I've read everything Dickens ever wrote," Caitlin said.

"I never read anything," said Jamey. "Part of that one about the beggar boy, I think."

"*Oliver Twist?*"

"I guess." He patted the bed for her to sit down.

Caitlin felt a rush of emotion go through her as sudden as a spill. He seemed so spoiled, so distant from any sense of effort, or responsibility.

It was not like being with a real person. He was someone in a story, someone you made up.

"You should be ashamed of yourself," she said, sitting next to him. "You go to college, with every advantage. You should at least read. I just finished *War and Peace*. It explains everything."

"What I'd really like to do is spend all our money."

"Are you trying to sound crazy just to be interesting?"

"We're running out of it anyhow. My grandfather knew about business but my father doesn't and I don't even care about it. One day we'll be poor anyhow, so I figure spending the money fast would be like shooting a wounded horse. To take it out of its misery."

"I would have given anything to go to college."

"You wouldn't have liked it, Catey."

"How do you know?"

"You've been living here all your life. I guess I know you pretty well."

"I don't think you know me one slight little bit, Jamey."

"Oh yeah? Then how come I feel the way about you that I do?"

"And how is that?"

He put his arm quickly around her and pressed a hard, ardent kiss onto her lips. His weight tipped her over and she stopped herself from falling by putting her hand down behind her, which thrust her breasts into his embrace.

He moved back to look at her face. Are you going to do anything about this? his eyes asked.

"I think your parents must be getting curious," Caitlin said.

"My parents are getting *drunk*."

"So are we," said Caitlin. Jamey reached for the bottle. It had rolled off the bed but she hadn't heard it when it hit the floor.

"You must hate my parents," said Jamey. "I mean really despise them." He put his arm around her shoulders and let it drape, touching her breast.

"Not as much as you do, Jamey," she said, removing his hand. She did it the way girls did, holding him around the thumb and lifting his hand as if it were a drowned rat.

He flushed red and she felt a jolt of compassion. He was so nervous, so undefended. He put the bottle to his lips and drank enough to half fill a highball glass. She was impressed.

Then the bottle was in her hand again, and when she drank from it she could feel drunkenness coming on like the sound of a parade getting closer.

"Caitlin," he said, his voice a ball of knots. He moved closer to her, lowered his head onto her shoulder.

And she did feel a terrible urge to cradle him. There was a pulse of desire in her that had been beating for a long while, but the desire was without a subject, or an object, or even a target. It simply was, like signals from a radio tower in a world without radios.

"I watched you all our lives," he murmured.

"Don't make more of it than it is, Jamey," said Caitlin. "You don't have to. You're a college man home for the holidays and this is what you guys do."

"That's not true, Catey. All your life, watching you. In the quarry. You swam in your underwear. I saw your breasts beneath your undershirt. I . . . I saw everything. I'll never forget."

He gestured up for her, waving his fingers like Congressman Stowe reaching for his drink.

She couldn't decide if she was drunk or if she was about to use drunkenness as an excuse for whatever happened next.

She did not feel that Jamey was a good man. He was handsome, however. His cheeks were shaved and smooth; he was wearing cologne that smelled of lemon and spice. The hand that reached longingly for her was softer than her own.

She placed the nearly empty bottle on the floor and said, "Tonight's your lucky night."

She lay next to him and their bodies trembled in a *petit mal* of desire. Something like a sob broke in his throat and Caitlin felt as if the bed were swallowing her. She opened her eyes; the ceiling looked one hundred feet high.

Jamey rolled over and draped a leg over Caitlin, rising on his elbow to look down at her. He placed his lips upon hers. The kiss was dry, formal. He seemed to be going back to the very beginning, like a piano student who flubs a note and then goes back to the first measure.

Eventually, his kiss softened into something tender and expressive that sent roots of sensation deep into Caitlin. But then his hand fondled her breast and the root of feeling died and began to recede.

"We're not alone, Jamey," she said, but as soon as the words were out they seemed to make no difference.

He rolled onto his back and she missed him immediately—or at least the warmth of his body. Her own skin was burning and without him near the air felt too cold.

She slid next to him and kissed his forehead, the tip of his nose, and then his mouth. Her kiss was moist and enormous and she felt it scaring him—but leading him forward, too.

"Caitlin," he said. "Maybe we should—" He pointed to the door.

"Shhh," she said. She returned to him as if to a meal after a disturbance—still hungry but aware that the plate had cooled.

She pinned his shoulders and kissed him again and again and again. She pressed herself against him.

He wrapped his arms around her and turned her over. It was meant to be masterful but it embarrassed Caitlin in some obscure way. She did not want him to be on top, but she knew it must be like that. He kissed her with a passion that trailed off into something near violence. And then, because he must, he ground his genitals into her.

She felt he had done this many times in this very bed, alone.

She opened herself to him out of a combination of wanting to find a more comfortable position and wanting to help him. He was thrashing around but then his motion became deliberate, solemn, and he began making a low, stunned animal noise that seemed so tender and universal. She was half trying to listen for footsteps, but all she could hear was his breath and the sounds of their clothes, and the rustle of horsehair in the mattress, the creak of the wooden floor as the old bed shuddered upon it.

A memory began to surface in her, rising from some great liquid darkness within, but then it disappeared and all that was left was Jamey, his weight, his smell, his hardness, and the movements of his body.

He came. For all the thrashing that preceded it, the completion of his desperate dance was rather secretive. The bottle had been knocked over, and it rolled across the uneven floor toward the bookshelf and then rolled back. She felt his spasms. She imagined an icicle breaking off an eave and dropping into the snow.

She hadn't bothered to lift her skirt but she felt naked for a moment. He was looking down at her with exhausted, guilty eyes.

"Caitlin." He held her in his gaze. It seemed as if someone had once told him he was supposed to. Then he flopped onto his back with an enormous sigh.

She looked at him. He was breathing rapidly; he seemed infinitely happier and more satisfied than she. And so she leaned over and kissed him on the mouth, as if brocaded within him was the secret of his happiness. He made a low hum of sleepy assent, touched the side of her face. He may have thought she was congratulating him on a job well done.

But then she climbed on top of him and grabbed the hem of her skirt, hiking it up as if to ford a stream. She positioned herself, as if it were her God-given right, as if this need and the power it magically bestowed were as familiar as the feel of her own skin. She opened herself, not to Jamey, altogether, but to the heat she sought, to that gnarl of sensation that buzzed within.

Instinct told her to rise higher and change the angle of contact, and the ticking of her suddenly powerful sexual metronome measured the duration of every downward thrust. This pleasure, this sexual justice was finally a thing she could ask for, a thing she could claim. And now her eyes were open and Jamey was staring up at her. He gripped her hips and pressed down to increase the power and specificity of her movements and part of him seemed to be trying to stop her.

Something within her felt as if it were growing immense and falling into pieces at the same time. The drunkenness burned off her, flambeaued by lust. She made a high keening cry of surprise and abandon and all at once her back and her legs were cold and her face was scalding. Her arms went weak and she began to collapse on Jamey's chest, but she held herself up above him, because she wanted to move some more.

"OK, OK," Jamey said.

"Sorry," she said, lowering herself onto him. She took comfort in the rise and fall of his breaths.

"God," he said.

"What?"

"I mean. You know. It's like a whore."

"I'm like?"

And it was then, before he could answer, though probably he would have ended up denying that was what he had meant, it was then that the door to his room flew open and the space it had once filled was occupied by the looming figure of Fulton Fleming. He stood with his arms folded over his chest.

"I heard the creaking of the bed springs," Fulton said.

"Get out of here!" Jamey's scream was wild, infantile. "This is my room."

Caitlin was smoothing her dress over her legs. She had gotten off the bed so quickly she didn't remember doing it. She just found herself standing there.

"I think you better run along now, Caitlin," Fulton was saying. His tone was reasonable, he looked amused, faintly aroused. He wet his lips, smiled.

Caitlin felt as if she were speaking not only for her own dignity but for the dignity of every Van Fleet who had ever worked on the estate when she said, "Thank you for a lovely evening, Mr. Fleming." She pushed right past him and walked down the front staircase, directly to the foyer and out the door.

She walked home without her coat, only intermittently aware of the cold, and she had not even reached her parents' house before the Flemings had begun to arrange with Congressman Stowe to hire her to work in his office in Washington, D.C. It was just as simple as that. She crept into the house, built the fire up in the kitchen stove, let it burn for a few minutes, banked it, and then went upstairs. She lay in her bed, remembering every word that had been said, every silence, every caress, and before she was asleep her life had changed forever.

TWO

It was winter, dead winter, the very core of the coldest time, and Caitlin was on a slippery, snow-packed path, guiding a man named Joe Rose and Joe's friend Gordon Jaffrey. The three of them moved swiftly because the cold came up through the soles of their shoes and entered their bones. The winter sun was a circular smudge in the white sky, a fingerprint on a pane of glass.

They'd hidden Joe's car, a black Ford with runningboards and a back seat filled with books and film cans and blankets. The car was left behind a billboard on County Road 30, right at the turnoff to Camp Sunrise. The billboard showed a happy American family eating their steaming-hot farina—though this family was now peeling, torn in long strips by the clawing cold winds of winter.

The path they walked on was narrow. Frozen treadmarks went down the middle of it. The hemlocks stood in a line like the pattern on a sweater.

Caitlin walked behind Joe and Gordon. They were both city boys and their tread was at once arrogant and awkward;

they walked too quickly and lost their balance. Their feet shimmied; they grabbed onto each other to keep from falling.

"Will it be too cold for that camera to work?" Joe Rose asked. His eyes scanned the horizon and he patted his breast pocket, feeling for his notebook and pen. He was handsome, right up to the edge of beauty, without being precisely attractive. He had the air of a man who was always thinking too many things simultaneously, trying to balance too many conflicting ideas, and for whom things could not quite come together. Caitlin considered him a victim of his own intelligence.

"How many times are you going to ask me that?" Gordon said.

Gordon and Joe had been friends for a couple of years. They worked at *Fortune* together. Gordon looked up to Joe and they both had secrets, complicated memories, and a day-to-day life that for the most part excluded Caitlin. Yet today they needed her.

"I don't know," Joe Rose said. "Maybe if you put the camera under your coat, gave it a little protection anyhow."

Joe and Gordon were not a natural pair. Joe was from Philadelphia; he was Jewish, the son of a successful lawyer. He was an edgy man and there was, even at the age of twenty-four, something mournful, wounded in his expression. He was pale, thin, and until recently he had had dark, wavy hair. Now he had had it cut short, straightened, and dyed light brown, to support the necessary fiction that he was a Gentile.

Gordon was large, broad, with reddish skin, freckles, and dark yellow hair he combed back in a single, good-natured wave. He had been raised in Chicago—his father was a cop, and Gordon was one of nine children. He had learned photography from a mail-order course and now made a living out of sheer energy and a willingness to go anywhere or do anything to get a photograph. He had sold pictures of a walrus giving birth, of slag being dumped; he had followed a cop onto a ledge where a mother with a child in her arms was threatening to jump—and indeed she did jump, and that last image of her sailing toward the street with the amazed child looking up at the camera made Gordon's reputation.

Caitlin, Joe, and Gordon came to a thick, icy chain strung up between two giant hemlocks. On one tree a sign said, "CAMP SUNRISE—PRIVATE." On the other tree the sign said, "BEWARE—AREA PATROLLED BY DOGS." Beneath the sign, someone had drawn a cartoonish picture of a dog licking its chops, with exclamation points of saliva flying all around it.

Joe gestured at the chain across the road, the signs on the trees, and Gordon took his Leica out from beneath his overcoat and took two quick photographs.

"We never would have found this place without you," Joe said to Caitlin. He patted her on the shoulder, and his eyes for a moment stopped wandering, stopped calculating, and he looked at her, showed himself, his frailty, his gratitude.

She breathed in deeply. Joe was the bravest man she knew, had ever known, and it made her weak with happiness to have his praise.

"What time does it get dark around here?" Gordon wanted to know.

"Same time as it does in New York City," said Caitlin. And she thought to herself: If these guys are going to save the Republic they ought to know what time it is.

She was the local. It was her spotting the man named John Coleman that had brought Joe and Gordon up here. They thought they could force Coleman to answer questions, to admit he was a German agent, or to perhaps deny it in a way that would reveal something more, perhaps something they hadn't even considered. And now it was Caitlin's job to guide them around over the frozen back roads. Gordon and Joe were nervous in the countryside. The barns and silos and knots of cattle melting the snow with their body heat while they chewed on bales of hay seemed exotic and unsettling to the men. To Caitlin, these were merely oppressive sights. She enjoyed having Joe depend on her, but she wished it was about something else. Being the one who feels most comfortable in the sticks was winning a game she would rather not have played, like winning at who is the poorest, the most naïve.

Caitlin had worked for Congressman Stowe after leaving Windsor County and now Stowe was dead and she was back where she had begun. Joe Rose was keen to prove that Stowe's death was not an accident but that he had been killed by the man calling himself John Coleman. Joe had come to her, had not even asked her to help, but had just begun giving her assignments—asking her for names, papers from Stowe's files, phone numbers. He assumed her cooperation. It was not in his nature to court and woo. In that way, the times were perfect for him. When you are enlisting someone to help win a war, all you have to say is what you want done, you don't have to say please and you do not have to be charming.

And she had lost someone she had loved when Stowe's plane turned into a throbbing, smoking ball of flame in a Virginia pasture. Her best friend, a woman named Betty Sinclair, had been on that plane, too.

They walked in single file and the soles of their shoes made a noise like a dog chewing a chunk of charcoal. Dense pine groves stood on either side of the path. An occasional blue jay flitted between the snowy boughs. The snowdrifts were marked with a latticework of fallen pine needles.

"Are you absolutely sure you saw Coleman in town?" Joe asked Caitlin. Furls of steam poured from his nose and mouth as he spoke.

"He was sick," said Caitlin. "Coughing. He walked around with a handkerchief rolled up in his hand."

Gordon suddenly stopped and aimed his camera at the tops of the trees, snapped a picture.

"Now what?" Joe asked. His voice was irritated, raw. Caitlin wondered if impersonating an Aryan had affected his character, spoiled his gentleness.

"The way the light was coming through the branches," Gordon said, shrugging. He seemed to be used to Joe and all his permutations.

"We didn't come for that," Joe said.

"I'm an artist, a terribly sensitive artist," Gordon said, putting his hand on his massive chest.

"We just have to save film, is all," said Joe.

"Over that hill," said Caitlin, pointing to a piny rise a quarter mile away, "there's an estate called Locust Manor. My father knows the man who runs it."

"I always figured," said Joe, "that everybody knows everyone in a place like this."

"There's two kinds of people around here," Caitlin said. Joe was at her side. They were the same height and now they had the same-color hair, too. "There's the rich who live on the estates and then there's us. And what we do is wait on them or make things for them or look after their children or milk their cows. But we're fascinated by them. We think of them as gods. And we talk about them all the time. Gossip is what we do for mythology."

Joe smiled. "You've given this a lot of thought," he said.

Caitlin was a water witch when it came to the hidden springs of snobbery, and she realized that it was not an altogether good sign that Joe was impressed—it meant he had assumed she was dull. But still she could not resist feeling a little jolt of pleasure, an internal rise and fall such as she would feel going over a bump in the road.

Her heart already knew that its destiny involved loving men who would not really see her very clearly.

"Hey," said Gordon. "We're here." He took the lens cap off his camera with the gravity of a man taking the safety off a gun.

They had come to a trio of empty flagpoles. In the summer, when the camp was going full tilt and the outdoor fireplaces were pouring fragrant smoke, and large, serious-looking men in khaki shorts were cooking meat on the grill, and the lake was filled with the sharp laughter of Die Mädchenschaft, which was the affectionate name given to the youngest and fairest of the camp's women, in the summer when the parade grounds were full of good earnest, hearty, Sieg-heiling marchers, these three flagpoles flew three banners—the orange-and-yellow flag of Camp Sunrise, the beleaguered flag of the United States, and the proud banner of the new Germany. But now the flagpoles were empty, skinned over with ice, and they stood in a perfect white field of snow.

On the eastern rim of the parade grounds was the main house of the camp, which also served as a restaurant and an inn. It was an old Victorian house painted brown and white. It had a wide, circular porch, whose roof sagged beneath the weight of the snow. The shades were drawn, turning each of the windows into a mirror, most of them reflecting only snow and trees but those on the west catching the first rays of the sunset in the rippled glass.

Two upward-angled, empty flagpoles were above the doorway of the main house, and beyond the main house were rows of modest, prim, well-kept cabins, each one sprouting an empty flagpole.

"Must be like the World's Fair when all the flags are up," Gordon said.

"The World's Fair if all that was invited was Germany," said Joe.

The house looked deserted. It had seemed unlikely that they would find John Coleman but there had been something compelling about the possibility. Coleman was in trouble in New York, in Pittsburgh, in Minneapolis—his name had come up during investigations of a bombing in a Brooklyn shipyard, an explosion in a steel mill, a fire in the offices of a small Farmer-Labor newspaper. Perhaps he did need a place to recover from some illness, a place where no one would look. Perhaps in this frozen landscape hid the man who killed with fire. Yet why would he be here? Why would he stay?

"When you thought you saw him . . ." Joe said to Caitlin.

"I did see him," said Caitlin. She was looking at the house, seeing there were no lights burning, no car nearby, feeling certain it was empty and wondering if Joe would now think she had concocted the sighting to bring him up to Leyden, to make her life important again, as it had been when she lived in Washington.

On the broad, circular porch there were two pairs of skis and a small stack of white-birch logs—enough for only a fire or two. Tacked to the door was a sign lettered in fierce Teutonic characters, red on black: SEE YOU IN APRIL.

"Friendly," said Gordon.

"Photo," said Joe.

"Right," said Gordon. He focused his Leica on the sign and photographed it.

"Often," Caitlin said, "caretakers leave an extra key above the door frame." She got up on her toes and felt above the door. She found the key, long and cold. Its teeth were barely ridged; it looked like an equals sign. She held it proudly for Joe and Gordon to see but they didn't seem impressed. They seemed to have expected as much from her.

Joe took the key from Caitlin and tried to fit it into the lock. But his hands shook from the cold and nerves, and he kept missing the hole.

"Reminds me of the night I lost my virginity," said Gordon.

Joe gave him what looked like a disapproving grimace but Caitlin was quite sure his frown expressed shyness. When she loved somebody she made up reasons for them.

There was a high, raw noise. They all turned, alarmed. Blue jays. Five of them, squawking over husks.

Joe got the door open. The darkness of the house was waiting for them, ever so patiently.

It was not much warmer inside and the foyer smelled of cleaning solvent and disinfectant. They stood before the beginnings of an elaborately curved staircase, and on either side were closed French doors leading to dark, wooden-beamed rooms.

"Oh, look," said Caitlin, pointing up.

Joe took a flashlight out of his overcoat and pointed it at the ceiling. There was a map of the stars painted on, with the stars of the constellations connected.

"Hitler believes in astrology," Joe said. "Astrology, mythology, bonfires, mass arrests. An interesting mixture."

"I'll bet you Frank de Cisto did it," said Caitlin. An image of de Cisto presented itself to Caitlin—a man on a motorcycle wearing dark-tinted goggles. He had been the muralist of choice for the better households. He had painted an arbor in the foyer of one of the Vanderbilt cottages, a view of the Parthenon for the Delanos, and the Flemings had asked him for a scene of New York Harbor.

At the foot of the staircase was a small mahogany table upon which lay a neatly folded newspaper. Caitlin picked it up but Joe took it from her. It was the *Deutsche Weckruf und Beobachter*, in German but printed locally.

"Well, well, well," said Joe, with the pleasure of a boy who has found a nest of snakes beneath a rock. "The good old *German Awakener and Observer*." He opened it with a flourish and showed it to Caitlin.

Wedged between long columns of German text were advertisements in English, boxed off and strangely innocent, like uncomprehending children at a funeral. The ads were for Windsor Coal and Lumber, the New Harmony Restaurant, Sunnyside Duck Farm, Rankin's Pond Rowboat Rentals. Caitlin felt queasy, but she would not say that she knew every business that had placed an ad in the paper.

"I would say that amongst the locals the goals of the Bund are not exactly reprehensible," Joe said.

They were whispering.

Joe turned the pages of the paper. They sounded like fire in the stillness of the house. "Here's something about *Grosser Filmabend*," Joe said. "Translation—Big Film Night." He read rapidly in German to himself.

Caitlin could feel his mind working. She liked the expression of his face when he concentrated: his eyes seemed to darken, his lips pursed with solemnity, and the overall effect was one that combined selflessness with virtuosity, like the expression of a great violinist.

"OK," said Joe, "listen to this shit. 'It was with hearts full of pride that we watched the great German martyr Horst Wessel, who died by the hands of a Jew while fighting the Communists of 1930.' I presume she means *in* 1930."

"Who's the writer?" asked Gordon.

"Some living doll named Henrietta Smith."

Caitlin had that feeling you get when you drop a dish.

Joe continued to read, now in a high, absurdly proper, sentimental voice. " 'Who of us will ever forget the pictures of his saddened family, his brave brother in the SA—' "

"Jesus," said Gordon. "Let's find her." He glanced at Caitlin; he seemed to sense she knew Miss Smith.

" 'This is a film reported to be Herr Goebbels's personal favorite and it is no wonder,' " Joe continued. " 'It is also a film which the anti-Aryan forces in Hollywood have sought to suppress, and those of us who braved the bad weather last week to attend Big Film Night now know why.' "

He put the paper down and grinned at Caitlin. Their

friendship had begun with his constantly proving to her that people and life itself were far worse than she realized, and he kept at it. Yet most of his life had been much more comfortable than Caitlin's. What gave him the right to treat her as if she were naïve? Even his bravery was hitched to inchoate notions of career—one day soon he would reveal to America what he had learned about the groups he had penetrated.

"I know Henrietta Smith," Caitlin forced herself to say. "She taught me in high school."

"And just what did she teach you?" asked Joe.

"Fascism 101," said Gordon.

"English," said Caitlin. And she let it go at that. She didn't tell them it was Miss Smith who urged Caitlin to go to college, who had brought her brochures from nearby schools where the tuition wasn't overwhelmingly high, who had urged her to take summer jobs, apply for scholarships, and do anything but waste the talent for learning that Miss Smith saw in Caitlin. She was a bosomy woman, with curly auburn hair and round, surprised eyes. Her voice was a wavering contralto, and when she turned her back on the class they waved their arms, made faces. It used to break Caitlin's heart. Miss Smith hadn't seemed as if she hated anyone. Her scorn was saved for split infinitives, illegible handwriting, and, in some general way, the twentieth century.

"Are you all right?" Joe asked Caitlin. He touched her arm, furrowed his silky eyebrows.

She put her hand on her stomach. She felt within her a hollow, churning dankness. Nerves? It was a pressure within, starting at her navel, radiating out toward her hips, sending a hard, corroded taste of itself up to the back of her throat.

"I don't feel well," Caitlin said.

Gordon was shining his flashlight through the french doors into the cavernous meeting room to the left. The long tables were pushed together and the chairs were stacked on top of them. Hanging from one of the exposed oak beams was a large full-color portrait of Hitler.

"What a face," said Gordon.

"A headwaiter in a place where you'd never want to eat," said Joe.

"And the pictures along the walls," Gordon said. He shone the beam at a line of eight-by-ten framed photographs: here and there, from beneath the burst of reflection on the glass, showed the face of a jowly man, a formally dressed crowd, someone coming smartly down a ski slope.

"Are you sure you're all right?" Joe murmured to Caitlin.

"I'm OK," said Caitlin. "I just need to go to the bathroom, if you must know the awful truth."

Joe blushed. "Then go," he said.

"Gordon," said Caitlin, "can I use the flashlight?"

Gordon clicked it off and handed it to her. In the sudden darkness she could not see their faces and it was like dying.

Through the window, however, she saw the field of snow, blue in the twilight, and along the horizon a long flaming crack of orange, over which a rubble of clouds lay like a field of broken stones. The darkness was moving in, faster and faster, like an old workhorse hurrying those last hundred yards back to the barn.

She turned the flashlight on again. It extended a long silver arm of light up the stairs, and she followed it, leaving the men in the darkness below.

On the wall leading up the stairs were framed photographs, and purely on impulse Caitlin anointed each of them with the soft, fuzzy beam of light. There were more pictures of skiers, a photo of a sleek wolverine of a man in a tuxedo exhorting an audience, a portrait of a smiling woman with marceled hair and a diamond necklace, a jowly, small-town-looking man wearing one of those little caps worn by boy scouts and soda jerks.

And then a familiar face. Congressman Stowe sitting at his desk in Washington, the same desk upon which Caitlin had once placed the morning mail, the day's typing, cups of coffee. He was dressed in a suit and a dignified striped tie, and for the purposes of this portrait the desk was empty, save for a bright wedge of sunlight. Stowe was smiling; his little cheeks looked as hard as crab apples. The bottom of the picture was signed with a flourish—"Best regards from the Hon. Elias J. Stowe, U.S. Congressman, New York"—as if it had been sent to a fan, some earnest boy who would put it between pictures of Lou Gehrig and Dizzy Dean.

She experienced a rush of rhapsodic malice, glad that Stowe was dead, forgetting for a moment there had been others on the plane when it had skidded across that Virginia pasture, scorching the earth, and that next to Stowe, screaming as he screamed, surrendering her mortal soul as his was snatched, was her friend Betty Sinclair, whom Caitlin had cherished and loved, and whose death was for Caitlin the true beginning of human knowledge, which is sorrow.

The bathroom was just to the right of the top of the steps. It was the only door that was open in a line of ten rooms on either side of a narrow corridor. The flashlight revealed the checkerboard black-and-white tiles, the claws of a tub. And then she moved the beam across the smooth cryptic surfaces of all those closed doors; they were painted white, or pale green, or perhaps sky blue—impossible to say in that light.

The bathroom was particularly cold. The copper towel racks were empty. Opposite the toilet was a framed painting of two little boys in short pants urinating into a pond while a family of mallards looked on. Caitlin went to the iced-over window and pressed her hand against it until some of the frost melted away and she could see outside. The snow was iron gray; the last of the sunset was being sucked into the night like a strand of spaghetti. She stood there until her handprint filled with ice again and the world outside disappeared.

But it was only after her skirt was hiked, only after her skin adjusted to the icy toilet seat, the still, dark air, with its faint scent of oatmeal soap, only then with the pressure within her beginning to subside and a smile of true human relief spreading over her face that she processed what she had seen in the corridor. Beneath the fifth door to the right, between the bottom of the door and the floor, was a narrow ribbon of pale light—not really bright enough to be immediately noticeable, but brilliant now in memory, like a gold coin on a field of dark velvet.

Caitlin got up to flush the toilet. She pulled down on the chain but the only sound was a hollow metallic rattle—the tank was empty, the pipes had long been drained. Her urine lay in a little golden puddle at the bottom of a commode that was as steep as a shot glass.

Caitlin's heart beat swiftly, shallowly. She pictured that light coming from beneath the door and she reread the memory, frantically, doubting it and finding new things in it at the same time—the light suddenly appearing, as if a lamp were being switched on, a moving darkness fluttering across that four-foot line of light, evidence of someone pacing back and forth.

She stood there wondering and then it wasn't necessary to wonder at all because she heard footsteps—feeble, shuffling. And then a low phlegmy moan, the despairing song of a man who believes himself to be utterly alone.

She reached for the door, as if there were still time to flee. And the sufferer, who himself was an inflictor of suffering, had his hand on the door handle, too, and as Caitlin turned it to the left he was turning it to her right and they stymied each other mid-arc.

Fear went off in her like a flashbulb, illuminating an internal structure of rigid nerves.

She let go of the door, stepped back. She looked around the room for something with which to defend herself. There was a wooden cross, the size of a hammer, on the wall, and Caitlin reached for it. But it was fastened tightly to the clammy plaster. Her cold fingers ached from the effort of trying to wrench the cross free. She brought her hand to her mouth, blew on it. And as she did so the door slowly opened.

It was John Coleman, his brow wrinkled with confusion, his lips pursed, his head jutting forward. Caitlin was shining the flashlight directly into his face and he slowly, with every evidence of confusion, brought his hand up to shield his eyes. In his other hand he carried a candle in a porcelain candlestick; the wick was off center and a huge tumor of wax had congealed on one side of the slim, tapered candle.

"Who is it?" he said. His voice was webbed and unstable. Not at all the piercing drone Caitlin remembered from her first meeting with him, at lunch in Washington with Stowe and Betty Sinclair. Caitlin was still quite new to Washington that afternoon and she still could remember Coleman's unashamedly appraising stare, as he blatantly judged if she was someone who could be trusted, and then if she was someone who needed to be taken seriously. He had been all sharp angles and immense sensitivity that day in his dark blue suit and long dark hair, parted up the middle, as if he were an emissary from a previous, finer era.

But now his hair was not pomaded, it was disheveled, and his eyes, which had once seemed to register impressions with the cold crunch of an adding machine, were watery and timid. The hand he used to shield his eyes from the flashlight held a handkerchief, and just as it had been when Caitlin had seen Coleman in town, the handkerchief was pink and brown from the blood he was apparently coughing up.

"Who is it?" Coleman said. "What are you doing here?"

Strange then to think of a man who served Adolf Hitler, who had sabotaged factories, and had, if Joe was to be believed, killed Congressman Stowe and Betty Sinclair, as a lonely soul in his thirties, a man with a frail constitution and no one to look after him, someone pathetic, who convalesced like an animal in a cold, deserted house.

He thrust the candle toward Caitlin, hoping to see her face. If he was frightened, he seemed now to be recovering his bravery.

She stepped back. She thought she could hit him with her flashlight and she arced it back. The light moved, swinging the room with it.

"I am a sick man. How dare you intrude on me."

"Get away from me," she said, horrified at the note of sheer pleading in her voice.

Her fear gave Coleman confidence. He moved quickly toward her now. His breath churned in his chest like the blades of a flour sifter. He dropped the candlestick. It shattered on the cold tiles, and the candle, severed from its waxy tumor, rolled toward the sink; the room shuddered and jerked, drawings in a flip book.

She wanted to call for help but she didn't want to show Coleman any more of her fear than she already had. She hit him with the flashlight. The blow shook the batteries, extinguished the bulb. The candle went out and they were in darkness. She raised the flashlight to strike him again but, sensing her movements, he grabbed her wrist hard. She tried to wrest herself free, but his grip was powerful. It seemed as if he could hold two or three of her.

He held her close to him. She felt his breath, reptile cool but ripe with the rot of his disease—he smelled like fermenting apricots, and curled within that sick sweetness was a scent of something fecal. "You have come here to my aid?" he asked her and then he repeated the question in German, this time filling his voice with mockery and then with malice. His fingers were steely, uncompromising.

Caitlin called out Joe's name. She shouted it, with the consonant barely pronounced and the vowel a long and frightened wail.

"So you're not alone," Coleman said. He gripped her all the tighter, with a desire now not only to keep her but to hurt her. Yet his voice sounded less masterful. He was turning away from her a little, wondering what would happen next.

They heard footsteps coming up the stairs.

"Where are you?" It was Gordon.

"In here!" she called.

Coleman slapped her across the face, incredibly hard. It made her cry out, and then he shoved her back. Caitlin slipped on the tiles, fell against the tub. She hit it in stages, first her shoulders, then her neck, finally the back of her head. She tasted blood on her lip where her mouth had snapped shut.

A moment later she could vaguely see Gordon's massive silhouette in the doorway.

"Are you all right?" he asked.

"It was Coleman," she said, pointing to the left.

"Where's the flashlight?"

Caitlin, still sitting, felt along the tiles and found it. Gordon was at her side, twenty degrees warmer than the room. He took the flashlight from her, whacked it against his large, hard palm a couple of times and the bulb lit again. He shined the light in Caitlin's face.

"Go on, he's getting away," she said.

Caitlin slowly made her way out of the bathroom, into the corridor, and, holding on to the banister, down the staircase. She could hear Gordon charging from room to room, throwing doors open, heedless of any danger. "Come on out, you son of a bitch!" he shouted into one empty room, and "I see you, shit face!" he shouted into another.

When she made it to the bottom of the stairs, Joe was waiting in the darkness, more or less hidden in a dark corner beneath the steps.

"Joe?" she said, only able to see his faint outline, a certain residual spark in the whites of his eyes.

"Shhh," he whispered. "Come here."

She walked toward him, hitting with her hip the table where they had found the *German Awakener and Observer*.

"Was it him? Was it Coleman?" Joe asked her.

"Yes," she whispered. Upstairs, the noise of Gordon's slamming the doors grew more distant, fainter.

"I'm sorry, Caitlin," Joe whispered, and the words, and the way he said them, held some rare perfume of intimacy that even in the frightful frigid darkness of that house struck her as an exaltation. "I wanted to help, but if he saw me . . ."

"I know, I know. It's OK, really it is."

"It's just that if he saw me then I'd lose all my effectiveness."

"I wouldn't want that, Joe."

"I wanted to go up there. I mean especially when I thought you might be in danger."

"I was only scared."

He was silent for a few moments. Caitlin stood close to him, yet in some strange way his body did not acknowledge her presence. It was not as though he avoided her, stepped away; it was just a failure to register. And then at last he said, "Thank you."

Gordon came pounding down the stairs, the beam of the flashlight sweeping in front of him.

"I can't find him. Anywhere. There's probably rooms in this place . . . tunnels, I don't know."

"We'd better get out of here," said Joe.

"Then he's still in this house," Caitlin said.

"We'll lock the place up and set it on fire," said Gordon. He shined the light on their faces, saw the shock. "I'm from Chicago," he said, by way of explanation.

Yet Caitlin and Joe had no arguments against burning Coleman alive. He had killed many and would kill more.

"Are you serious?" Caitlin asked. "You'd really do that?"

"What do you mean, would *I* do that?" said Gordon.

"We'll all do it," said Joe. "He deserves to die. He must die. If we don't do it then we'll be murdering the next people the Germans send him out to kill."

Caitlin felt a tumult of anticipation in her stomach. She knew it was a trivial comparison but it reminded her of how she felt only once before in her life: in Washington when Betty Sinclair clicked cocktail glasses with her and then kissed her full on the mouth.

In the corner where Joe had retreated there was a door, locked with a dead bolt. Gordon asked Joe to move and he opened the door and there was a steep wooden staircase going down to what was surely the cellar.

"Keep an eye out for him," Gordon instructed, the brusqueness of his voice announcing the fact that he felt himself in control now. He disappeared down the stairs. A cold humid air rose from the cellar.

"They'll find our footprints in the snow," Caitlin said to Joe.

"They won't be able to make anything out of it. Anyhow, they'll find three sets. So they'd be looking for three people who work together and Gordon and I will be out of here. They'll never figure it out."

"Have you ever done this before, Joe? Or anything like it?"

"I know what you're thinking. But it's our morals and theirs, don't you understand? A gun has no morality. In the hands of a fascist it's evil, in the hands of a freedom fighter it's good."

"Well, I always thought it was hard for anyone to know for sure *what* they were."

"I sure as hell know I'm not a fascist," said Joe.

The face of Gordon's flashlight appeared at the bottom of

the stairs. "I found what we need," he called up in a passionate whisper. He came quickly up the stairs, holding an oblong gasoline can. When he was next to Caitlin and Joe he shook the can back and forth. A frothy slosh of fuel echoed inside of it.

"Let's go," he said.

They made their way to the door, leaving the nearly unanimous darkness of the house. The moon had risen and cast its pale light on the snowy field. Gordon shook the gasoline onto the porch, along the outer windowsills. Joe found the key above the door frame and locked the door and then replaced the key.

Caitlin noticed the cross-country skis. They were no longer propped against the house but were strewn over the porch.

"We better take the can along with us," said Gordon.

"We'll wait right here until he comes running out," said Joe.

"But you just locked the door," said Caitlin. "He couldn't get out if he tried."

He glanced at her. There seemed to be scorn in his eyes. But he retrieved the key and unlocked the door. "There," he said. "Feel better?"

Gordon took a box of matches out of his coat pocket. He held them up. "Who would like to do the honors?"

"I will," said Joe, grabbing the matches. Caitlin was certain he was making himself hard because he hadn't run up the stairs when she had cried for help.

He struck the match so violently it snapped in two. "Step back," he said to Caitlin and Gordon, as if everything were going according to plan.

They stood on the edge of the porch and Joe struck another match and threw it at the spot Gordon had soaked with gasoline. It burst into flames with the startled, hollow sound of a man who's had the wind knocked out of him. A chaotic bloom of bright orange. They jumped off the porch and watched. The flames raced across the porch, as if to get a closer look at the ones who had given them life, and then they seemed to turn and head back toward the house.

Caitlin stepped further back to see the windows on the second floor, to see if Coleman's face would appear, or the shadow of his racing form as he frantically tried to rescue himself. She saw nothing.

She stumbled over a ridge in the snow and looked down. There were ski tracks.

"Joe!" she called out. "Gordon. He's already gone. He took a pair of skis and just—" She moved her hand in a smooth arc to describe an escape.

They didn't answer. She was pointing now to the ski tracks and they came to see for themselves.

"There must be another way out," she said. "All these old houses are full of secret passages." Her voice sounded high, excited; she forced herself to calm down.

The flames that had so rapidly crawled up the side of the house were now suddenly losing intensity, growing smaller. It seemed that not even that would work out.

Joe shook his head. He squeezed his hands together and seemed to want to appear distraught, but there was something in his eyes that Caitlin recognized: a shimmer of sheer relief. It was not really in him to kill a man, or even a monster.

Gordon took pictures of the burning house that was no longer a burning house.

Caitlin turned away, first toward the moonlight and then toward a distant rise in the snowy field. And there she saw a figure, perhaps three hundred yards away, a man on skis. He seemed to be looking at them, but when she stepped forward to get a better view of him, he quickly turned, stuck his poles into the snow, and with a heave propelled himself forward, up over the rise, down again, and out of sight.

FEBRUARY 3, 1952

Caitlin was sitting in the living room–dining room–bedroom of her apartment on Barrow Street, New York City. It was snowing outside; the city was quiet, even beautiful. Now and then the sun would appear, and the ground, the automobile windshields, and the windows of all the apartment houses would vibrate with light.

She was being interviewed by two FBI agents, one of them with a pocked, vaguely Mexican-looking face, but who spoke with no accent, and the other a tall redhead with a small Band-Aid on his massive chin—a chin as blunt as a knee.

She was not in grave trouble herself; it was all about other people. She had been working in an organization that had helped refugees come to this country, and now some of the refugees and anyone who had helped them were under suspicion. Some of them were Communists, some of them were not anti-Communist enough for this particular era.

Caitlin was, in her own estimation, handling the two agents beautifully. She was wearing a woolen skirt, a sweater, nylon hosiery, black pumps. She gave every appearance of someone who was in a hurry to get to work, though the truth was that the baby sitter had been stranded in the Bronx by the snowstorm and Caitlin was going to take this day off anyhow, to be with her little boy. She was acting vague, formal, slow; she was boring them to death, making them restless. She could remember no one, nothing. She pretended to be the sort of person to whom specifics are an anathema.

Then the red-headed agent pulled one in from left field. All of the questions had to that point been about the Combined Emergency European Relief Committee, but then he asked, quite casually on the surface, but with a glance at his partner, "How about Gordon Jaffrey. Ever see much of him?"

"Who?" asked Caitlin. She smiled when she felt the slightest fear and that usually seemed to work.

"Gordon Jaffrey, the photographer. He used to be quite a good friend of yours."

"He was?" asked Caitlin, indicating confusion, and a willingness to be let in on an absurd joke.

"It would be really a shame if you held the truth back from us," said the Mexican-looking agent.

"Shame?" said Caitlin. "I used to feel shame all the time, now I never do, practically never."

And that was exactly when the kid waddled in. He was four years old but not terribly coordinated. Poor thing, he already wore eyeglasses. He had been going through his mother's dresser drawers and found, hidden away in one of those accordion files made of brown cardboard, a cache of photographs. Gordon's photographs, taken at Camp Sunrise, exactly eleven years ago. The Fee-bees never guessed but the pictures were all there, right under their noses—the empty flagpoles, the zodiac ceiling, the last of that day's sunlight making a Bethlehem-star pattern in the tangle of empty branches.

"Mama," the child said, holding the pictures before him, his belly showing beneath the hem of the blue flannel shirt he had outgrown, the sunlight flashing in his glasses, his roseate mouth in its characteristic querulous pucker. "Can I have these pictures to keep?"

THREE

It was the day after Caitlin's birthday. She was eight years old, tall, graceful, with long, already shapely legs, delicate fingers, and her eyes had an element of virtuosity to them— they could accuse, appraise, they could even, in some childish, innocent way, smolder.

Her parents had imbued the story of her birth with a sense of drama that floated in Caitlin's vague sense of herself like a long curl of blood in a glass of water. They thought at first that Annie was barren and then there was a miscarriage, and then another—Caitlin's vision of miscarriage was based on the still-born calf she once saw: a liver-and-white creature glistening with its mother's gore, which the other cows stomped on their way through the barn.

For Caitlin's eighth birthday, Annie made a vanilla cake and spelled her name on the icing with nasturtium petals, which Peter had saved from the summer, pressed in his copy of *Ivanhoe*. Caitlin had wanted a dog or a cat, but the Flemings were strict about the families in the tenant houses keeping animals—the Flemings had expensive hunting dogs and an Abyssinian cat to whom they gave the run of the property and

which they didn't want polluted by the sperm of lesser animals. And so Caitlin was given a thick green sweater, which
her mother had knitted, a smooth wooden bracelet, which her
father had carved out of cherry, and a subscription to the *Saturday Evening Post*, which would come every week in a brown
envelope and be placed in the tin mailbox on River Road and
which would have her name typewritten on the wrapper—
and this was paid for with cash money.

Now, the day after, she was in her bed, in the cold room
at the north end of the house, wearing over her nightgown the
new green sweater and wearing on her wrist the smooth, bur-
nished oval her father made. A rime of ice was on the window
and behind that was the faintly silver darkness of a winter
morning without sun. Caitlin gripped the hem of the quilt;
beneath her bed, currents of cold air twisted and turned like
eels under ice. The window glass rattled in its pane.

She must go to school today, a journey of two miles,
which she must make walking backward against the wind that
would pant in her face like an eager dog no matter which way
she turned.

But for now she could be still. She did not have to worry
about oversleeping because she knew her father would come
in when it was time.

He minded her now, after leaving the first years to Annie.
Caitlin was like a baton that had been passed and now Peter
was running with her. He had taken over her upbringing, if
not her care. He showed her sunsets, the stars; they went
often to the woods with a torch to see what went on in the
night. He taught her the names of the trees, flowers, grasses,
and weeds. She knew where the morels grew, and next year
he said she could take them to town and sell them for money.
He taught her poetry and chess. He made her a pair of real
Dutch wooden shoes, and when she was too shy to wear them
he made a pair for himself and together they walked the

muddy fields, leaving in the soft earth marks that looked like small anvils.

It had been a disappointment for Peter when Annie did not produce a son—even as it was for Annie, for whom manhood was not necessarily exalted but for whom womanhood was a state of danger and humiliation. Peter had wanted one day to pass along the tools and costumes of his trade, the outfits that meant as much to him as caps and ribbons would to a soldier. He had wanted a boy to give the green-and-tan gum boots one wore when working in a mucky barn, the moleskin trousers one wore when clearing the brush, the heavy wool birding pants, the gloves, the hickory-handled hammer, the brilliant little carbon-toothed saw that could cut through lead, the thick and aged ropes. These were the things that represented a way of life, a way of doing things Peter respected; they were a part of a harmony he found comforting and even beautiful, though of course it drowned out whatever his own personal song might have been.

Caitlin heard the door below her room open with a groan. She slipped out of bed and ran to the window. She pressed her hand against the ice until a palm-shaped peephole melted, and then she looked through and saw her mother on her way up the black frozen path to the Flemings'. She must be there early to roll out dough for bread and to make the breakfast in case someone in the main house got up early. There was barely any snow on the ground, just a little crust here and there nestled into the bare branches of the forsythia or mixed in with the dead leaves along the stone walls. Annie wore a long black coat over her white uniform, and black rubber boots with the snaps open, and they seemed to want to come off her feet as she trudged up the incline.

In front of her, rising out of a wreath of mist, was the brick mansion with its towering, narrow chimneys, which seemed to impale it, pins through a butterfly. In the summer,

Caitlin might spy her mother walking barefoot on this path, suddenly girlish, swinging her white, square-heeled shoes in her hand as she breathed her only free breaths of the day. But in the winter speed was all. Annie walked quickly, with her head bowed against the wind, and Caitlin watched as she got further and further away, in a landscape shaped by Caitlin's small hand, until the ice formed again in the handprint, the fingers filled in and then the palm, and then the glass was opaque and Annie was gone.

Caitlin ran back to her bed, pulled the covers up to her chin, and closed her eyes.

It was Peter's job to awaken Caitlin, feed her, get her off to school. The Flemings could never complain about what time Peter started working—everyone knew he did more than his share on the property, did the work of two men, maybe three, and barely got the pay of just one.

He liked to wake her gently, recalling and recoiling from the raucous risings of his own Dutch childhood—his mother beating a spoon against a pot, his father simply throwing open the windows. Peter wanted his daughter to have mornings that allowed contemplation, gratitude for life, reverence, pleasure. He would say, "Only a still pond can hold a reflection."

Sometimes he woke her by merely sitting on the bed and letting his thoughts stir her. Sometimes he stroked her hair until she opened just one eye, a dolphin breaking the water's surface; she would smile at him, reach for him. And then there were the times when he would slip into the bed with her, the small bed that he had made with his own hands and he and Caitlin had lacquered one distant afternoon in an equipment barn while the rain had drummed on the tin roof, drummed and drummed and drummed.

This was one of those frigid winter mornings when even the wind is too cold to make a sound. Peter had made oatmeal—he believed in hot breakfasts, just as he believed in hard work. His long face was raw from a cold-water wash and the scrape of the straight razor; he smelled of brown soap and the strong coffee he had poured into himself. His hands were always cold, with something waxy and pious about them. He blew on them to warm his fingers. He was wearing dark brown boots that laced almost to the knee, and he was careful not to get them on the quilt as he stretched out next to his daughter and whispered in her ear, "Caitlin, rise and shine."

She had a slight cold, she'd had it since the harsh weather settled in, and her breathing was raspy, belabored. It was only ten years since children died by the thousands from influenza and winter colds were still occasions for dread. Peter listened to her phlegmy breaths and he spun between the magnetic poles of concern and rapture: her beauty was braided around her vulnerability and it broke his heart.

He loved Caitlin with the core of his being. It was a love so deep, so alive, so boundless and incoherent that there were times he was lost within it. He walked through his love like a man through a blizzard. And he would never mean to hurt her, or frighten her in any way. But he must lie next to her; he must feel the abrupt curve of her spine through the quilt as she lay curled into herself.

His love of order bent beneath the burden of his love and he felt fear this morning, real fear. There was something lonely within him, something ravenous, and he didn't know what this beast of appetite required of him. He wanted to cover his little girl's face with kisses but he knew he must never. Desire came to him like a traveler from a distant land: he didn't understand its language, he couldn't communicate with it except for pleading, impatient gestures.

He was perfectly suited for running a large estate and there was not one man who worked under him who felt he ought to have Peter's position. He knew every stone and tree on the property, his Dorset lambs, his Guernsey cows, his horses. He knew the proper mix of ash and oak and cherry to make a perfect sugaring fire, knew the exact direction to place the bales of hay for the best drying in July and how to change the angle slightly in August. He knew carpentry and plumbing, and was lucky when it came to wells. He knew everything on this property except his own heart, but this was the moment when everything else fell away and it was only this mysterious muscle with which he had to contend.

He stretched out next to his sleeping daughter and slowly brought his fingers closer to her hair, never knowing, never even suspecting, that though Caitlin's eyes were closed she was entirely awake.

Maybe some men who dream of fondling their children, who want to press them close in a long, forbidden embrace, do so out of some need to debase and defile the innocence before them. Or perhaps they are compelled to reenact some childhood wound—a moment, perhaps, when an adult did the same to them. But in Peter's case it was largely the consequence of a heart and a conscience unprepared for the love that was thrust upon it. His view of himself was small and tidy, and now he carried within him too much passion. He stumbled beneath it, just as a man staggering down the road beneath a load of kindling on his shoulders can drift far from the path and end up in the briars, the bog, in a world of trouble.

"Caitlin?" he said in a whisper like a flame guttering in a candle.

She pretended to sleep.

"Caitlin," he said again, this time louder.

And she knew, without exactly knowing why, that he was testing to see if she was asleep and, if so, how deeply. She slipped her arm beneath her pillow and breathed herself deeper into the mesh of the mattress.

He moved closer to her and then closer still, until he could not be closer without being on top of her. "Shhh, shhh," he said.

And then he pressed himself against her, hard, and he was

hard, too, though it would be some years before she could remember that part of it, that hardness at his center.

"Shhh," he said, "sleep. I love you, my darling. I love you."

It was an incantation, and as he said it he was pressing against her and moving, rubbing, once, twice, again and again. And then he rolled away and got quickly out of the bed, ran from the room, and out of the house.

She heard his footsteps going away and she heard his voice. His voice was low, it sounded stunned, he was talking to himself but she could not understand the words. The wind carried them away.

She lay there for a long while, lonely for him, confused, feeling queerly ill at the pit of her stomach, the way she once did when she heard something she was not meant to—her mother saying to Peter: "It hurts when I pass my water. Do you think I should see the doctor?"

It was cold in that room and she pulled the covers over her head to be away from the air, which moved everywhere, looking for someone to make miserable. The darkness beneath the quilt was cold, too, but at least it was still and soon she was asleep again, thinking as consciousness faded that if no one came to waken her then she would not go to school.

When she did awaken, it was well past the time to go to school. The sun had streaked the icy window; long ovals of blue showed through the gray glass. She heard voices below, excited. She heard Shorty Russel saying, "Put him down here—careful now, careful."

She sat up in bed, knowing something awful had happened. And then someone said, "Go up to the house and tell Mr. Fleming."

"Yes, and Annie, too," another voice said.

"My leg is broken," she heard her father say, his voice filled with anger and wavering with the effort to remain calm.

"You're lucky you ain't dead," Shorty Russel said. "What

could be the matter with you? And what were you doing with that tractor in the woods anyhow?"

"I was bringing in some wood, the red oak we cut down last week."

"Well, I think you must be crazy. You just drove that tractor off that ledge as if you was blind. Here, I'm going to put your leg up here to make you more comfortable."

And more than anything else that day, she would remember sitting up in her bed and holding her ears as her father made one final strangled shout of pain.

FEBRUARY 21, 1940

Years later, Caitlin would learn that today the Germans began building the concentration camp at Auschwitz. But in her own life this day seemed only the beginning of her first true adventure, the day she left Leyden for Washington, D.C., the day when the restless and grandiose part of herself that had always dreamed of a life away from the estate, a life full of sleek errands and witty friends, a life of real importance, had suddenly to find a heretofore undiscovered internal ally—a self who could actually manage such a life.

Her parents brought her to the train station. Mr. Fleming had loaned Caitlin's father the Buick to take Caitlin to the station and eighteen dollars to buy the ticket, which Fleming had handed over in a flour sack into which he swept spare change from his bureau at the end of every week—the eighteen dollars was in pennies, nickels, and dimes and weighed as much as a fieldstone.

Peter drove slowly, with his knuckles like bleached stones from gripping the steering wheel so tightly. Caitlin sat beside him, watching the snowy countryside go past in fits and

starts. Annie sat in the back, checking through the wicker basket full of provisions she had packed for the train journey.
Fleming had neglected to give Peter the key to the trunk, so
Caitlin's trunk and suitcases were also in the back; Annie sat
precariously perched on the suitcase with her feet propped on
the trunk while she touched now the apples, now the jar of
pickled green beans, now the little tin of biscuits.

They were silent. It was six in the morning; dawn was
two red furrows in an ice-gray sky. Peter drove the car over a
slushy pothole and gasped at the thought of having damaged
Mr. Fleming's car. "What did Dr. Freeman have to say for
himself?" Peter Van Fleet asked, as he took the turn off River
Road. They were just a half mile from the train station by
now.

"That's funny, I was just thinking about him," said Caitlin.

Peter smiled, pleased and regretful—he always said they
had a special communication, and now it was ending.

"A clean bill of health and all that?" he said.

"He said I should eat more," said Caitlin.

"As if we didn't feed you," said Annie, from the back seat.

It struck Caitlin then that her mother was always a voice
from the back seat, or the next room, someone just out of
earshot, someone not entirely included. She turned to look at
her mother but it was difficult, wearing such a bulky coat,
sitting as she was. She straightened herself out and felt her
heart grow heavy.

"We may as well face it," said Peter. "Freeman's a quack.
He moved here from the city. Running from something, I'll
bet." As respectful as Peter was toward the Flemings, he was
just that scornful toward everybody else.

"Then why did you make such a fuss about me going to
him?"

"Well, with you going off halfway across the country . . ."

"I'm going to Washington, not Kansas City."

"You got that right," Peter said, smiling. "Kay Cee. Half-way across the country."

"If I put it on your plate and you don't eat it, I don't think it's my fault," said Annie.

"I know that, Mama," said Caitlin. This time she did not attempt to turn around. She just said it and left it at that.

"Everything else check out, though?" asked Peter. "Ticker?"

Caitlin had had scarlet fever when she was ten and there had been persistent concern about her heart since then.

"Ticker's great, pulse is the cat's pajamas."

"I always actually see a cat wearing pajamas when you say that," said Peter, grinning happily. He had been sullen for days, dreading this goodbye at the train station, but now his spirits were rising like a fever.

Caitlin was thinking about the look on Dr. Freeman's face—he was a small, dapper man, with a pencil mustache and brilliantined hair—when he said, "Are you still intact?" She had told him it was none of his business and he smiled, smoothed his mustache down with his forefinger, and interpreted her little flash of temper as a kind of confession.

The train station was simple, a little red brick waiting room where the stationmaster sat smoking his hand-rolled cigarettes behind the bars of the ticket window, looking like a convict. There were two long benches for the passengers waiting for their trains. A few years before, there had been no place to get out of the weather or to buy a ticket. The brick structure had been built with the use of private funds—the river families had chipped in a few thousand each to construct it. It had been quite awful to see how the Flemings had campaigned to be asked to contribute.

Peter pulled into the station. The tracks went along the river, south to New York City, north to Canada. The ice on the river looked like shattered glass; here and there it was melted and steam rose up toward the morning light. The snowy, still lawns of the great houses swept down to the river. On the west side of the river, where there were more workers, a cement factory, closed during the worst days of the Depression, was going again, and its smokestacks sent up puffs of gray smoke that looked somehow colder than the sky.

Caitlin peered out the car window at the tracks. She could see the southbound train a mile away. It was burning coal and the smoke was black. The train was slowing down now and the smoke trailed over the engine and then the next car, and then the next, like a long vaporous scarf.

"We better hurry," said Caitlin.

Peter was looking at his pocket watch and shaking his head. "Either they've changed the schedule on us or the train's early."

"Maybe the Flemings paid extra to get rid of her that much sooner," said Annie. As she often did nowadays, after saying the worst, she laughed.

"Annie, what kind of thing is that to say?" The voice Peter used when he addressed his wife had within it the tone of a teacher who is only biding his time before his new position comes through, a teacher who has nothing left to say and only wants to avoid anything that will impede his departure.

"I'm only saying what is true," Annie said. "And what we all know to be true."

"Annie—"

"She's right, she's right," said Caitlin, opening the door. "I'm sorry I embarrassed you."

"It's not embarrassment, it's disgrace," said Annie. Her arms were folded over her bosom. She was wearing her black overcoat with the fur collar. Her face was too narrow for her large, staring eyes.

The train sounded its whistle. That whistle had always

been a howl of loneliness to Caitlin, who would hear it from her bedroom and long to be on her way somewhere or other. Yet now it was calling to her and she did not feel joy. She did not feel fear, either, or sadness, or even excitement. All she felt was vague tension, as if she were at the sink washing her hands and wondering if she might be late to work.

Caitlin grabbed her suitcases—plaid cloth, brand new, a goodbye, good-riddance present from the Flemings—and Peter dragged the old battered blue metal trunk by its parched and crumbling leather handle across the snow-packed parking lot. They had to hurry; the pressure of the moment overwhelmed whatever impulse any of them might have had for last-minute embraces, promises, tears. Caitlin scurried down the steep, icy stairs toward the track. Annie trudged behind her, grasping the handrail, with a faraway, faintly amused expression on her face, the wind ruffling the fur of her coat collar so that it touched her creased white face. Peter was last, limping, frowning each time the trunk bounced against a step as he dragged it behind him.

Caitlin had her ticket in her purse. She was the only passenger getting on in Leyden this morning. The train was coming from Albany; it would be full of politicians and well-to-do housewives, on their way to the city. In New York, Caitlin would change trains for Washington. She had three quarters in a new leather change purse so she could tip Red Caps at Grand Central and not have to struggle with her luggage. She was looking forward to that particularly. She had never before paid someone to do her work for her.

The train's headlight was on, shining pale gold in the gray morning air. The engineer was having fun with the steam whistle; Caitlin imagined people rolling over in their warm beds for miles around, heeding the train for a moment, and then pulling the covers over their heads.

They had just one moment for their final goodbyes. A conductor was hanging out the open door as the car pulled into the station. He pointed at Caitlin's trunk, gestured for her to just leave it there.

"I'll write you tonight as soon as I'm there," said Caitlin.

"Mr. Fleming said for you to sit on the right side, so you can watch the river," said Peter.

"I think I've seen enough of this river," said Caitlin, and then immediately regretted it.

He shook his head. "It's changing so fast, though. Factories, houses. Poor Henry Hudson wouldn't recognize it."

Steam poured off the train. The enormous iron wheels were white with frost.

She saw the men inside the train reading newspapers, smoking, talking to one another. Caitlin quickly glanced down a row of windows looking for a woman's face but saw none. Ah: there. An older woman wearing a silly feathered hat, reading no newspaper, smoking no cigarette, talking to no one: just sitting there in perfect unmoving profile.

A man in a blue cap and uniform, handlebar mustache and bushy eyebrows, had taken her suitcase in. The conductor, an older man with a round face, wire-rimmed spectacles, leaned out again and called, "All aboard!"

"Is it OK if we see her to her seat?" Peter asked.

"No visitors!" the conductor called out.

Peter saluted. Understood.

Caitlin turned quickly and hugged her mother. It was the first time she had touched her mother intimately in many years. She felt she had to take Annie by surprise.

"So now they've taken my only child," muttered Annie into Caitlin's painfully cold ear. Instinctively, Annie hugged her tight—but then quickly let go and seemed to push Caitlin away, in a gesture that might have meant "Hurry up" but which Caitlin knew more likely meant "Leave me alone."

She turned to her father, embraced him, kissed him lightly on the cheek. He needed a shave; he smelled smoky from the wood stove. He clasped her hands and looked down at her. He was becoming stooped but he was still enormously tall. His eyes filled with tears. He looked mortified, as if someone had just slapped his face.

"Don't be surprised if I turn up one day in Washington to pay you a surprise visit," he said. "Both of us."

"I'd give all my wishes away if that one would come true," said Caitlin, hugging him one last time, backing toward the retractable steel steps that led to the mysterious amber warmth of the waiting train.

"That's from a poem, isn't it?" Peter called out.

The engineer let the whistle howl one last time. A fierce burst of steam hissed from the belly of the train as it started to roll. Caitlin looked back at the platform; her parents were enshrouded.

"Tickets," said the conductor. He had looked friendlier when he was hanging out of the train; now that she was under his jurisdiction, he looked displeased with her.

Caitlin opened her purse and gave the conductor what he wanted. He tore pieces of the many-paged ticket out, put holes in others with his paper puncher, and handed it back to Caitlin.

"Second class, two cars down," he said.

She nodded. "I was told if I wanted to change this ticket to first class I could do it on the train."

He nodded, frowned. She was making work for him. "To New York, or all the way to Washington?"

"First class, all the way to Washington."

"We have a club car, too," the conductor said, meaning to be sarcastic.

"Is that better than first class?"

"Oh, much."

"Then I'll have that." The car was swaying back and forth as the train picked up speed. Caitlin looked out the window a last time to see her parents. Peter was waving, unsure if he was being seen, and Annie was moving closer to him, touching him lightly on the sleeve, as if to reclaim him. She was still holding the basket she had packed for Caitlin's journey.

"You should have got what you wanted in the first place," the conductor said, handing Caitlin the blue-and-white ticket that would allow her into the club car.

"The person who made the purchase wasn't aware of my requirements," said Caitlin, opening her purse and counting out crisp dollars that were being spent for the very first time.

And so she traveled with the rich, on a dark velvet seat, adjusting and readjusting the footrests, and watching through her own reflection as the miles went by. The man sitting next to her worked in an investment house in New York. He was coming back from visiting his sister, who had married a farmer and was living upstate. The stockbroker was upset over the life she was making for herself. "The cold, the filth, everything stinks of horse or cow." He had a way of folding his newspaper so it was no larger than a book. After he had had enough of decrying his sister's new life, he asked Caitlin where she was going and she told him she was on her way to Washington.

"Family there?"

"No, I'm going to work for a congressman." This was her first time out in the world with this new fact of life and she tried it on proudly.

"Say, that's all right. Which crook? No, just kidding. Who'll you be working for?"

"Elias J. Stowe."

"Say, Stowe's all right." The man tapped his forehead, apparently pleased he knew who Stowe was. "What we need is politicians with the guts to stand up to Roosevelt in case he tries to get us into a war against Germany."

"I don't think Mr. Stowe wants war."

"You can say that again. He's got guts. You know, like in Shakespeare, 'Discretion is the better part of valor.'"

Caitlin turned away. As they headed south, parts of the

river were already thawed. An old European-style castle was built off a little islet in the river and it was in ruins, its tower crumpled, its windows blue with sky. She felt the sudden pressure of tears in her eyes: she was just getting a glimpse of herself as a free woman riding a train, sitting in the best seats, next to a stranger quoting Shakespeare.

"You just tell your boss that Teddy Collington—here's my card, by the way—is behind him all the way. You know what I think? Basically, Roosevelt's too shrewd to get us mixed up in that war. You see that Gallup Poll the other day? Seventy percent of the country wants us to keep our noses out of it." His eyes darted for a moment. "The only ones who want war are the crazy Army generals who have nothing to do but march around in the stink and the mud. And the Jews, who seem to think that this, like everything else in the world, is really all about them."

He settled back in his seat, propped his feet up on the footrest, and bit down hard on a peppermint candy.

"I hope I haven't gone on too much about it," he said, smiling at Caitlin. There was something searching, vaguely and ominously flirtatious in his eyes suddenly. He seemed to be scrutinizing her for some possibility of sex—it struck her in the pit of her stomach because she had sensed him as a prissy bachelor type and now it seemed she had been wrong.

"No, not at all," she said.

"I assume your views are the same, then?" he said, smiling.

"I'm not sure," she said. "I don't think I've given it much thought."

"Not much thought? There's no more important question facing us now."

They parted in Grand Central Station. Collington carried a small leather suitcase, draped his topcoat over his shoulders. They were underground, in a smoking, acrid tunnel. "You be sure to wish your boss good luck, now!" Collington called out as he walked out toward the circle of white clear light at the end of the platform.

On the train to Washington, Caitlin sat next to a priest who smoked a pipe and read a book in French. He never once glanced at her; even when she squeezed past him to go to the bathroom, he kept his eyes on the page.

The claustrophobia and exhaustion of traveling overwhelmed her high spirits, and she was suddenly weary and afraid of all the strangers around her, all the houses with the unknown lives taking place within them, the factories and fences, the unfamiliar skies, the lengthening shadows, the incessant chug and sway of the train, the fermented-apple aroma of the priest's tobacco.

She closed her eyes and slept and the rest of the journey slipped away. None of it even lodged in memory. The unfriendliness of the priest, the smell of his pipe, the coils of an electrical generating station in New Jersey flashing red as they caught the rays of the sun, the thump of her head against the thick window glass as she dozed off, the distant voice of a conductor calling out the station stop in Philadelphia, and then a dream, oblique, just of light, of a jar full of violets, a trembling square of sun on the floor intersected suddenly by a shadow, and then she awakened as if from a nightmare, disoriented, trembling, waves of panic rippling through her like wind over the wheat.

Union Station was chaos. She walked behind the porter who dragged her luggage. She stared at the trunk's handle, wondering if it would snap. Everywhere there were trains sweating in the tunnels, and the steam gathered around the travelers, who moved like phantoms. Here were people of all colors, speaking all the languages of the world—businessmen, lawyers, journalists, men in white suits with beards like Georgia colonels, Negroes, women in pillbox hats with cigarettes plugged into their brightly painted mouths. They had arrived on the great lurching and howling locomotives of the Atlantic

Coast Line, the Southern, the Pennsylvania, the Fredericks-
burg & Ohio. Peter had told her that over two hundred passenger trains pulled into Union Station every day.

She walked through the tunnel, into the light. The Red
Cap was a young black man with a deformed back. The skin
beneath his fingernails was bright pink, like a calf's tongue.

She had asked the Red Cap to take her to the information
booth, where, by prearrangement, she was to meet Betty Sinclair, who was then nothing but a name written on a piece of
paper to Caitlin. "Miss Sinclair will be wearing a tan coat and
a dark green hat," the instructions from Stowe's departing secretary read. "She will see to your lodgings, as well."

Everything echoed in the station: voices, footsteps, even
her own heartbeat. She stopped for a moment, to calm herself. People streamed past her like rushing water past a boul-
der in the streambed.

"It's just up here, miss," said the Red Cap. "Information."

Caitlin nodded her head. Her breath was shallow and felt
useless. She had never spoken to a black person before.

Then a voice said, "Are you Caitlin Van Fleet?" It was a
deep, melodic voice, and though Caitlin did not think of it as
seductive at the time she would come to remember it so.

She turned toward the voice and faced Betty Sinclair. She
was dressed in a trenchcoat and a green hat that looked like
something Errol Flynn would wear. She was tall, angular,
with blond hair, bright, aquamarine eyes.

"I knew I'd recognize you," she said, smiling at Caitlin.
"And it's a good thing, too. There's at least ten women in this
place wearing hats like mine. You could have ended up going
home with *anybody.*"

She looked at Caitlin, squinted her eyes a little, and then
took her by the arm. "Long ride, isn't it?" she said. She waited
for a response, though surely she could not have cared what
the answer to her question was. Betty Sinclair was verbally

taking the pulse of the beautiful young girl who stood before her and who seemed not to possess the power of speech.

"Are you all right?" Betty asked, softly. She gestured for the Red Cap to follow them with Caitlin's luggage. "I've got a taxi waiting for us outside."

The porter was dexterous with Caitlin's luggage. He carried the suitcase with just the index finger of his left hand hooked through the handle, and he suddenly hoisted the trunk onto his shoulder. He walked in front of them and weaved through the crowds.

"It's like being on safari," said Betty.

Caitlin stopped. She felt so short of breath that even the mild exertion of walking seemed a risk. She had such a clear vision of herself sinking to the floor of the station and the patterns the people made as they shifted this way and that to avoid treading over her that it seemed to be not dread but some real prescience, a vivid memory of the future.

"Are you all right?" Betty asked again.

"I just can't believe I'm here," said Caitlin, the first words she'd spoken to Betty.

"You'll get used to it," said Betty. "Really, it's not so bad."

"I just can't believe I'm here," Caitlin said again. She felt vaguely the comforting weight of Betty's arm around her but more than anything she was conscious of a voice that resonated like a drum within her and the voice said, I'm free, I'm free, I'm free.

FOUR

The day before Easter, a day in which winter usually still lay furled in every hollow of Windsor County, but this year the spring was early, extravagant—flowers were scattered everywhere like coins from the purse of a drunken sailor. The sky was dark blue, and seemed to tremble, a sail filled with warm wind.

Caitlin was twelve years old. She wore a loose-fitting shirt to camouflage the changes in her body. Her hair was cut short in that practical, not terribly becoming way of a country girl. She was not being raised to believe that adornment was a sin but only that it was foolish. "As stupid as a rooster with its feathers spread," was how her father had described a friend given to expensive, store-bought clothes, and surely the barbs directed against a preening woman would be sharper still.

It was Saturday and she was with her father in one of the barns. Peter was organizing the hay left over from the winter, hay that they would not need now that the snows had melted and the fields were already pale green—though the sheep, he told her as he hauled the bales of rye and timothy hay, had to be pastured gradually, or else they would get diarrhea from the rich new grass. Caitlin's parents were either silent or oblique about matters of the body and even the heart—they were always fully clothed; her father ran water in the sink when he urinated; menstrual supplies were nowhere to be found in the house—but they exercised whatever frankness they possessed in casual, graphic talk about the estate's animals. Bitches in heat, runny cow stools, a nanny goat with an infected teat, all were discussed openly and at great length.

Her father was lax about making her do Saturday chores; in fact, he discouraged it. But he did like her company and he was content to stack the bales of hay along the north end of the barn while Caitlin sat on the floor, her legs stretched out before her, her back against the slightly warped wagon wheel. She was reading the *Saturday Evening Post*.

She read every word in the magazine. Because it was sent to her it seemed to have been written for her—the stories, even the advertisements.

Now she was looking at a picture of the Empire State Building. The picture was taken from the base of the building and it looked like a fountain that had erupted from the sidewalk and then turned to stone.

"The Empire State Building is one hundred and two stories high," Caitlin said to her father.

He turned to face her. Little sticks of hay clung to his shirt like porcupine quills. He wore a red handkerchief over his mouth and nose because the dust from the hay made him choke. He was tall, bony, with large, hard hands and deep, wounded eyes. In the house, he wore cardigans and wire-rimmed reading glasses, but when he worked he wore overalls, greenish gum boots, and no glasses—it made him seem like two separate people to Caitlin.

"Lot of little rooms to rob people blind," he said.

Caitlin watched his mouth moving beneath the handkerchief, moisture appeared, disappeared as he spoke.

"Wish we could go to New York," Caitlin said, detecting

the note of petulance in her own voice. She hated to sound whiny and childish but sometimes desire kicked so hard within her she couldn't really help it. It was like being thrown from the saddle by a wild horse—there you were on the ground before you knew it.

"What are you looking at there anyhow?" Peter asked. He walked across the worn gray plank floor. He was about to crouch down in front of Caitlin but then he remembered his stiffened, scarred leg and stood up, very, very straight, as if pain were his commanding officer calling him to attention. He yanked the kerchief off his mouth and it draped around his long neck.

"Does it hurt?" Caitlin asked. She felt oddly accused by her father's injured leg. It made her feel guilt, despair, and it seemed to create within her a path she dared not follow, a path of shame.

"Just a little stiff."

Caitlin closed the magazine and stood up. The blood seemed to leave her head like water down the drain—she stumbled a little, feeling dramatic, rapturous, about to faint.

"I don't see why you can't be estate manager anymore," she said.

"Shorty's doing a good job. He's a good worker."

"But it was always your job, and your father's before you had it."

"And his father's, too." Peter smiled. He had large white teeth, which he took good care of, scrubbing them with salt and baking soda. He said there was nothing so low class as a mouth full of bad teeth.

"So it isn't fair."

"The fair is at the end of the summer."

"No, I really mean it."

"It's fair. Until my leg's better I can't get around as easy as I used to."

"Do you think it will get better?"

"It's slow. But it gets a little better every day." He took the magazine out of Caitlin's hands and thumbed through it. She wondered what he was looking for.

"Well, are you mad at the mister for taking your job away?"

"Don't call him the mister," said Peter.

"Mama does."

"She's from Ireland. I would call him Mr. Fleming."

"That's what I do, to his face."

"Well, you see, that's the whole thing right there. There should be no difference between what you say to his face and what you say behind his back."

"So then you do like him," said Caitlin. She smiled but there was something in it that disturbed her. She would have liked her father's relation to the Flemings to be somehow clever, concealed, like one of those humble, treacherous clerks in stories who manage to take over the business secretly before anyone gets wind of what they are doing.

"The Flemings have been good to us, Caitlin," Peter was saying. "You read about what's going on. There are men everywhere nowadays who can't feed their families. With business so bad and the banks holding on to every penny. It's happening right here, in our own hometown. Boys and girls in your own school without shoes on their feet. I think we're pretty lucky, don't you? We all eat and have a good house, with a good roof, and plenty of firewood, and we get to live in the most beautiful spot on earth. We live like real gentlemen, without all the worries."

"We do all the work," said Caitlin.

A thin bar of sunlight, with a swarm of dust captured within it, poured down from a pinhole in the barn's metal roof.

"It's good work, Caitlin—"

But that's all he said because just then they heard a sound that opened the day and emptied it over everything it once held, like a knife slitting a sack of feathers. They heard Mr. Fleming calling Peter in a loud, commanding voice—with that undertone of mirth that always seemed to be there, as if Peter, or Mr. Fleming's relationship to Peter, was somehow humorous, like the relationship between a man and a chimpanzee.

Fulton Fleming drove straight into the barn, crushing a scythe that had been left on the floor. He was in his shining maroon Hudson, without a top, and he wore a blue suit, a white shirt, a yellow tie. His hair was wet, shining, slicked back.

"There you are, Peter," he said, exasperated. "Get in."

Peter looked himself up and down and gestured apologetically at his dirty clothes.

"Never mind that," said Fleming. "Just get in back."

Without waiting to be asked, Caitlin followed her father into Mr. Fleming's Hudson. There were vases attached to the doors in back, with fresh daffodils in them.

Mr. Fleming threw the car into reverse and ran the scythe over a second time. His eyes looked boiled and he didn't move them when he wanted to see more but only opened them wider. Once he had backed out of the barn and turned the car toward the main house, they sped along, exploding the clouds of dust that seemed to be curled into every rut like genies in bottles.

"What seems to be the trouble, Mr. Fleming?" Peter asked.

"Annie," said Fleming.

"Mama?" said Caitlin.

Peter patted her hand, counseling her to keep silent.

"Did she hurt herself?" Peter asked.

"No, no, nothing like that," said Fleming. "Mary's cousin asked her to do something and the next thing we knew—" He was about to make a helpless gesture when the car hit a heave in the road and he gripped the wheel hard with both hands. "She simply went berserk."

"What happened?" asked Caitlin. She leaned forward and shrugged her father's hand off her shoulder.

"You must handle her, Peter," said Fleming. "Calm her down and do whatever needs to be done." And then, softly, to himself: "I knew something like this would have to happen. We have people in our house who have *never* come to see us before."

The house was at the top of the drive, on a breezy knoll, with a view of the valley and the iridescent ribbon of river winding through.

They followed Fleming into the house. The marble floors shone like water in the sunlight. Their footsteps echoed.

Fleming opened the french doors to the music room. Sitting at the piano was a good-looking young man in a blazer. He had placed a newspaper on the music stand and played the piano as he read, as if the letters in the headline—"German National Socialists Call for Moratorium on All Other Political Parties"—could be played as musical notes. The tune he played was like circus music.

Sitting on the floor was a woman with long red hair. She had one arm wrapped around his legs; she supported herself with her other arm and she cocked her head and smiled at Mr. Fleming.

The lilac branches were scratching at the window.

"Where's Mary?" asked Fleming.

The red-haired woman pointed straight up at the ceiling. Fleming took a deep breath, and then nodded formally. He closed the doors.

"They're upstairs," he said to Peter. He made his way toward the staircase, with Caitlin and Peter following. The local muralist had painted a scene of New York Harbor on the curved wall going up the stairs, where Morris Fleming, upon whose labors the family fortune was based, had made millions in the maritime trades—importing, exporting, insuring ships, storing cargo, and gaining a reputation for rapaciousness and easy morals that Mary and Fulton Fleming were still trying to escape.

"That was William Porter in there," Fleming said to Peter as they climbed the stairs. "His family was one of the first to build in Windsor County—over two hundred years ago. They have really seen people come and go." He breathed a sigh and shook his head.

As they made their way upstairs, Caitlin saw a man and a woman dressed for tennis leaving through one of the side doors, the one that let out onto the bluestone terrace, which sprouted ironweed no matter how many times Peter cut it back. Following them was Jamey, holding two snowy-white tennis balls. He was saying, "I get to play, too, you know."

"Oh, there you are," said Mary Fleming, as they reached the second floor. She was wearing pleated trousers and a billowing shirt. Someone had done her hair so it curled at each temple. Even at thirty-two, she seemed like a woman straining to act young.

"Bill and Daisy seem like they're doing just fine downstairs. Bill's playing the piano," Fulton said. His inflection seemed to be asking Mary to back this observation up.

"I'm glad you think so," she said. "It took us a year to get them over here."

Fulton turned to Peter, finding solace in easy commands, stable lines of authority. "I think you had better look in on your Annie."

"Is she in there?" Peter asked, pointing to a gray door in a corridor of blue doors. It was the room in which the linens and cleaning supplies were stored, as well as wooden valets, chamber pots, footstools, wicker baskets, dry sinks.

Fulton nodded. "She won't open the door."

"I'm sure she will for Peter," said Mary, and Caitlin mar-

veled at this woman's hideous facility to combine in a few
words so many conflicting emotional clues: mockery, nonchalance, panic, and threat.

Peter rubbed his hands together and made a loud sniffing
noise. There were moments of coarseness that Caitlin always
felt her father produced for the Flemings, as if he sensed they
were expected of him. At home, he was reserved, diffident,
almost elegant, but in the main house he was jittery, a Rube
Goldberg contraption of jiggles and shrugs.

He walked to the gray door of the west-wing supply room
and tried the handle. It was locked.

He tapped the door with his large, raw knuckles. But
softly.

Softly.

The way he tapped on Caitlin's bedroom door to wake her
for school in the morning, now that he no longer just came in
and lay with her as he once had. In days gone by.

Caitlin felt shame tumbling through her like a barrel down
a flight of stairs.

"Annie," her father said, "open the door. It's Piet." He
glanced over his shoulder to see if the Flemings had noted his
reversion to Dutch—and Caitlin could not tell if he wanted
them to, or not.

"Should I leave?" Caitlin whispered to her father. She felt
suddenly light-headed, trapped in the force field created by
the ominous impatience of the Flemings and the increasing
nervousness of her father.

And behind that door was Annie, whom Caitlin now
imagined to be in a state of nightmarish duress: a she-devil,
with her hair huge and erect, her eyes empty of everything
but madness.

"Open this door now," Peter whispered frantically. He
shifted his feet and Caitlin sensed that what he would like to
do was kick at the door, break it down. But he didn't dare. He
had to respect that door as he respected the Flemings.

And then from behind the locked door came the raw heaving sound of Annie weeping.

"Do you think I should leave?" Caitlin asked again, making herself stand so straight that her knees ached.

"Annie?" Peter said. He must have thought it was going to be easier than it turned out to be. He must have thought that hearing his voice would heal her.

But now he didn't think it was easy. He had always known his wife as a woman of extravagant moods: a glass of beer could launch her on a fit of laughter; an early snow could make her want to die. But these emotional outbursts were contained and they had always been private. He had served as her confessor throughout their marriage. She would whisper to him of her grievances against the Flemings, her hatred of her work, her loneliness for Ireland and that fading photograph of near-strangers she called her real family. He had listened and absolved her by simply not judging her harshly. She was always ready to do what was expected and that was what counted. She was, finally, a good worker.

"Daddy?" Caitlin said. She touched him on the arm, not certain he could hear her.

He waved her away from him.

All of his suppressed impatience and scorn were in that gesture. It did not say, Move back; it said, Go away.

"Annie," he said, "come out."

And then she spoke. "I'm resting, now, Peter." Her voice shook as if she were speaking into the blades of a whirring fan.

"You can rest at home," said Peter. He glanced back at the Flemings and they nodded yes, giving their permission to let Annie go home.

"I don't want anyone to see me," said Annie.

She sounds like a normal person, thought Caitlin. And now she imagined her mother behind that door not as a haunched hag but as a woman in repose, someone enjoying herself, someone who had been given one task too many and who had decided on her own to change the lives of the Van Fleets forever, to get them thrown off the estate and into some amazing, transforming, resurrecting adventure.

Caitlin thought of the Empire State Building exploding out of the sidewalk, rushing up toward the little tufts of cloud and then right through them like a beanstalk in the fairy tale.

"I'm all dirty," said Annie. Now her voice had a gruesome singsong quality, ancient and deranged. "Oh-oh-oh," she wailed, and the way her voice came forward and receded made Caitlin think that her mother was being swung back and forth on a rope, like someone about to drop into the ice water of a quarry. "I think I'll die now. Yes?"

"Annie," Peter said, like thwacking a hatchet into the chopping block.

Annie heard the anger in his voice and it frightened her, made her let go of the last strand of good behavior—there seemed no more point in holding anything back.

She rushed to the door and flung herself against it. "Let me alone!" she said, her voice a shriek. "Don't you understand anything, you horse's ass, you horse's ass opening, you hole. God, I hate you. I am too dirty to come out of this room."

Caitlin felt as if her bones had been removed and replaced with breath.

I should not be hearing this, she thought to herself, at first censoriously, as if she were witnessing a species of bad behavior, and then with a sense of peril, as if the words were really a form of infection, and could kill her. When was one of the adults going to realize she was there? When was someone going to grab her by the arm, turn her around, point her down the steps and send her off?

She could almost see her mother pounding at the door from the other side, as if it were not made of wood at all, but canvas, or gum.

Caitlin glanced over her shoulder at the dark curve of the

staircase leading down to the entrance hall, the front door, and, at last, to the silence and privacy of the warm afternoon. She stepped back away from Peter and was about to turn when he took her by the hand.

His eyes were bright with desperate hope. His smile, usually so subtle, almost withheld, was large and awful and the falseness of it made her afraid of him for the first time in her life.

"You talk to her, Caitlin," he said. Terror made his breath sour; he held her much too tightly.

She shook her head No. That was all she could do; she couldn't speak.

"Yes, yes, she likes you, it'll be *goot*." He held onto her with his right hand and patted her shoulder frantically with his left.

The sound of Annie's crying grew fainter, but Caitlin couldn't tell if she was getting herself under control or had just moved further away from the door.

"Annie?" Peter said. "Caitlin is here. She wants to see her mother. Open the door for her, Annie. Caitlin needs you."

There was silence.

The birds were terribly busy outside.

"She doesn't seem to be answering, Peter," Fulton Fleming said. He folded his arms across his chest and pursed his lips.

"Peter?" Annie called, softly.

"Annie," Peter answered, his voice having that At Last quality of someone coming to the end of an ordeal.

"Peter, I want to rest, Peter." Annie's voice was young, pleading. "They tell me to do this and then the next thing and then another. And so nothing ever gets done, nothing is finished. Everything is half done all over the house."

Peter looked back at the Flemings. He seemed to be apologizing for his wife's complaining.

Caitlin couldn't believe how low they were sinking, her family, and taking her with them.

"Your daughter is here," Peter fairly crooned to the door.

"I have no daughter!" Annie screamed this and her voice assumed an actual shape in Caitlin's mind: a cat with its back curved, its fur up, all claws extended. "I have no daughter, no daughter!" Annie continued to howl. "She came out of my ass. I shit her. Oh. I said it. I said a bad thing. But it's true."

Caitlin was knocked backward by the force of the words and the hatred of that laugh. She covered her ears but her mother's voice tore them away and she heard every word, even the dank vibrations at the back of her mother's throat, the sound of her swallows.

Caitlin turned away and with only one thought in mind: freedom.

But Peter did not let her go. After having led her to the door, he blocked her passage.

Annie was still raving. But it was more of the same: morbid, foul, heartbroken visions of excrement. It was a transcription of the dull roar that fills every corner of hell.

"Move," said Caitlin, pushing at her father.

He didn't know why he kept her from fleeing, he only knew he must. He wanted to master something. He gripped her tight and his hard, capable hands branded her with the pain they could inflict.

She twisted free, and ran down the stairs. She almost fell; she saw the steps rushing toward her, but she righted herself, continued. She hit the ground floor at a dead run and raced across the foyer and out toward the side door, which led to the bluestone patio.

Jamey was just walking in. His face was red and his upper lip was like a generous slice of purple plum: he'd been hit by a tennis ball. He was sniffling about it and didn't see Caitlin, and when he did and tried to get out of her way it was too late. She ran into him as if deliberately and left him there, sprawled like a toppled chess piece on the black and white marble squares.

And as she ran across the long, sloping lawn she realized she had no idea where she was running. She happened to look up and there was the sky, still deep blue but filled with more clouds than before, and in the clouds, as if riding upon them, riding a chariot of heavenly vapor, was an angel, or a spirit, or a vision: a being wrapped in white, with a calm, serious face, holding an immense sword with both of its hands and aiming the glistening tip of the sword down at the earth, down at Caitlin really, and when Caitlin moved the sword moved, too.

She stopped and looked around to see if anyone else was there to see what she was seeing. She could hear voices coming from inside the house, but outside she was all alone. She looked back up at the sky, expecting that in the moment her attention had strayed the angel had left her. But it was still there, moving its sword back and forth, breathing quietly as its vaporous robe blew gently west toward the river.

APRIL 8, 1939

Caitlin was in her room, reading *The Grapes of Wrath*. She had woken that day with a headache, a vague sense of uneasiness. She felt as if she hadn't slept; her nerves were raw. And so she did what was for her an extraordinary thing: she simply did not go to work.

Annie was working in the mansion, and she said she would call the George Washington Inn to tell them Caitlin was ill, but Caitlin knew the chances were Annie would forget to make the call. She had only used the telephone a few times in her life; it tended to be an ordeal for her. She gripped the

receiver with one hand and that hard black lily of a mouth-
piece with the other.

Caitlin didn't care if the call was made or not. She knew
the hotel would never fire her; she got as much work done
there as any three other employees. She had inherited her
father's tragic capacity for diligence.

It felt strange and so wonderful to just lie in bed. A light,
rather brittle rain was falling. The trees were bare but some
of the branches were budding. It was windy; the single pane
of glass in Caitlin's window rattled in its frame. Her father
had gotten some violets from the Riverview Greenhouse and
they were in a Mason jar on the windowsill. Their petals were
as purple as royal robes against the cold gray window pane.

She wore a flannel nightgown, knee socks, and green
woolen gloves. She had cut the fingertips off the gloves so she
could comfortably turn the pages of a book.

She had been reading since eight that morning. She was
the first one to have taken the new Steinbeck out of the Leyden Free Library. She had never read a book whose pages
were so white, so crisp; they seemed to resist her each time
she turned one over.

And the book was breaking her heart. She was in a melancholy rapture from Mr. Steinbeck's notions of the open road
and hobo camps, soft, idealized pictures of the Joad family,
and, most of all, from the fact that the writer was out there in
the great unknown world, with his tweed jacket and his pipe,
his carefully combed hair, his neat mustache, and the look he
must have had in his eyes while he wrote this all down, the
creased forehead, the glass of warm whiskey, the old dog
sleeping at his feet, the pen flying across the page.

It was noon. The sun was over the house and its pale
golden light touched the water in the jar of violets. The
shadow of the jar and the violets shimmered on the bare
wooden floor; the sunlight passed through the flower petals so
that even the shadow showed pale blue.

And then the pathos of the book was unbearable. It toppled from her hand as she covered her face and wept. And when she felt it had gone on long enough, she did something she had learned a few years before. Whenever she cried she asked herself: What are you crying about? And the question would stop her cold, because there was a difference between the generality of sorrow and the specificity of the answer to that question, and that difference was like digging up the ground around a fire—the flame would extinguish itself when it came to the circle of barren earth.

I'm crying for the Joads, she thought. For the Okies, for farmers everywhere, for Mr. Steinbeck's enormous heart, I'm crying for the want of someone to tell my story, too, because I am in this room, and the sun is moving over the roof and it is the warmest part of the day and soon it will be afternoon and cold again. I am crying for some reason I cannot discover, a wound I can't remember.

FIVE

Morning began with a paroxysm of desire. The soul long-
ing, the body yearning, the ego pacing back and forth like
a beleaguered old auntie left in charge of two incorrigible
children.

She lay in her bed and watched the morning light shimmer like reflections of water against her wall. She was covered
by a single sheet, with a bare foot extended to keep her a little
cooler. The mattress beneath her molded to her form, held
her loosely but possessively.

Strange, still, to awaken so deeply alone, to be raptur-
ously bereft of the familiar sounds of Twin Ponds—the wind
through the hickory trees, the hysterical squabbles of domestic geese, the careful clinking of her father's flowered coffee
cup in its cracked but matching saucer. Her alienation from
her own desire had had a symmetry then; the familiar surrounded sensual hunger like sentinels, with orders to shoot to
kill. Yet here, in this strange room, this strange house, somewhere in the vast circular chaos of this strange, sultry city, the
familiar, dreary regime of denial had been subtly but inexo-
rably subverted.

Caitlin lived now in a converted attic room in a house owned by a family named Zweig. Thomas and Hilda Zweig were one of the many families who let rooms to government employees. They were Austrians who ran a small wine-importing company. They were elegant, rather formal people. Mr. Zweig wore a coat and tie to breakfast, Mrs. Zweig wore gloves whenever leaving the house, even in the summer. In the evenings they sat in their parlor listening to music and reading newspapers and magazines (though Mr. Zweig had a taste for private-eye novels as well) and they referred to Caitlin either as Miss Van Fleet or Dear. Caitlin had chosen to live at the Zweigs' house her first full day in Washington. She had been given a typewritten list of houses in which single young ladies could room, and the Zweig house was closest to Betty Sinclair's apartment, where Caitlin had spent her first night in Washington.

"Zweig," Betty had said, "could be anything. German, Jew, not that it matters, but it's fun to try and guess."

Caitlin's room was slanted, high in the center and cramped at the edges; she had to practically get on her knees to look out the small diamond-shaped windows. The walls were pale yellow; the floors were dark, and little Persian rugs were scattered here and there. Her narrow bed was in the center of the room. Next to it was a night table with a porcelain lamp in the shape of a French lady walking a dog. She had an easy chair with a floor lamp next to it, a dresser with eight drawers—mostly empty still—and a mirror that made her look fat. There was a half-bath down the hall from the Zweigs' bedroom that had white tiles and butterscotch-painted plaster and that Caitlin had all to herself. If she wanted to bathe, however, she needed to use the Zweigs' bathroom, and the near intimacy of being with their towels and lotions and aspirin tablets, their razors and witch hazel and tooth powder, their tweezers, their laxatives, made her feel confused, and strangely ashamed.

It was Saturday. In Leyden, Caitlin used to sleep until noon on days she didn't have to work, and her parents, though they disapproved of late sleeping just as they did of early drinking, allowed her this luxury, feeling it was the least concession they could make for a valedictorian. They could not afford to give her travel or college but they could keep the house quiet on the weekends.

In Washington, however, she awakened with the first light and waited for the day and her life to begin. She pulled the pillow out from beneath her head and placed it over her breasts; she ran her hand over the pillowcase until she found a patch of linen that had not been heated by her body heat, and this cool spot sent a spiral of pleasure through her as if it were a stranger who had slipped into bed beside her.

She wore a pair of pale green rayon pajamas she had bought with Betty Sinclair. She had never owned anything made of rayon before; it made her feel affluent, modern. Suddenly scornful of her own reverie, she turned on her reading lamp—free electricity came with her thirty-dollar-a-month rent—and read for a while in the Anne Morrow Lindbergh book Betty had given to her. Then, not wanting to awaken the Zweigs, but unable to stay in bed any longer, she put on the dark green, rather Oriental-looking robe she had bought along with the pajamas, and went down the narrow stairway that connected her attic room to the rest of the house.

She went to the bathroom, washed her face and hands, brushed her hair, her teeth, and then crept down the carpeted second-story corridor, past the Zweigs' closed bedroom door, past the straight-backed upholstered chair placed reverentially beneath a painting of a young Mr. Zweig wearing the tan uniform and ludicrous pointed steel helmet of the Austrian Army.

It was just eight in the morning. The heat never really left the house any longer. If she raked her fingers through the air she could practically feel it.

Caitlin walked barefoot down the stairs toward the parlor. Though she rented only the attic, the Zweigs had made her feel welcome everywhere in their house. A breakfast of coffee and fruit was included with her rent and Mrs. Zweig, who had a cleaning woman but no cook, had from the very beginning of her tenancy asked Caitlin to prepare her own breakfasts on the weekends.

"It's our only time to pretend we are just newlyweds, with no responsibilities in the world," Mrs. Zweig had said, smiling.

It had struck Caitlin as an almost shocking intimacy, and she often imagined her somber, sedate landlords in bed together, wrapped in each other's arms, fully clothed.

The kitchen was large, with blue-and-white linoleum on the floor and a bay window against which honeysuckle nuzzled. Caitlin had never been alone in a kitchen that wasn't hers before she'd moved into the Zweigs' and their food was an unexpected source of temptation. She had felt at first that she wanted to taste their food because she had never tasted that sort of noodle or that kind of pastry before, and then, as time passed, she craved the things she had developed a taste for and might never have an opportunity to try again. There was always a pitcher of orange juice in the refrigerator and Caitlin was in a perpetual struggle between appetite and conscience— how to slake her thirst for the sweet, pulpy juice without taking so much that her pilfering would be noticed. And there were always strange doughy cookies in the bread box, which Caitlin counted daily, having devised the rule that if there were twenty she could take two, and if there were ten she could take one, though there were times when she counted out eight and took three. Sometimes her curiosity about the Zweigs' food lurched toward utter avidity. She once found herself peeling the binding from a leftover chunk of sirloin roast and chewing the burned fatty flavor out of the string.

Today, she filled the percolator basket with Chase & Sanborn coffee and then drew water from the tap. The Zweigs liked the way she made coffee. Then she surveyed the refrigerator. They must have had company the night before while Caitlin was at the symphony with Betty Sinclair. There were hunks of various cheeses wrapped in waxed paper and a platter of sliced salami and some sort of white meat—it turned out to be smoked goose, which Caitlin did not care for; she spit it into her hand and then threw it into the garbage can beneath the sink.

Caitlin checked the bread box. Yesterday, there had been two cinnamon buns in a small brown-paper bag. When Caitlin had reached in to see how many there were, a bit of honey and pecan had stuck to her fingertip and after she licked it off she could not resist eating an entire bun. She admonished herself with every bite but she could not control herself. She had developed a palate that could only be satisfied by other people's food. Surely if there were only two cinnamon buns left then she was eating half of them and that would certainly be noticed. What a humiliation that would be! Yet no one mentioned anything to her and this morning the bag was still there, holding the last bun. Perhaps they've forgotten all about these, thought Caitlin, and, after making a half gesture to return the bag to the bread box, she shook the last bun into her hand, crumpled up the bag, and threw it away. She wanted to save the cinnamon bun for her coffee, but suddenly she just ate it while standing in the middle of the kitchen.

She had, in fact, put on a little weight. Betty had squeezed Caitlin's upper arm, which had always been hard, almost unyielding, with the biceps of a young boy, but which had of late become soft. "Jewish cuisine," Betty had said, furrowing her brow in a burlesque of disapproval—yet the words themselves tended to outlive the mitigating mockery.

It was summer and Congress was on vacation. Too hot in Washington to think about any laws but those of nature. Even at night the heat still clung to the city like soiled bandages.

Men wandered around in seersucker suits with their collars open, women in sleeveless blouses, their armpits smooth. No one seemed to care.

With Stowe out of town and little to do in the office, Betty had been introducing Caitlin to museums and libraries, book-shops, perfumeries, parks, and a terrific record store on Connecticut where you could take a Duke Ellington record or an old Bessie Smith into the listening booth and play it for as long as you liked without so much as a glance from the tolerant, music-loving Swede who ran the place. Betty knew all the jazz and blues singers, and she'd sing along with them, making Caitlin blush because she never believed those booths were really soundproof.

In some strange yet entirely welcome way, Betty was circling Caitlin. If it had not been coming from a woman, it would have been nothing short of Caitlin's ideal of courtship. It had begun casually, with friendly gestures tempered by natural reticence and respect. Then it had become part of the rhythm of work—a shared lunch, a cup of coffee after work, a burst of heartfelt confiding that did not insist on leading to a complete destruction of all barriers. Contact was uncertain, sporadic, but free of anxiety. They didn't have to make up a reason to see each other and they didn't have to invent excuses not to: work took care of all that.

Once Congress was in recess Betty began more regularly to suggest to Caitlin that they spend time together. It seemed as if Stowe's absence animated Betty. She smoked more, laughed more, took Caitlin away from her typing and filing tasks for earlier and lengthier lunches. They ate in cafeterias for the most part, but slightly off the beaten track because Betty didn't like meeting people she knew. Caitlin did enjoy meeting this congressional aide, that senator's secretary. People who had important jobs thrilled her and it filled her with pleasure and amazement to be treated as if she were on a par with them. But Betty treated every chance meeting as an arduous task, a combination of public relations and sheer endurance, and when the interloper was gone Betty would rub her eyes with her thumb and forefinger, as if she had just been reading pages and pages of fine print.

Yesterday, after lunch, Betty had taken Caitlin out to shop. Caitlin had bought a Leading Lady pocketbook, wine-colored, with a more or less alligator grain, for just a dollar. Then Betty talked her into some fancy soaps. "It's the cheapest way to make a working girl feel like a debutante. Take the Woodbury. Recommended by Mr. Cholly Knickerbocker." She had tossed a bar of the soap to Caitlin while the saleswoman looked on in prim disapproval—but that was part of the fun. Betty had a way of creating a private world that others couldn't understand. Then she had Caitlin buy some Kayser hosiery and then, finally, she somehow talked Caitlin into a Playtex makeup cape. The cape was an outsize bib; it was meant to protect your clothes while you did your face. It cost a dollar and it seemed a ridiculous waste of money to Caitlin. "But oh it's so sheer, so chic, so terribly feminine," Betty had said, her voice alive with laughter. She brought you close to her, made you want to discover the joke, too. "And look, a swing pocket to hold your powder puff. Now come on. I may not always be there to hold your powder puff, you know."

That evening, Betty drove them in her new Ford out to Maryland to see the Roadside Players perform some old play about boyfriends, a lost wallet, switched blazers. Caitlin had always felt there was something inherently solemn and meaningful in anything that deserved to be called drama and she surprised herself with her own laughter. Afterward, Betty said, "I love old plays. Not just the classics but really dumb ones you can make fun of and enjoy."

They drove home. The night was so hot it seemed the stars might melt and turn the sky silver. It was a long drive and the sway of the car had lulled Caitlin to sleep. When she finally woke up they were parked in front of the Zweigs' on Peabody Street and Betty was leaning back in her seat, smoking a cigarette and looking at her.

"How long have I been sleeping?" Caitlin had asked.

"Awhile."

"You should have—" She sat up, rubbed her face. She felt unaccountably nervous.

"You looked so peaceful." Betty put out her cigarette. The car was full of smoke.

Caitlin was getting a cup when she heard the sound of human movement behind her and she turned quickly, startled.

"Oh, hello," Joe Rose said. "You must be the boarder."

"Who are you?" asked Caitlin. She made certain her robe was closed. She felt suddenly and morbidly aware of her body. Her breasts felt heavy; there seemed a kind of gravitational pull in her womb. She placed the empty cup on the counter near the stove while the coffee beat like blood in a vein against the glass cap of the percolator.

"I'm Joe Rose. Hill's brother."

"Hill?"

"Hilda." He smiled. He was dressed in pleated slacks and a clean white undershirt. His face was freshly shaved; his thick black hair was wet. He smiled; he had a space between his front teeth. "Mrs. Zweig, to you, I guess."

She looked him over. His handsomeness inflicted on her an agitation that was almost like pain, as if something that had been closed within her was suddenly being pried open. He was, like her, barefoot. His feet were very white, his toes long and graceful. He was slender, even a little delicate. His arms didn't come close to filling the sleeves of his tee shirt. Though he was merely standing there he gave the impression of quickness, and though he had barely spoken he gave the impression of wit. He stood straight, his shallow chest extended, and rubbed the knuckle of his ring finger, as if he had perhaps banged it against the banister on his way down the stairs. She felt within her the intimations of kinship—yet it was difficult to say, really. Was that voice across the valley another person or merely your echo? Yet she sensed within Joe a turmoil that was somehow sympathetic to her own—an uncertainty of direction, an intelligence cut down by a desire not to be altogether noticed.

He had just shaved and his skin radiated the scent of his cologne. He breathed deeply and smiled; he seemed to be smelling the coffee.

"Can I pour you a cup of coffee?" she asked.

"Sure can," he said. There was a forced note of heartiness in his voice. He was pretending, as if he had seized on the notion that this was how a man spoke to a strange girl.

He sat at the kitchen table. He had gathered the morning mail, which came early on Saturday. There were several pieces of mail and he spread them out before him like a fortune-teller arranging cards.

"Thank God, it came," he said, finding a square light-yellow envelope, surely containing an invitation.

When Caitlin came to the table with two cups of coffee, Joe slid a large envelope toward her. It was bulky, secured with twine; her name was written in large block letters and there were eight penny stamps, glued on neatly in two rows.

"Caitlin Van Fleet. Sounds fancy."

The envelope was from her father. She looked at it without touching it while Joe tore open the envelope addressed to him. He pursed his lips and nodded with a satisfaction she suspected was slightly ostentatious. It was an invitation and after he read it he flicked it with his fingernail.

"It's from Sumner Welles," he announced and looked at

Caitlin, assuming she'd be impressed. When she said nothing, Joe narrowed his eyes and asked her if she knew who Welles was.

"Orson's brother?" she said. It struck her as something Betty would have said and she smiled.

"He's Under Secretary of State and one of the few people in Washington who know which end is up."

Caitlin in fact vaguely remembered either Stowe or Betty talking about Welles in the office. He was one of those men who were encouraging Roosevelt to get America mixed up in the European war. She seemed to recall Betty saying something like, You can bet Sumner Welles won't be getting his dainty little hands bloody in any war.

Joe folded the invitation and placed it in his back pocket. His own hands were not dainty but they didn't look as if they had done much real work, either.

"Hill tells me you work for old Elias J. Stowe," Joe said. He sipped his coffee and his eyes gazed at her over the rim of the cup. He had dark eyes, a mixture of gray, violet, and black. They seemed the eyes of someone who was used to watching others, eyes that at once recorded and concealed.

"That's right," said Caitlin. Joe's tone of voice had made it abundantly clear that he didn't think highly of Stowe. "And I happen to think I'm awfully lucky to have the job. It's not as if I had a degree in political science."

"Now, now," said Joe, with his hand raised in a peaceful gesture. "I don't blame you for Stowe. Look, I work at *Fortune* and I don't want people blaming me for Henry Luce. Sometimes you just get mixed up in something before you have a chance to realize what it is." He took a long drink of his coffee; he seemed immune to its heat. "Will you excuse me for a moment?"

"Of course."

He stood there for an extra moment, trying to extract with a smile her promise to wait in the kitchen for his return. Then he turned and left the kitchen. His shoulder blades protruded like a young girl's breasts.

Caitlin listened to his bare feet pad up the stairs, and when his footsteps disappeared she opened the envelope from her father. In it were a bouquet of violets and a note written lightly in pencil. (Peter's letters were always delicately composed, as if he wanted to give Caitlin the opportunity to erase what he had written and use the paper for something else.)

Dear Caitlin,

I hope this letter finds you well. Your mother and I are busy, as the summer has been one of many important social occasions up at the house, as well as one of unusual heat and elm blight on the farm. Just last night, the Flemings had a dinner for a real Russian count named Vonsiatsky and his wife, an American woman with sad eyes and a private fortune. They live over near the Connecticut border and the Count is teaching Cossack-style horsemanship to all the families around here. He cuts quite a dashing figure, though Mother says he looks like a big baby in his coat with all those Russian ribbons and eagles on it. The party for the Vonsiatskys went on until all hours and Mother had to walk home in the moonlight, carrying her shoes. Her feet had swollen up to twice their size! But the laugh was on me because after dinner the Count and Mr. Fleming and a few of the others went out shooting and ended up frightening the cattle, who took it upon themselves to stamp down the fence along River Road. It took me three hours to get the heifers in and three days to repair the fence!

The Flemings ask after you all the time. They are very proud of how well you are working out. Mr. Stowe has told them many times what a good worker you are, and how you've learned all the office systems and the typing and filing and even a bit of diplomacy in the way you handle others.

We miss you. Your mother wishes you would write more often. Your last letter arrived three weeks ago. We would certainly be happy to hear your news.

Do you have a nice vase you can put these into?

Your Father

The violets were dark purple. Peter had wrapped them in wet newspaper and then dry newspaper and there was still some life to them, though half of the petals were crushed. Caitlin stared at them, only partially aware that her heart was pounding like a fist. The flowers, the feel of her father's voice had brought her back to Leyden. Caitlin had imagined that once she moved to Washington she would never return to Leyden, that the town and its memories would fall away like milk teeth.

"Are you all right?"

She looked up from the flowers. Joe had put on a light brown shirt with a long, wide collar. He wore his trousers belted high.

"I'm fine," she said. "I hope you didn't dress on my account." She gestured toward her robe and pajamas.

"Some young suitor send you flowers?"

"They're from my father."

She stood up to find a vase. Mrs. Zweig, a bit of a horticulturalist, kept a row of simple glass vases on a shelf over the sink.

"Say, I don't suppose you'd be interested in going to a party at the French embassy tonight. Would you? Mr. Welles sent me an invitation and I can bring someone if I like. In fact, to tell you the truth, it would look a lot better if I had a date for it."

"Well, you see—"

"No, sorry, sorry, Hill told me you were a country girl."
Joe's face was flushed and he waved his hands up and down at
Caitlin as if he were trying to calm her. "You must think I'm
very forward, which as a reporter I am, but not as a person.
As a person, I'm backward."

"It has nothing to do with being a country girl," said Caitlin. She walked back to the table and placed the violets in the
center, on a faded white doily. "I'm just busy tonight. There
must be plenty of girls in town who would love to go to a
party at the French embassy."

"I don't know any. I live in New York. I only came here
to do an article about Mr. Welles and his views about the war."

"I don't have the right kind of clothes for a party like that
anyhow," said Caitlin. "The whole purpose of having a
woman on your arm would be completely undone if she didn't
look right."

"You'd look beautiful. I have to rent a tuxedo for tonight.
I never owned a monkey suit in my life."

"Well, it's not as simple for a woman." She imagined Betty
saying those words and how she would make them funny,
how she would clasp her hands in front of her breast and bat
her eyelashes in a burlesque of the simpering female. Betty
knew how to hit those notes, how to claim the prerogatives of
femininity and mock them at the same time. She had a way
of putting imaginary quotation marks around words like girl,
lady, nice, giving them an emphasis that made them absurd
and harmless and somehow touching, too.

"What we could have done," said Joe, "was rent a tuxedo
for you, too. That would have given the Washington diplomatic community something to wash their caviar down with,
don't you think?" He smiled, captivated by the picture he had
put in his own mind.

They talked for a time. Joe spoke of Sumner Welles. He
said Mr. Welles was not only brilliant but a man of unusual

elegance and grace. "He thinks the way Fred Astaire dances," Joe said. Joe had a radio announcer's baritone. He smiled often. But, despite this, he seemed ill at ease. He went on about Welles, about the article he planned to write about Welles, about the objections his editor had about running an article about Welles.

Finally, he stopped talking about Welles and looked at her gravely. "Sorry," he said.

"Sorry for what?"

"I don't like men who do that—and they always do it to women, too. You know, just talk about themselves and call it conversation."

"You weren't, you were talking about Mr. Welles."

"It's kind of you to say so."

They were silent for a moment. Caitlin heard the Zweigs stirring upstairs. Footsteps. The sudden animation of the pipes as tap water was summoned.

She glanced up at the ceiling and then noticed that Joe's eyes looked upward, too, simultaneously.

It was not a major emotional event in her life, sitting with him in that kitchen. It was comfortable, vaguely promising of something further, no more than that. His hands seemed to want to gesture when he spoke but he kept them folded. He looked directly into her eyes. He wanted to know her and she wanted to know him, too.

When she finished her coffee Caitlin stood. Out of restlessness, she stretched her arms out, not remembering she was wearing only pajamas and a robe. The robe opened and Joe looked away.

"Hill didn't tell me how beautiful you are," he said, looking at the floor.

"I've got to be going," said Caitlin.

The sun went behind a cloud just then, and a layer of darkness fell through the kitchen, as if reality were a photograph that was suddenly starting to fade.

"If you see your boss," said Joe, rising from his seat and making a playful, formal bow, "tell him *Sieg heil* for me."

JULY 11, 1967

Twenty-seven years later, Caitlin sat at her desk. Behind her was a huge semicircle of window, spotted with rain, and before her was Marlene Draper, a small, dark woman of twenty-five. Marlene's inky hair had been chopped severely; it looked as if she had done it herself. They were in the offices of the World Refugee Alliance, fourteen stories above the corner of Eighteenth Street and Fifth Avenue.

It was a large office, harshly lit and disorderly. The walls were lined with file cabinets, some of them metal, some cardboard. The art works on the wall were organizational. Every year the WRA produced a poster, which was sent to anyone who donated more than twenty-five dollars. The most cheerful of these posters was a hundred small snapshots in rows of ten showing the faces of people who had been brought to America thanks largely to the work of the Alliance. Most of the other posters were dark paintings of battlefields, barbed wire, border patrols.

The one anomalous poster was a photograph of a golden saxophone lying in the snow. Above that was: "WELL, YOU NEEDN'T." A PLAY IN TWELVE BARS. THE NEW YORK UNIVERSITY ENSEMBLE GROUP. The play had been written by Caitlin's son, whose name, in the spirit of collectivity, did not appear on the poster. There was nothing else in the office to suggest Caitlin's personal life, or that she even had one. Her old steel desk, with a keyhole on every drawer, had been bought from the Marxist splinter group that had rented the office space before the World Refugee Alliance took over the lease, and it held only a phone, an old Royal typewriter, a couple of manila folders, and an ashtray filled with paper clips.

"I'm taking so much of your time," Marlene Draper was saying.

"We're here to help you in whatever ways we can," said Caitlin.

She looked at the girl. Her youth and beauty were there—fine, clear skin, delicate but prominent bones in the face—but sorrow had dulled her spirit as a stony field can dull a scythe.

Marlene had come to America from Austria in her mother's womb. Her mother, Lena, a gifted pianist, who, because of a touch of arthritis, earned her living as a piano teacher. She had fallen in love with and married a Gentile named Otto Schilling. Schilling owned a small steel mill in Austria. He had been, when Lena met him, a widower, with a young child, a boy to whom Lena was hired to teach music. Otto and Lena married and had a few happy years. But when anti-Semitism became the overwhelming reality of life in Vienna, Otto, feeling he was going to be persecuted for marrying a Jewess, sold his factory and disappeared, leaving not only his pregnant wife but Otto, Jr., the issue of his first marriage. When Lena escaped Vienna, she took Otto, Jr., with her. They slept in farmhouses, in spare rooms, in the holds of freighters; the boy died while in quarantine on Ellis Island. Two months later, Marlene was born.

Now Lena was working as a secretary for two psychoanalysts, elderly brothers who shared a suite of offices on Central Park West, and Marlene was studying biochemistry at Brandeis University.

"My mother doesn't know I'm doing this," Marlene said to Caitlin. There was a fan on the floor behind Marlene, and every few moments the warm breeze it stirred agitated her long earrings.

"I'm surprised you'd want so badly to *see* your father," Caitlin said. "He didn't behave very honorably."

"I know, I know. He abandoned my mother. And his son. But he didn't abandon me. He didn't even know me."

"Marlene," Caitlin said.

"He never even saw his own daughter," she said. Her face reddened from the throat up, but the blush stopped at her cheekbones and her eyes remained logical. "And now he is in trouble with the authorities."

"He was convicted of many offenses, Marlene. And nothing that anyone can construe as having anything to do with human rights. A public nuisance." Caitlin said this with some gentleness in her voice, but it was not easy. She could not understand why this girl wanted to worry about a father she had never known, a father who had betrayed her and her people.

She could not help but think of her own fatherless child: what agonies of self did *he* endure? What was the little begging bowl he held, asking her, asking friends, asking the world for alms in the form of identity?

"I have reason to believe he is not a well man," Marlene said.

"Physically?"

"In every way."

Caitlin was silent. The rain scratched against the window. Traffic sent up its desperate noise, mechanical sinners beseeching heaven.

"You're very forgiving, Marlene," she finally said, folding her hands, raising her eyebrows.

"Because of you I can be. We lived, we escaped, we have made a good life here. I know he was a coward, but he was not the only one. There were many who did worse things than hide. And he's been punished. He lost everything, his business, his friends, his pride. When he works he works as a common laborer. He's been in the hospital with tuberculosis, anxiety, and depression. He is blind in one eye. And now he writes me and says he would like to come here and I wrote him back and said I would help."

"Let me make something clear, Marlene. It wasn't because of me that your mother could come here. It was many people."

"My mother thinks it was because of you."

There was a knock on Caitlin's door and Mrs. Rosenthal came in without waiting for an answer. She was stooped, with a permanently startled expression on her face. She carried a cup of tea. Mrs. Rosenthal's right leg was six inches shorter than her left; though her left shoe had a lift in it, her gait was nevertheless uneven and she covered her teacup with her hand.

"You have a visitor, Miss Van Fleet," she said. She had known Caitlin for twenty years and still rarely used her first name.

"I'll get out of your way," said Marlene, standing quickly.

"Who is it?" asked Caitlin.

"Mr. Jaffrey."

Ah, Gordon. She could not think of him without a stab of sadness that was peculiarly comforting.

"Ask him to wait a minute, Mrs. Rosenthal."

Marlene was looking around the room. Her eyes stopped on the poster advertising *Well, You Needn't*.

"It's a play," said Caitlin. "My son wrote it." She got up and stood next to Marlene, put her arm around the girl's shoulders. It was the best she could do.

"I didn't know you had a son, or even that you were married," said Marlene.

"Yes, a son, just the one child," said Caitlin.

"Your son? He's in college?"

"Yes," said Caitlin. It was something she was proud of: he was the first person in her family to go to a university.

"Then he's my age. How come you never introduced us?"

"I don't know," said Caitlin. "I think you would find him . . . I don't know. I think you are much more serious than he is."

"I'd like to find someone to help me become less serious," said Marlene. She quickly, almost furtively embraced Caitlin; she was small and had to rise up on her toes to place the kiss on Caitlin's cheek.

Caitlin sat at her desk for a few minutes after Marlene left and then went to the waiting room to collect Gordon. He was standing next to the aquarium, with its few indolent goldfish floating about the murky green water. He moved his fingers on the glass and one of the goldfish followed as he did.

"Hello, Gordon."

He turned around. He had grown a beard. His face was heavy, deeply lined, but he had a rapt expression now.

"He likes me," said Gordon. "That fish really likes me."

He walked toward Caitlin, who had her hands extended toward him. He clasped her and kissed her on both cheeks. He was courtly, though there were still nights, infrequent though they were, when he would show up at her apartment very late and very drunk and talk of nothing but his loneliness.

"You look beautiful, Caitlin Van Fleet," he said.

He was wearing a summer suit. The right side of his jacket was wrinkled from carrying his camera case around.

He followed Caitlin back into her office and closed the door, took the seat where Marlene had been, slouched back, thrust out his long legs.

"Guess who I saw today," he said.

"Can you give me some sort of hint?" She often felt prim around Gordon, as if it were up to her to maintain social barriers, tact, felicity of phrase.

"OK, a hint." Gordon pretended to think it over. "All right. Here's a clue. He's your son."

"That sort of narrows it down. How is he?"

"Amazing."

Caitlin nodded, gestured, as if to say, Go on.

"Hair down to here," said Gordon, touching his shoulder.

"That really is impressive," said Caitlin.

"Oh, come on, give the kid a break, why don't you? He's lively, he's creative. He's *young*."

"I worry about him. I don't know what he's doing."

"You see him, don't you?"

"I see him all the time. But I still can't figure out what he's doing. He's a playwright, he's moving to California, he wants to work with the Indians, he wants to open up a restaurant on Cape Cod. He has no beliefs. His compass is all screwy."

"We were luckier," said Gordon. "We had the war."

"There's a war right now. Plenty of wars."

"Vietnam," said Gordon, with a dismissive wave. "We had a real war, with no one on the sidelines. We would have been just as screwy as the kids today. But."

Suddenly, Caitlin leaned forward on her elbows and covered her face with her hands.

Gordon was silent for a moment and then asked, "Caitlin? Are you really that worried?"

She shook her head No, but did not uncover her face.

"It's July 11," she said. "This is the day I met Joe for the first time."

"The world traveler," said Gordon, with so much contempt it bordered on the comic.

"I wasn't very nice to him," Caitlin said, finally removing her hands from her face. Her face, older now, but still lean, still with its fierce feminine bearing, was wet with tears. "He asked me on a date and I said No."

"The first time he met you?" asked Gordon. "Not the Joe I knew."

"The French embassy, no less."

"Fancy that."

"Do you think about him?"

"Yes."

"I mean often."

"It's the great thing we have in common, dear. Do you think he's still in Europe? Do you think he'll ever come home?" Gordon smiled; his politics made him embarrassed to call America home, but really it was how he felt.

"He has no home. He's an exile, a permanent exile," said Caitlin.

"It's strange, isn't it. You've helped thousands of people come to this country, running for their lives."

Caitlin reached across the desk and took Gordon's hand. Their fingers braided and squeezed tightly.

"What do you say we go to someplace very very air-conditioned and have a stiff drink?" said Caitlin.

"I know just the place."

In the elevator going down, they were alone. They could hear the chains clanking in the old elevator; the ride was slow, full of shudders.

"I'm glad you stopped by," said Caitlin.

Gordon was preparing to unfurl his umbrella. His camera case hung down to his knees and he stood as crookedly as Mrs. Rosenthal.

"Do you think I'd leave you alone on July eleventh?" he said, smiling. He had new teeth; it gave him an eerily youthful smile.

"You knew?"

He shook his head. "Every year you do this, Caitlin. And every year you say: 'You knew?'"

The elevator bumped to a stop and the door slowly slid open. They walked through the small, scuffed lobby, toward the door to the street. Caitlin stopped for a moment to watch the passersby in the rain, some of them with their collars up, some holding soaking newspapers over their heads, some of them seemingly led by umbrellas that had filled with wind. So many, many people.

And no trees anywhere. The little snip of river filled with garbage, bodies. Concrete buildings like factories producing lives.

"Gordon," she said, "would you do me a favor and just hold me, hold me before we go out?"

He didn't say a word. He dropped his open umbrella on the tile floor and took Caitlin in his arms. Pressed her chastely close to him, breathed the scent of her slightly grayed hair, felt the articulation of her.

And she held on to Gordon, as if he were a childhood friend. He had gotten so large she wasn't sure she could get her arms all the way around him. Oh Gordon, she thought, go away, get married, make a life for yourself.

SIX

One of Caitlin's jobs in Stowe's office was to sort the correspondence from people back in Windsor County. The letters were brought in a stack by a boy named Eddie, who had a blood disease that made him cold all the time—even in these sweltering dog days.

Today Eddie was wearing a tight sweater with a diamond pattern; his orange-red hair was combed up in a high loopy wave. He was a winker, a tongue clucker, an eyebrow wagger. He was the legendary bellhop from Niagara Falls. Yet for some reason Caitlin adored him. She cherished his dependability, his promptness, and the frailty that made his roosterish demeanor something like bravery. And somehow knitted into this fabric of regard was the fact that she did not know his last name, or where he lived, and he knew nothing about her except she worked for Stowe, sat at this desk, was young, smiled.

Eddie dropped the morning mail onto Caitlin's desk. Congressman Stowe was back in the office and the informality of the languid, steaming summer was suddenly gone. Caitlin was at work by nine, lunch was an hour, she didn't leave before five.

Eddie made a soft, harmless version of the wolf whistle and winked. When he placed the mail before Caitlin she noticed his hands. The skin was pale, peeling, as if he had been soaking in a tub for hours.

"Thanks, Eddie," she said.

"You look out of this world today, Catey," he said, in his wise-guy voice.

The letters he had delivered were bound by a piece of twine. There was one that was separate, however, and he held it in his hand and fanned himself with it.

"This one's for you," he said, skimming it across the desk at Caitlin.

It was from New York City; the return address was *Fortune* magazine. Her name was typed by a typewriter with a half-broken letter A.

As Eddie left, Caitlin looked out of her small office. Stowe was in his office with the door closed. Betty was in with him, along with a young man, a lawyer, who had come in with Stowe this morning. The lawyer had been introduced to her briefly. He had sunken cheeks, dark, staring eyes, his hair was swept back and thinning. His name was John Coleman.

Caitlin opened the envelope. She knew it must be from Joe Rose. She knew no one else who worked at *Fortune*, she knew no one else who lived in New York City. She opened the letter carefully, as if it were for somebody else and she must be undetected.

> *Dear Caitlin,*
>
> *I was going to send this note to my sister's house but fact is she has been urging me to "ask you out" (you must forgive her: older sisters fret over unmar-*

ried brothers) and I think if she saw a correspondence from me to you she would lose her mind with happiness. (You haven't seen that mind-losing-with-happiness part of Hill yet, I suppose.)

I only wanted to add something further to the words we had about your boss down in Hill's kitchen. I hope you have forgiven my Sieg-heiling like that. These days, Hitlerite salutes are hardly a laughing matter. But most of all I didn't want you to think that I was grouping you with your boss. I may not have had the right to criticize your working where you work. Working for Fortune isn't exactly making the world safe for democracy. But I'll be leaving Fortune soon to work on a book. (Every hack journalist says he's going to be writing that book, pretty soon, but what makes my claim more creditable is mine ain't The Great American Novel and, also, that I've already served notice.)

Caitlin, what I mean to tell you is keep your eyes open. Your boss might not be a dangerous character himself but he pals around with some pretty unsavory types. He's in control now and everything he says about keeping us out of the war and even about being more "understanding" about the New Germany might sound OK, but one day, I hope, it won't. It'll sound rotten through and through and everyone will know what these guys are really made of. And when that happens, I don't want to see you caught on the wrong side.

I suppose I sound pretty arrogant. Don't worry, I'm used to being thought of as a know-it-all. Look, I've been wrong about a lot of things. I thought Paris would stand up to Hitler and I thought the Phillies would win the pennant. But I'm damned sure that one

day Stowe will show his true colors. If there's an
ounce of justice left in this terrible world, one day
every decent person will know that the man you work
for is a moral gangster.

Caitlin folded the letter in half, and then in half again and
shoved it into her wine-colored handbag. She clicked the bag
closed and sat there quietly, without moving.

Suddenly, she felt a hand on her shoulder and she turned,
startled, as if she had been caught at something.

And there was Betty Sinclair. "Boo," she said, in her
round, amber alto. She was wearing a green skirt with a broad
belt, a white blouse, a strand of her grandmother's pearls. She
was tall, blonde, very, very blonde. The down on her face
looked silver in the sunlight.

Caitlin looked at her friend with a feeling of relief. There
was no feeling of loneliness that Betty could not dispel, no
feeling of doubt she could not make seem absurd. Betty was
as confident as Jamey Fleming but without his snobbery, his
petulant insistence that the world owed him the seat by the
window.

"What's wrong with you?" asked Betty. "You're pale."

"You startled me, I guess."

"I hate it that he's back," Betty said, gesturing toward
Stowe's closed door. She pulled a pack of cigarettes from her
skirt's hip pocket. She smoked mentholated Spuds in the summer, Chesterfields when the heat broke.

Betty had been working for Stowe since she was twenty-
three years old. She'd come to Washington with a degree in
history from Temple University and the job in Stowe's office
was her second on the Hill. (The first had been with a Michigan congressman named Eliot Conners, who had kissed Betty
hard on the mouth one evening while they were both working
late and then had stood there in crimson astonishment as
Betty had stalked out of his office, forever.) Now she was

twenty-eight. Officially, she was Stowe's administrative aide; she made fifty-five dollars a week. But there was no one who was closer to Stowe than Betty. Half the day she was in his private office with the door closed. They traveled the chicken-and-peas circuit together, going to Windsor County, New York, Philadelphia, St. Louis.

She offered Caitlin a cigarette and Caitlin accepted. She wasn't buying her own yet but Betty had gotten her into the smoking habit. It was all a part of life as Betty's pal: Scotch and soda, club sandwiches, theater in the round, listening to old blues records.

"Elias just loathes being here, and this Coleman character he's brought along—this is a chap who makes Bela Lugosi look like Will Rogers." Betty laughed and waved the smoke away from her face. She had the gestures of a girl who had sneaked a lot of cigarettes.

"But you like him, don't you?"

"Elias? Sure. Compared to most of the guys in this city, he's a prince, a philosopher-king. At least he sticks his neck out for what he believes."

"Would he stick his neck out for Hitler, then?"

"Hitler. Oh, please. No one gives a hoot about Hitler. I mean, the mustache alone. Old Adolf is strictly a transitional figure, there's no doubt about it. He's like a charwoman sent in to clean up a mess."

"But—"

"The important thing, Caitlin, is to keep out of the war." She smiled. "It's really pretty elementary."

"But the President's already said we aren't going to get involved, at least not militarily. It would just be a matter of helping out the democracies—"

"Roosevelt's better than Edgar Bergen in talking without moving his lips," said Betty. "He says he wants peace but in the meanwhile he's getting ready to spend *billions* sending planes and ammunition to the Brits. He says it's a loan. But how do you loan someone an antiaircraft shell? It's like loaning someone a piece of gum." She pantomimed taking a piece of gum out of her mouth, handing it to Caitlin. "Here, thanks ever so much."

The door to Stowe's office opened and a stocky, middle-aged priest came out. He went to the water cooler, filled a paper cup, and then dabbed his handkerchief in it. He mopped his face with the wet cloth and then drank the water, crumpled the cup, and went back into Stowe's office.

"Who was that?" Caitlin asked Betty.

"Father Coughlin," said Betty. She made a face; she never had much use for Catholics.

"The radio priest?" Caitlin said, for a moment genuinely impressed. Sparked by the sound of a familiar name, a name connected to the vast invisible hierarchical world of celebrity, she had forgotten she had once actually heard Coughlin on the radio and thought he was hateful. One of her father's friends back home, Russ Sauer, listened to Coughlin on the radio, quoted him. Sauer claimed the Jews manipulated the wholesale prices for apples and made him lose his farm. Then, after that, he found work as a low-paid handyman in one of the Jewish resorts across the river, and used to leave copies of Coughlin's magazine *Social Justice* in the cabins he cleaned out before the next wave of Jewish vacationers would arrive from the city.

"Father Coughlin is a sentimental, scheming old windbag," Betty said. "Elias took me to one of his mass meetings at Madison Square Garden and I swear it, Caitlin, if you added the IQ of everyone in the hall it would have come out to a hundred and six. He plays to the rabble. Like a ham actor, so vulgar, pitching his gestures to the cheap seats in the back rows."

"Then what's he doing here?"

"Talking to Elias. Coleman arranged it." Betty tapped her

finger against the side of her head and raised her eyebrows, as if to say Smart Move.

"I don't understand why Mr. Stowe would even let him in the office, if he's so disgusting."

"Coleman's point is, with Roosevelt already dipping his quill into the ink getting ready to loan England all that money, we need all the help we can get. Stopping short of the Reds, of course, who now claim to be against America getting into the war, too, but they'll change their tune when Moscow tells them. I mean, really, Caitlin, do you want American soldiers spilling their blood over in Europe?"

"No. But my daddy always said you have to be careful who your friends are." This was a locution she had picked up recently from Betty: you could always express an opinion with no fear of contradiction if you preceded it with "My daddy always said."

"Well, your daddy would have made a lousy politician," said Betty. "Elias isn't the only man of taste and breeding—" Betty could put words within quotation marks with only a quiver of an eyebrow "—Coughlin is seeing here. He's got friends all over Washington. Lemke, Patman, O'Conner."

"And what's this about my illustrious colleagues?"

Caitlin and Betty were both startled to hear Stowe's voice. He had come in without their noticing and now stood there in his shirt sleeves, his maroon suspenders twisted on the left side. Betty had once said that Stowe wore elevator shoes, but if he did it was hard to say what they did for him. He looked like a very independent, wizened child. His gray hair was combed neat as a puppet's and there were deep grooves in his narrow face.

"I was wondering where you'd disappeared to," Stowe said to Betty in his inquisitive tenor.

"I thought you boys wanted a little privacy," said Betty, sliding off Caitlin's desk, smoothing her skirt.

"Malarkey," said Stowe with a wave. He glanced at Caitlin for a moment and noticed the residue of emotion on her face. "What's with you?" he asked, in a voice not wholly lacking in kindness.

"Nothing, sir."

Stowe shrugged. His insights were penetrating but hit-and-run. He left the follow-through to others.

Turning back to Betty, he said, "Coughlin's going to pay his respects to a few of the fellows and then he's coming back and we're going to meet the Russian for lunch, around noon. I need you to arrange a table."

"How many will you be?" asked Betty. She was pliant with Stowe, but never subservient. She served efficiently, willingly, and most often spoke with a playfulness and irony that implied a larger purpose beyond the routines of the office, a more profound hierarchy in which Betty and the congressman were equals, collaborators.

"Me, Coughlin, the Russian, the Russian's besotted bride, and Coleman," Stowe said.

"And will we be setting a place for the Holy Ghost?" asked Betty.

"No, but you may as well come too."

Betty hesitated. "Four Feathers?"

"Yes. Make certain Raymond takes care of us and let him know to water the Russian's drinks."

"Are you kidding?"

"Yes, but I hear the Russian's a lush and the last thing I need in this heat is some Slav slobbering on me."

"How about Caitlin here joining us, Elias?" asked Betty. She took a pencil off Caitlin's desk and tapped the pinkish eraser against her own chin, smiled at Stowe, challenging him.

"Why not?" he said. He took his railroad watch out of his vest pocket and held it importantly in his small hand. "I'm going down to see what we can do to keep those damned gun-boats out of the North Sea," he announced.

At the Four Feathers, Caitlin was seated between Stowe and Anastase Vonsiatsky, the man Stowe called the Russian back at the office but whom he now referred to variously as Count, Alex, and Annie. An elderly Negro in a white jacket filled their water glasses with ice water.

Caitlin's hands were trembling. She had an overpowering sensation of not belonging.

But there was rapture, too: the surging, egotistical joy of the outsider finally allowed in.

Betty had prepared her, telling her that all she was required to do was act young and charming. ("Should be easy for you, being rather young and charming anyhow. And to these old geezers and that little drip Coleman charm in a woman consists of listening to them with a rapt expression while they say whatever pops into their minds.") Betty had warned her that Vonsiatsky's wife, the former Marion Stephens, an heiress whose purse was bursting with Baldwin Railroad Works money, was obsessed with Vonsiatsky and thought every woman was mad over him, too. "And as for Coughlin, just stay downwind from him and you'll be safe. He's just a dumb, well-meaning, musty old priest. Coleman? Don't even make eye contact. I suppose it's rather late in the game to believe in evil, but that one frightens even old Betty."

The Four Feathers served but did not exactly welcome women and the décor made that clear. The wood was dark, the prints in the heavy gilt frames and dark green mats were of the Charge of the Light Brigade variety—horse soldiers, dying comrades, all rather upsetting and strangely tiresome in Caitlin's view. A congealed galaxy of cigar smoke hung over the center of the dining room, and the confluence of all those male voices bragging to each other simultaneously sounded indistinct yet powerful, fueled by an overwhelming sense of purpose, like the sound of the trains Caitlin used to listen to in her bed back home.

Their waiter, Raymond, brought each of them a Tom Collins. Count Vonsiatsky kept an eagle eye on the women's glasses, never allowing them to remain empty, and Caitlin drank slowly. She didn't want it to go to her head.

Then Raymond placed a green-tinted glass plate full of olives and tomato slices before them and Caitlin let herself go a little and ate as many of them as she pleased.

Across the table, Father Coughlin had been questioning John Coleman about his religion. Coleman was from Yonkers, New York. His mother was Catholic and his father, a policeman, was a mixture of Lutheran and Baptist.

"Ah, but you see . . ." said Coughlin, smiling. His glasses caught the light as he cocked his head; he seemed very aware of his own impishness. "Predominantly you're a Catholic."

"No," said Coleman. There was something forceful but hollow in his voice.

It reminded Caitlin of listening to the radio with her ear pressed hard against the fabric-covered speaker.

"Ah, but when you think about it," persisted Coughlin. He wagged his blunt finger at Coleman.

"I have thought about it," said Coleman. "The trouble with Catholicism is that it gives consolation."

"But we need consolation," said Coughlin, as if in triumph.

"Exactly," said Coleman. "But some of us have decided to forgo it. Some of us would rather struggle here on earth and not let our minds go fat with fantasies of paradise later on."

"Now that's a novel idea," said Betty. "Religion as some sort of intellectual bonbon."

"Let those who need a splash of holy water now and then

have it," said Coleman. He barely moved his lips when he spoke. "I love Christ and I accept Him as my savior, and I despise the Jews who took His life on Calvary. Look around you, you see it's happening all over the world. The sins of the Jews are being punished, but not by priests—by warriors."

"I think in recognition of where we are right now, we could all be more discreet in our remarks," said Stowe, tapping his ringed finger against his cocktail glass.

There was a moment's uncomfortable silence, which gave Vonsiatsky the opportunity to begin talking about the friends with whom he was in an international league to defeat Communism. Vonsiatsky wore a khaki uniform of his own design, with a broad black leather belt around his waist and another from the waist to the shoulder and back to the waist again. His buttons were emblazoned with tsarist eagles clasping arrows in their talons.

"The great German army will crush and humiliate Stalin and freedom will be restored to the great suffering Motherland," Vonsiatsky said, with the slight irony of one who has said the same thing too many times. He seemed at once a man in the midst of a feverish dream and a man retelling the dream. He had colorless, thinning hair, inquisitive blue eyes that looked rather small in his large childish face. "We have made our headquarters in the charming town of Manchouli, in the northwest of Manchuria. Very carefully chosen, very important spot, just three kilometers from the Red frontier."

"That's less than two miles," his wife told the others. Marion Stephens was a graceful, dark woman, with modest curls and eyes that radiated emotional excess. She spoke with a sad lilt.

"Yes, in American, two miles," said Vonsiatsky. He turned to Caitlin and rested his very warm hand on her wrist. "You must try to imagine. Every evening when the sun goes down, my friends turn on the lights of the swastika that rests on top of their building and the lights shine deep into Russia, proclaiming freedom and *defiance*." He smiled. His teeth showed evidence of hard times.

Stowe sighed, tilted back in his chair. "Raymond!" he said, beckoning the waiter.

Vonsiatsky moved his foot so that his boot touched Caitlin's shoe.

She placed her hands in her lap and squeezed them together. She felt disoriented, as if the room were slowly turning.

The waiter came to take their orders. He needed no pencil and pad. Similarly, no one had consulted a menu but the orders were made nevertheless. When it came time for Caitlin to order she felt a surge of anxiety, as if she were going to disgrace herself by ordering something naïve, or common. There was something in the way the elderly waiter looked at her that seemed to say he knew she was out of her class.

"I'll have your Waldorf Salad," Caitlin said. She had never had one but she'd read about them, believed they were labor-intensive, knew she would never make one for herself. She would always feel that every meal in a restaurant had to be special.

Vonsiatsky pointed at her empty Tom Collins glass and then snapped his fingers, glancing at the waiter.

"Will anyone else be wanting a drink?" asked Stowe, taking command of the table again.

"No," said Coleman.

"I don't see how I can refuse," said Coughlin.

Everyone but Coleman wanted another drink and once that was settled Stowe held forth on the Lend-Lease Bill. He knew how to speak without leaving any spaces for others to wedge in and interrupt him. His voice was steady and he filled the silence as a paint-soaked brush covers wood.

Caitlin told herself that Stowe was in a sense using the men around this table. Stowe's objective was to fight Roosevelt and keep America out of the war, and right now that meant striking some alliances. Betty had said more than once that politics makes strange bedfellows.

Betty.

Caitlin glanced across the table at Betty. She was listening to Stowe as if hearing all of this for the first time. It seemed she always knew when it was time to make a wisecrack and when it was time to sit raptly at the master's feet. Betty's strong face was beautiful in repose. Her eyes were the blue of a bright winter sky.

Peace, thought Caitlin. All Stowe wants is peace. In the end, what they were trying to accomplish was good. Even the Communists wanted peace. Caitlin had been walking down Pennsylvania Avenue with Betty a few days ago and they had come upon a Red rally. A skinny man with bristly hair was on a hand-fashioned stage in front of a microphone, leading the group in singing "The Yanks Aren't Coming." "With friends like these . . ." Betty had said, taking Caitlin's arm, hurrying her along.

She took a sip of her drink. She was further at this moment from Twin Ponds than she would have ever dared to hope. Even as a girl when she had studied geography and dreamed one day of becoming a cartographer, she had not imagined herself so far from Leyden as she had now come, in this restaurant, with its horse-soldier prints and tobacco smell, with its lazy ceiling fans. Treasury Department people at one table, Republican National Committeemen at the next.

She felt a flurry of gratitude and a kind of romanticizing of herself. And then she realized she would not be at this table were it not for Betty. Betty was shaping her as Caitlin had longed all her life to be shaped. She stared at her friend and thought her name over and over, louder and louder within her, until Betty looked over and smiled and Caitlin felt her own face scald with pleasure.

"I've never been more firmly convinced than I am right

now," Stowe was saying, "and the Gallup Poll bears me out on it, I dare say. Did you happen to see it, any of you? Betty? What were the percentages again?"

"Eighty-eight percent of the American people say they want no part in the European conflict," said Betty.

"Yes, indeed, I did read that," said Father Coughlin. "In fact, I read those findings well before they were published. In fact, I was the first person ever to read them." He nodded emphatically.

Marion Stephens touched her throat with her delicate, nicotine-stained fingers. "There is so much at stake, Congressman Stowe. Annie and I and the American people cry to heaven for peace."

Annie, thought Caitlin.

Vonsiatsky shifted in his seat and pressed his leg against Caitlin's.

"We've become so used to polyglot cities and outsiders running our lives," said Coleman, carefully placing his fingertips together, "I think we have forgotten the American dream. The American dream is alive, in me, and in others."

"We all believe in that dream, sir," said Coughlin, as if offended. He seemed to feel that Coleman was besting him in some way, claiming the territory Coughlin himself was used to occupying. "I think every man and woman at this table burns with the belief in that dream. But I must say I find it curious to hear you decry the mongrelization of America, as I myself have called it, when you are a confessed hybrid, religiously speaking."

Coleman tensed his jaw but smiled.

"And what's more," said Coughlin, as if preventing Coleman from speaking, though Coleman gave no indication he wished to reply, "I think it's in questionable taste to be making remarks about polyglut—"

"Glot," corrected Coleman.

The priest's stout, creased face colored for a moment.

"With a man who has graced our shores," he said, pointing to Vonsiatsky, "sitting right here with us at this table."

"I was hardly speaking about royal Russian blood coming here," said Coleman, with a small, tactical laugh.

"Oh, John and I are old friends," said Vonsiatsky. "Often Marion and I have had him home with us, isn't that right, John?"

"Annie," said Coleman, bowing his head slightly.

"We have showed to him our militia, our arsenal."

"I would say the finest private army in the land," said Coleman.

"And John has given us the benefit of his knowledge of munitions, sharp-shooting, and explosives."

"There is no one who shoots better than this man," said Coleman, pointing at Vonsiatsky.

Coughlin, apparently discouraged by this repartee, sank back in his chair. "Do you know Roosevelt used to call me Padre?" he said to Marion Stephens. "When I was organizing for the race against him in '36, he called me on the phone and said, 'Padre, I thought we were friends.' Asked me to see him, so I went to Albany and Joe Kennedy picked me up in a Rolls-Royce. First thing I saw when I got off the train was a headline saying Huey Long was dead. Bless his soul. Joe Kennedy and I shot the breeze all the way down to Hyde Park—"

Vonsiatsky's hands were beneath the table. He patted out a rhythm on Caitlin's knee, keeping a beat on music only he heard.

". . . And when we got to Hyde Park, it was five in the morning. The door was wide open, no servant or guards. Roosevelt was sleeping so Joe and I just went to the kitchen and helped ourselves to breakfast." Coughlin took off his wire-rimmed glasses and inspected them for dust, then brushed the back of his hand against his eye.

"The arrogant devil's got you hypnotized, Father," said Stowe with a laugh.

"You should have gone to his bedroom and shot him," added Coleman.

The waiter came with their lunches. Caitlin was the last to be served. It made her feel somehow exposed. She edged toward Stowe to put herself out of Vonsiatsky's reach. But it didn't discourage him in the least. He reached his long arm under the table until he was touching her again and this time with a brisk, utterly proprietary gesture, he flipped up the hem of her skirt.

"Your employer tells me you are a great reader of literature," Vonsiatsky said to Caitlin, looking at her brazenly.

She could only nod. She saw herself throwing her drink in his face, but she held herself back. She believed there were alternatives still open to her.

"What are you reading now?" asked Vonsiatsky.

Caitlin didn't say anything. His fingers touched her stocking and then playfully walked up her leg, like a fool skipping up the hill.

"Caitlin?" asked Stowe, raising his sparse eyebrows.

"*Listen, the Wind*," she said, in a voice so unstable that Betty put down her fork and looked at her inquisitively.

"Ah, Mrs. Lindbergh's wonderful book," said Marion Stephens. She was looking directly at her husband, who looked back at her and smiled in a false, cruel way.

"Charles Lindbergh is a great patriot," said Father Coughlin. "Where a lesser man would be resting on his laurels, Lindbergh has crossed this land a dozen times over, speaking of our historic friendship with the German people." He put his fork down with a piece of steak speared on the tines. "Charles Lindbergh is an aviator not only of the skies but of the soul," Coughlin said.

"And how that family has suffered," said Marion Stephens. She clutched her napkin; she hadn't touched the breast of chicken before her. "The loss, the tragic loss of their child. Oh, I think I know how they must feel."

"But how could you know, Marion?" asked Vonsiatsky, with a laugh. "*You* have no children."

Marion Stephens's face colored but she didn't respond to her husband's remark.

"But you must tell me," Vonsiatsky said, looking boldly into Caitlin's eyes. "Your most beloved book, not just what you are reading now."

"Ah," said Betty, "now you've got her number. She reads like a real bluestocking."

Vonsiatsky smiled at Caitlin, cocked his head, as if to say, Well? Prove yourself to me.

"My father and I used to read *Great Expectations* together," said Caitlin. She was aware that her voice sounded weak, nervous, as if nothing could have been further from the truth, as if she had had no father, or a father who was an ignorant brute.

"And that is your most beloved book?" said Vonsiatsky, seeming to lure her further into making a fool of herself.

"Dickens," said Marion Stephens. "The great Dickens."

"I don't know," said Caitlin.

"I thought *War and Peace*," prompted Betty.

"Yes, I suppose so," said Caitlin.

"*War and Peace*," said Coughlin, who seemed to be hearing the title for the very first time. "Sounds like a story of today."

A look of nostalgia that looked almost like a species of kindness spread across Vonsiatsky's wide, deceptive face. "Tolstoy," he said. "Tolstoy would be with us, working with us, were he alive today. You know, when I was forced to leave my home, to leave Russia, and live like a common refugee in strange and unfriendly lands, I carried Tolstoy with me, wherever I went. Yet I was for years afraid to open the book, I knew it would, it would—" He took a deep breath, shook his head.

"Then, in Berlin, preparing to come here, I cut the pages of an edition that I had taken from my father's library.

He had a most tremendous library. You would have liked him." Vonsiatsky was not even pretending to include anyone else at the table in his conversation. "And I opened it up, near the beginning, and I read these words." Vonsiatsky closed his eyes for a moment and then recited a line in melodic, though woodenly paced Russian. "And do you know what those words mean? They are nothing, of no great importance, they are trifles, but they broke my heart, Count Vonsiatsky's heart was broken as if these simple words were a message telling me of some great tragedy, that my mother had died."

"Suppose you give us the translation, Annie," Stowe broke in, with an annoyance in his voice he was trying to disguise as amusement.

"Those simple words meant this," Vonsiatsky said, moving still closer to Caitlin. "'It was after one in the morning when Pierre left his comrade. It was one of those luminous nights in June we have in Petersburg.' I read those words, and wept. It brought it all back, my youth, my country, the simplicity of our lives then, the smell of the new-mown fields, the sound of good Russian voices and the mystery of the Russian sky at night. It was pure then, so pure." Vonsiatsky's hand moved further up Caitlin's leg. "I wish I could take you to Russia, my Russia, but today it would be easier for us to go to the moon."

He touched the hard nubs of her garter belt through the tops of her stockings and then lightly caressed her bare thighs with his callused, corrugated fingertips. She grabbed his hand beneath the table but he resisted her. The effort shook the table and she quickly moved her hand away. She was trapped as if in a dream. The walls were closing in and somehow she was required not to scream. She must stop this man without drawing any attention to herself. She was certain that if anyone at this table were to know, she would be blamed, not the Russian.

She turned in her chair and glowered at him. He smiled. It seemed perfectly natural to him, a game.

"Mr. Vonsiatsky!" Caitlin said, her voice rising. Her heart was a barrel rolling down the stairs. His face, the room, everything was as unstable as a reflection in the water.

"Count," said Vonsiatsky. The legs of his chair squeaked on the bare floor as he slid it closer to her. He was not going to stop. Her thighs were clasped so tightly her hips ached. With a soft, barely audible grunt of effort, he jammed his hand between Caitlin's legs and slipped his fingers into her underpants, stretching the elastic, stroking her pubic hair, his fingers moving back and forth like the tentacles of a squid.

With a chaotic gesture she hoped looked accidental, Caitlin waved her hand and knocked her water glass, which was full, and her Tom Collins, which was nearly full, into Vonsiatsky's lap.

Reflexively, he withdrew his hand from her and half-stood. He began rapidly swatting at his trousers, as if all that liquid were a swarm of bees.

"Oh, I'm sorry, I'm sorry," said Caitlin, so passionately that for a moment she actually felt sorry. She stood up and handed Vonsiatsky her napkin.

He grabbed it from her. The front of his tight khaki trousers was soaked black. "Oaf," he said.

She looked at Stowe but did not say anything. Suddenly, she didn't trust herself to speak.

"Caitlin?" said Betty, softly. She was putting her napkin down, standing up.

Marion Stephens was rising too, coming toward her husband, still holding her napkin. She seemed rather relaxed about it, as if she were used to things like this happening to Count Vonsiatsky.

Caitlin realized the decorum she had hoped to preserve had been lost. Vonsiatsky had had his way with her; he'd made her into a fool.

The room throbbed. Once her life had been a solid thing, durable, but here in this city it was fragile and now it was broken, and what she had wanted, the person she had longed to become, drained away, in a mess, like the contents of a cracked egg.

"Caitlin?" asked Betty, but her voice was so far away.

"Annie," said Marion Stephens, reaching out for her furious husband. "Are you all right, Annie?"

Annie, thought Caitlin. She turned away. Someone was leaving the Four Feathers at that moment and she saw a wedge of sky through the open door.

"Excuse me," she murmured.

Her legs felt weak, unable to understand the suddenly foreign language of the synapses that commanded them.

She simply could not imagine sitting down at that table again.

Her mouth had a queer, hideously alive feeling, as if she had taken a huge gulp of hard cider but must not swallow. She felt elongated, ectoplasmic, cold. She tried to summon an inner voice that would calm her, but the creature who whispered within her was cross, frantic, entirely disoriented.

She only wanted to be alone. She walked toward the memory of the blue sky as if it would deliver her. She knocked into someone's chair, almost collided with a waiter. The last thing she saw in the Four Feathers was the face of the cashier, an elderly man with bright silver hair and an eye patch, who was just putting a pastel candy into his mouth as Caitlin staggered past him. Their eyes met. Caitlin must have been staring at him with apocalyptic intensity. He took the candy out of his mouth and smiled uncertainly at her, and Caitlin pushed her way out the door, and as soon as she was in the fresh air, with its scent of flowering oleander mixed with hot tar and traffic, she breathed deeply and burst into tears. She wept openly, choking on her tears and the vague sense that there was something awful deep inside of her, all the way to Peabody Street, home.

It was at least a half-hour walk to the Zweigs'. Caitlin was sweaty, exhausted; she had worn herself out trying to decide what to do next with her life. There was no question but that she had humiliated herself before Congressman Stowe and that she was going to be fired. Her rent was due in a week; she could pay that. It would give her another month to find some other work, and stay in Washington. She could not go back to Leyden.

As she walked, she passed department stores and imagined working inside them. She passed the Canadian Embassy, a library, a Woolworth's, an art gallery, and projected herself into each of them. Then she passed private homes with sprinklers sputtering water onto the smooth manicured green grass and the wind blowing a bit of the spray onto the soft gray screens around the porch, and she imagined herself working in one of those houses—a secretary to a writer, reading Brontë to an elderly woman, even working as a maid. The speculation gradually returned her to herself, and by the time she mounted the steps to the Zweigs' house she was clear-eyed, even feeling slightly defiant.

Screw them, she told herself.

Her thighs grazed each other as she climbed the steps, and suddenly she felt Vonsiatsky's fingers poking toward her center. A passing image: his finger inside her up to the knuckle, and then she turns quickly, violently, snapping it off.

I should have ground my water glass into his face, she thought.

She had had no idea how deeply she longed to be accepted, and it was this realization above all that made her burn with shame. The shame was so vast it was like a river overflowing its banks, irrigating heretofore fallow fields of grief. It was beginning to impress itself upon her that for her entire life she was going to feel as if there were something about her that was not good enough, that she did not truly belong in the places she wanted to go. There was a code of belonging that she could not crack. And knowing she would always be without it was like realizing you will never get a decent night's sleep, that the hours of darkness presented to others as a smooth, unbroken ribbon night after night fall into your hands as a jumble, tatters, confetti.

It was quiet in the house. Caitlin only wanted to sleep, but before she climbed up to her attic room she stopped in the kitchen. She was thirsty. She let the water run for a while until it became cold, but when she filled the glass she no longer wanted it and she poured it down the drain. Then she opened the refrigerator and saw that Hilda Zweig had made a fresh pitcher of orange juice. It was in a blue-and-red-striped pitcher; there was a piece of waxed paper held tightly over the top by a thick rubber band. Caitlin stared at it for a moment and then removed the pitcher from the refrigerator. She moved the rubber band down the pitcher until the waxed paper was loose, and then she picked up an edge of the waxed paper and drank a long swallow of Mrs. Zweig's carefully strained juice straight out of the pitcher's spout.

"Oh, hello there," said a voice from behind her.

She raised her shoulders, as if in response to a blow, and replaced the cover on the pitcher, smoothed out the rubber band, wiped the corners of her mouth with her knuckle, and closed the refrigerator.

It was Joe Rose. He was wearing a sleeveless undershirt, pleated brown slacks; he was barefoot, holding a notebook. His shoulders were smooth and rounded like a child's. The hair under his arms was glistening black.

"What are you doing here?" she asked, her voice a little sharper than she would have wanted. "I thought you were in New York. I got a letter from you, from New York."

"Oh. I was hoping to see you before you read that letter. I think I was a little out of line. Bad habit, minding other people's business."

"I don't think you realize how much my job means to me. But then, how could you? You don't really know me at all."

"Are you all right?" he asked.

"Yes. Of course I am." Caitlin walked away from the refrigerator, sat at the kitchen table.

"You look a little . . . I don't know. Pale."

She was pale. She had been frightened to be seen stealing Mrs. Zweig's orange juice. But rather than reveal this small thing she thought it somehow preferable to give a vaster and ultimately more revealing reason for her discomfort.

"I think I may have just lost my job," she said.

"Your job? What happened? It wasn't because of my letter, was it?"

"We were having lunch with some of his friends. I behaved like a fool and now he's furious with me." But it wasn't my fault, she wanted to say.

"Stowe's friends are half the trouble with Stowe. Who were you with?"

He asked the question in an offhand way, a boy tossing stones into a pond. He didn't even make eye contact with her.

"Father Coughlin," said Caitlin. "And this Russian. Vonsiatsky."

"Ah," said Joe. "Him." He went to the refrigerator and took out the pitcher of orange juice, then to the cupboard for a glass. "Thirsty?" he asked.

"No, thank you." She watched him as he poured a glass of juice, just like that. But of course he really belonged there.

"Was Vonsiatsky with his wife?" asked Joe.

"Yes."

"She's bankrolling him, you know. He's got the largest private militia in the history of America. Jerks, for the most part, but a jerk with a gun can kill you just as thoroughly as a genius can. Was that it?"

"And a guy named Coleman," said Caitlin.

Joe was quiet for a moment. He ran the glass beneath the faucet. "John Coleman?" he asked, his back to Caitlin. Steam rose from the sink, clouding over the window, making the yard with its weeping willow tree disappear. Joe turned the water off, put the glass in the rack to dry.

Caitlin had never before seen a man perform the slightest domestic task.

"You know him?" she asked.

"No," said Joe, "but I'd like to." He walked slowly toward her, sat at the table, turned his chair, and faced her, let his knees graze against her. "Can you introduce me?"

"I don't know him."

"Nobody does. He has names, extra names. What do you call them?"

"Aliases."

"Yes, aliases. Earl Kingsbury. William Mason. He has pretended to be a Jew. He knows Hebrew. He's studied it, he knows the Torah. Better than I. Morris Fiegenbaum. He wears a black overcoat, a homburg."

"Not today."

"Morris Fiegenbaum was for Cleveland."

Caitlin conjured up Coleman's face, the hollow cheeks, the moody eyes, the prim, somehow girlish smile. She saw his long fingers on his water glass. She remembered what Betty had said: That one is evil.

"Is he a spy?" Caitlin asked.

"I don't know who he works for," Joe said. "I'd like to. He may work for the Germans; he certainly gets some money from them. I can prove that. But he may be independent, for the most part. Wherever the Nazis operate they find men like him, men with poison in them, willing to do anything. Coughlin, Vonsiatsky, they're the same, but not so selfless.

They want their roast beef and their feather bed. Coleman could sleep on nails. He doesn't have a cynical bone in his body. In his own mind, he's a hero. He sets a bomb and feels as if he's cleaned up something dirty."

"A bomb?"

"I can't prove any of this."

Caitlin nodded, not wanting to seem too curious, not entirely wanting to know. It was too large; she had no structure to contain it.

"I love this country," she found herself saying, apropos of nothing.

"So do I," said Joe, without a moment's hesitation. He moved his hand toward her, but they did not touch. "But so what? John Coleman does, too. And the Soviets are saying fascism is a matter of taste. It's like musical chairs out there and when the music stops Hitler ends up on your lap."

His voice was soft, his eyes intimate. He had a deep, slightly sharp masculine scent, new-mown hay, an iron skillet drying in the sunlight.

The phone rang in the front hall.

"That might be Sumner Welles's office," said Joe. "I'm supposed to meet him. For cocktails, tonight." His voice was suddenly youthful, reedy. The phone rang again; he didn't bother to excuse himself.

Caitlin sat at the kitchen table and listened to Joe's voice on the telephone. The late-afternoon sun cast a shimmering square of light on the table's polished surface. She moved her fingertips into the light and they became translucent. She could see the blood beneath her fingernails, pink and bright. Her heart was beating out a steady telegraphy of sadness and exhaustion. What would she do if Stowe were to send her home?

"Well, whatever would be most convenient for Mr. Welles," Joe was saying in the foyer. "Five o'clock, six, I'm at his disposal."

She heard the phone slide off its mahogany table and could picture Joe nervously pacing back and forth, then reaching for the heavy phone as it swung from its black cord, suspended above the loomed lions of the maroon-and-purple Oriental runner.

"Just a second, just a second," Joe was saying. "Let me, ahh, straighten something out here."

Caitlin got up. She was light-headed, her extremities were cool and heavy. She took a deep breath and then walked slowly out of the kitchen, into the dining room, the parlor, and up the stairs to the attic.

Once in the attic she closed the door behind her. Even in the middle of the day, the diamond-shaped windows let in little light. Now it was nearly five o'clock and the late-afternoon shadows were on everything, soft as moss. The heat filled the room like smoke. Caitlin sat on the edge of her bed and turned on the rotating fan. She called it her man in an iron mask. The beige blades pushed the warm air around the room. She slipped off her shoes and let them fall to the floor and then she pulled back the dotted Swiss bedspread to expose her parsimoniously stuffed pillow and then she stretched out on the bed. She pressed her heels into the mattress and held her toes straight up. They looked hard and wooden through the dark-brown of her hosiery. . . .

Caitlin awakened with a gasp. Someone was touching her arm. She opened her eyes. The lamp screamed yellow light. Then Betty's hand reached for the lamp, turned it off, and the sloping attic room was indigo.

There was the smell of Betty's cigarette. The smell of Betty's April Showers talc.

"Were you sleeping?" Betty asked, taking the book from Caitlin's hands, gently closing it, placing it on the table.

"I guess." Her voice was webbed. She lifted herself on her elbows.

Betty touched Caitlin on the side of the face, tucked a strand of hair behind Caitlin's ear.

A feeling of sluggish unreality. She could not come properly awake.

"What time is it?" asked Caitlin.

"A little after six. I came as soon as I could."

"I guess I'm going to be fired."

"Never in a million years, Caitlin." Betty's voice was solemn; you could never break a promise made in that true and ardent voice.

"I just walked out."

"I'd call it running for your life. That goddamned Russian wanted to roger you."

"Roger?"

"The thought of that oaf touching you," said Betty, "that it would even cross his mind . . ."

"And Mr. Stowe isn't mad."

"He's completely humiliated." She tucked a few more strands of hair behind Caitlin's ear. "I saw to that."

"He's not going to fire me?"

"If you asked him for a raise tomorrow morning he'd probably have to give it to you." She clasped Caitlin's hand; slowly their fingers entwined. "Elias knew Vonsiatsky was flirting with you. We just need him right now. Anyhow, what kind of friend do you think I am? Do you think I'd let Elias fire you?"

And with that she quite casually bent over Caitlin and kissed her lightly on the top of the head, as if this sort of gesture was quite natural to their friendship. And perhaps it was to Betty, but Caitlin was raised in an atmosphere of emotional illiteracy, where tenderness was rare, and was followed by gestures of negation as the groan of thunder follows the ecstasy of lightning.

Yet here was this kiss, this gentle kiss placed on the top of her head in this virtually airless room. It shook her. She felt a wild and terrifying aliveness where Betty's lips touched her hair, felt her friend's breath. She looked up at Betty, who was staring at her with the great seriousness of love.

Betty seemed as if she was about to say something but instead she craned her neck and slowly, slowly moved her face toward Caitlin until their noses touched and then their foreheads, and Caitlin did not move, either forward or back, left or right, and Betty seemed to understand that remaining poised was assent because her breath broke within her like an icicle snapped in two and she grabbed Caitlin's shoulders, not to embrace her but just to hold on, as if she, Betty, were suddenly doubting gravity's promise to keep her in place.

"Oh dear? Dear?"

Caitlin and Betty turned toward the sound of Hilda Zweig's maternal soprano, with its slightly foolish interrogative swoop. A guillotine-shaped wedge of yellow light raced up the wall as Hilda opened the door to Caitlin's room. She held a pewter tea service; the teapot, cups, and saucers trembled as she walked. She wore a girlish summer dress, a small yellow hat cocked to one side of her head.

Betty turned on the bedside lamp. Her smile was regretful, conspiratorial.

"Joe told me you were feeling poorly, dear," said Mrs. Zweig, as she made her way across the room. The spout of the teapot spewed steam; Mrs. Zweig's heavy, creased face was perspiring. "And he also told me you had a visitor." She smiled at Betty, and made a little bow of the head.

"Oh, how very gracious of you, Mrs. Zweig," said Caitlin, as much for Betty's benefit as Hilda's. She sensed that Betty was looking on the landlady with a certain contempt, and Caitlin wanted to make it clear that this woman was elegant, generous, despite the clumsy intrusion.

"Oh, not at all, dear, not at all. After all, you are a guest in this house."

She placed the tray down on the beside table and heaved a sigh. She fanned her face with her right hand.

Betty stood up, smoothed her dress.

"Hello, dear," said Hilda, extending her hand. "I'm Hilda Zweig."

"Hello," said Betty. There was a small turn of amusement in the O. "I'm Betty Sinclair. I work with Caitlin."

"Oh, is it true that she's going to lose her job?" She spoke to Betty as if they were both elders, each entrusted with Caitlin's welfare.

"Like so much of what one hears in this city, it is completely untrue," said Betty. She winked at Caitlin.

"Thank goodness," said Hilda.

"So you won't have to evict her after all," said Betty.

"We would have waited for her to find another position," said Hilda. "You know that, dear, don't you?" she added, looking at Caitlin.

"I really must be going," said Betty.

"Oh," said Caitlin, not daring to say more. Yet what would she have said had they been alone? Stay? Stay with me?

"Work," said Betty, vaguely, but with finality. "I'll see you tomorrow, Caitlin."

"I don't know how to thank you," said Caitlin. Mrs. Zweig had poured a cup of tea and handed it to Caitlin. She accepted it and noticed a plate of cookies on the tray. Scottish shortbread—she had stolen a few from the tin late last night.

"It has nothing to do with thank you," said Betty. She raised her hand to stop Mrs. Zweig, who was about to offer to show her out. "I can find my way out," said Betty.

She walked out of Caitlin's attic room, down two flights of stairs. Joe was sitting in the living room, reading the late paper. The smell of a recently peeled orange was in the room.

When he heard Betty's footsteps he put the newspaper down and their eyes met. She was sure he had sent his sister up because he did not want her to be alone with Caitlin. And the way he smiled at her, nodded, and put the newspaper up again did nothing to lessen her suspicions, or her annoyance.

Upstairs, Caitlin was listening to Mrs. Zweig, but really all that she could attend to was thoughts of Betty. She breathed deeply before the aura of Betty's scent disappeared from the room. Her feelings were like the beginning of snow, the point at which you can still differentiate each snowflake but must do it quickly because soon it will be impossible, soon the air will be thick and white and the wind will be howling.

And so Caitlin sipped her tea and nodded politely as Hilda Zweig talked about her health, her husband's business, of a frightening letter they had received from relatives trying to get out of Austria. Caitlin did her best to pay attention but it was difficult: within her she felt the freedom and fright of a girl running through a corridor, throwing open doors that had never been opened. Caitlin thought of how Betty's chin wrinkled as she dragged on her cigarette, how she darted the tip of her tongue into her coffee to make sure it was cool enough to drink. She thought of what Betty said while they watched the Washington Sinfoniette Society: "The orchestra looks like the inside of the body. With all the violin bows going up and down and up and down, it's what it must look like when you're having an orgasm."

"You're still so pale, dear," Mrs. Zweig was saying. "Why don't you at least take a *zipp* of your tea?"

Caitlin looked at her, blinked, and felt her own heart accelerate. I'm in love, she thought to herself. At long last. She brought the teacup to her lips. The tea steamed in her face but tasted barely warm. She drank and then reached for a shortbread cookie. It felt strange to be eating them in front of Mrs. Zweig. She took a large bite. I'm in love with Betty Sinclair.

SEVEN

Betty Sinclair lived in a parlor-floor apartment on Dupont Circle. It was four large, high-ceilinged rooms, with wedding-cake plaster near the overhead lights. The furniture was gray, for the most part, and the walls were white. There was never the scent of cooking in those rooms; there was light, lily-of-the-valley cologne, and music.

Tonight it was raining. Headlights from passing cars flashed over the bay windows, revealing constellations of raindrops. Every now and then, there was a long groan of thunder that rolled around the black dome of sky like a marble inside an empty can. Betty's rooms were lit by wall sconces. They cast their light against the smooth plaster so that it looked as if bolts of pale linen were propped in every corner.

Betty had asked Caitlin to her house for dinner, and after dinner she wanted Caitlin to help her prepare a speech Congressman Stowe was going to give to the German-American Friendship League next week.

Caitlin had arrived just before the rain had begun. She wore a blue dress with a rounded cream-colored collar. Her hair was thick with the night's humidity. She was a little tipsy, too. It was Mr. and Mrs. Zweig's wedding anniversary and they had insisted she drink a glass of champagne with them before she left. Accustomed to Viennese ways, the Zweigs were dressed for an evening at the theater, Mr. Zweig in his black silk top hat, Hilda in a gold lamé gown. They had drunk Moët et Chandon out of heavy crystal champagne glasses. Mr. Zweig, who so rarely spoke, made a sentimental toast and Hilda's eyes filled with tears. The glasses themselves had once belonged to her mother, and this memory of family, of Austria, inevitably brought back the passionate confusion she had felt ever since receiving her sister's letter from Vienna, in which the terrors of the Nazi occupation were described with breathless Aesopian tact. "There will be no more crops harvested here, my dear sister. And all of the seeds have been destroyed."

"Well, who knows what that means," said Betty. "Anyhow, these Zweigs seem to have a lot of wine on hand."

"I told you. Mr. Zweig owns a wine-import company."

"Oh yes, right. I knew he bought and sold something."

Caitlin flopped into an armchair and stretched her legs. Betty went into the kitchen and came back with a bottle of champagne and two glasses.

"More champagne?" asked Caitlin with dismay.

"If you don't, you'll get a hangover. When you drink champagne you in fact commit yourself to drinking it all night. It's like plucking your eyebrows. Once you begin you have to keep it up for the rest of your life."

"I have to drink champagne for the rest of my life?"

"Yes, with me," said Betty. She smiled, wriggled the cork out, stepped back, as the effervescence overflowed.

Caitlin accepted the glass and waited for Betty to fill her own.

"If my friends could see me now," Caitlin said.

"Your best friend can," said Betty, touching her glass against Caitlin's.

They drank. The champagne was not cold and the bubbles churned in Caitlin's mouth.

"And now for our dreary speech," said Betty. "To be given by our dreary boss at a banquet for dreary old men with fur in their ears."

On the dining-room table there was a plate of cucumber sandwiches, a large Royal typewriter with clear glass casings for the typewriter ribbon, and a stack of coarse yellow paper. Betty picked up the sheets of paper, took another swallow of champagne, and cleared her throat.

"OK, I'll be Elias and you be the German-American Friendship League. OK?" She must have seen something hesitant in Caitlin's expression. "You're sure you don't mind doing this?"

"Who are they, though? This Friendship League."

"Businessmen, professors, professional people, people from good families. Some of them have been to Germany as tourists, or have family, or went to school there, and they want to preserve our ties with the German people. I mean, you should know. Windsor County is full of German-Americans. These were the people who helped settle this country."

Caitlin drank from her champagne glass. Within her, there were images, from the magazines, the newsreels, visions of Hitler, with his mad-assistant's mustache, his furious assistant's voice, his billions of soldiers throwing up their arms in unison. "What about Hitler?" she asked.

"Well, what about him?"

"He seems so crazy."

"I'm not his psychiatrist, personally. And if he is crazy, that's not our affair. I'll bet FDR sounds just as crazy to the Germans as Hitler does to us."

Caitlin smiled. She felt reassured Betty had acknowledged that Hitler sounded crazy to her, too.

Just then, Caitlin heard the piping song of a cuckoo clock,

though it seemed distant, muted. And following the song was a tap tap tap.

"What's that?" Caitlin asked, but as soon as the words were out she noticed an ornate wooden wall clock in the corner of the parlor.

"That, my friend, is a cuckoo clock," said Betty, with a small laugh. She was pouring more champagne into Caitlin's glass.

"But the bird can't get out."

"Correct. I nailed the door shut. I can't stand it when the bird just *pops* out."

Caitlin looked at her with amazement. "You nailed it shut?" It would have been hard to say why, but knowing this made her love Betty more than ever. Betty's eccentricities made her seem accessible and forgiving to Caitlin.

"I was going to give it away," Betty said, "but it was a present from Stowe. Apparently worth a king's ransom. And I do like it, but the bird is so obnoxious, with a loud voice and one red eye. It was made by the master clockmaker of Düsseldorf and the German trade minister gave it to Elias."

At last, the mechanical bird gave up trying to escape; its frantic calls and tapping were replaced by the steady, deeply authoritative tick of the clock.

"OK, now," Betty said, "I'll just run through it, you listen, and then tell me where the speech is most boring and I'll take those parts out. Elias is guest of honor, so he'll be speaking last. That means they'll have listened to five or six speeches already, so my figuring is he'll be a hero if he keeps it short. What do you think?"

"Me?" asked Caitlin.

Betty pretended to look around the room, as if there might be someone else there to whom she had asked the question.

"I don't know," said Caitlin, laughing. "It's not as if I go to banquets."

"Ah yes, the poor country girl," said Betty. "OK, ready?"

Betty cleared her throat and began to pace as she read. "'Thank you, Mr. Viereck. Ladies and gentlemen. It is a distinct pleasure to follow Mr. William Griffin, the New York *Enquirer*'s distinguished publisher.'" Betty quickly scanned the page. "And so forth and so on. This is all pretty standard."

"'There's been a lot of talk about nationalism here tonight,'" Betty went on, lowering her voice so it approximated the tone of a man. "'And as I sat here, I began to wonder just what we mean by this word *nationalism*.'"

"Don't read it in that voice, Betty, come on," said Caitlin.

Betty shrugged, as if to say, Why not?

"It makes me laugh," said Caitlin.

With mock admonishment and a shake of her finger, Betty said, "You see what happens when you let those Jews get you drunk?"

It was just a joke. But Caitlin felt as if she'd been slapped in the face. She recoiled a little, cast down her eyes.

"'*Nationalism*,'" Betty read on, her voice returned to its natural alto, yet with a tremor within it now, as if she knew she shouldn't have made that crack about Jews. "'What is *nationalism* but another word for *Americanism?* After all, our great country was born because brave men wanted to live their lives free of foreign, European entanglements. That was an honorable sentiment then and it is an honorable sentiment today.'" Betty looked up at Caitlin, who nodded at her. Betty smiled and returned to the text.

"'There are elements in this country who insist that our independence, our nationalism, if you will, is something we should throw like a piece of tinder on the fires that rage in Europe today. There are those, and I think you know who they are, who say that good American blood must be shed on the distant battlefields of Europe. There are those, and I think you know who they are, who seek day and night to poison the sacred wellsprings of German-American friendship.'"

Betty looked up from the script and shrugged at Caitlin.

"Elias loves rhetoric. Do you think I'm banging this 'and you know who they are' drum too vigorously?"

"I don't know. I'm not even sure of . . . of who they are."

Betty sighed. "Well, in truth, it's a lot of people—the Reds, until this nonaggression pact between Germany and Stalin, but soon that'll be over and the Reds will be clamoring for war again. And the European-culture crowd, who are up all night worrying a few paintings might get torn, and all the liberal sentimentalists, and a hell of a lot of international financiers, as well, though responsible people in the business community are perfectly happy to live in peace with the new Germany. And, of course, the Jews. They're very anxious to get us into the war, and people here are justifiably annoyed with them."

"So many people seem to have it in for the Jews, don't they?" said Caitlin.

"Well, I guess it's not very nice to say, but they bring it on themselves." Betty sat on the arm of Caitlin's chair and playfully fanned Caitlin's face with the pages of Stowe's speech.

"It's a whole attitude. They stand apart. You know, back home in Michigan Henry Ford is a great hero. I mean, you know, half the people in the state work for him, or do something that comes out of the automobile industry. And Henry Ford likes to give out copies of a book. Have you ever heard of *The Protocols of the Elders of Zion*?"

"I saw it in the office," Caitlin said. "I didn't really read it, something about rabbis in a cemetery, all plotting to take over the world."

"Well, I don't think it's necessarily real. It's a legend, a parable, I suppose. But people believe it, and I think that's interesting." She stopped herself, let her shoulders down in a show of self-mockery, rolled her eyes, as if to say, Listen to me going on this way. Then she simply tossed the pages of Stowe's speech into the air. They fell to the carpet.

"Let's just drink our champagne and listen to some music.

I bought a Bessie Smith record today, it's about ten years old, very rare. Been looking everywhere for it. You like Bessie Smith, don't you?"

"I'm not sure," said Caitlin. She held her glass out while Betty poured.

"I played you one of her records last week. The colored blues singer?"

"I've heard so many new things."

"Remember 'Empty Bed Blues'? 'Woke up this morning with an awful aching head'?" Betty was half-singing the lyrics, using that slightly discouraged yet boundlessly hopeful voice of someone who longs to be musical but who is nevertheless tone deaf. She wagged her head back and forth, metronomed with her open hand. "'Woke up this morning with an awful aching head. My new man had left me just a room with an empty bed.' I love that—'new man.' As if this had happened many, many times before."

"I think I do remember it," said Caitlin. She was enormously relieved that they had moved on from Stowe's speech, the war, the Jews.

Betty was at the Victrola now. She switched it on; the speaker breathed and crackled. Outside, the rain was starting to come down straight and hard, the way rain falls in the South, and the sound of the needle on the outer edge of the record made the same sound as the rain.

The record began with a delicate, syncopated introduction played by a violin and a piano. Betty turned toward Caitlin and swayed her body in time with the music, and when Bessie Smith's unrepentant alto emerged, Betty opened her mouth and pretended the voice was hers.

> *Tell me what's wrong with me.*
> *My man we can't agree.*
> *Now he tried to steal away.*
> *That is why you hear me say*

That I've got the blues,
Yes, I've got the blues
Gonna sing them night and day.
Ticket agent, ease your window down.

The violin filled in while Bessie Smith waited for the count of four. Betty bowed an imaginary violin, in perfect time.

Ticket agent, ease your window down.

This time, the piano filled in and Betty stretched out her long graceful fingers and played keys made of air.

Oh, my man's done quit me and tried to leave this town.

The record player spun around at approximately seventy-eight revolutions per minute, the steel stylus on the Victrola's brass tone arm rode the grooves of the record, and Bessie Smith's voice filled the apartment. When the song was over, Betty played it again, and when it was done a second time she played it a third. And when that was over she found her copy of "Empty Bed Blues," and she played it so many times that before the night was out even Caitlin knew it by heart. She liked the verse that went, "Oh, he's got that sweet something and I told my gal friend Lou," because somehow their three voices, Bessie Smith's, Betty's, and Caitlin's, braided in an eerily perfect harmony on the word *Lou*, and when they sang it twice and then sang the last line, the capper, the line that held both the joke and the rhyme—"By the way she's raving she must have gone and tried it, too"—they had their arms around each other's waist and they were shaking their hips and jerking their knees in one of those approximations of Negro dancing only possible among people who have never known a black person.

Time passed. Ten o'clock retired without being noticed

and then eleven slipped out unseen. The imprisoned wooden bird within the cuckoo clock banged its maple beak against the door, but who could have heard it above the slide trombone, the muted trumpet, or the thrilling clarinet that every time it played made Caitlin picture a schoolmarm trying to hold her skirts down in the wind?

And then it was nearly midnight. The rain had stopped and begun again and this time the storm was fierce, no longer falling straight down but at a windy angle, pelting the windows, rushing past the street lamps. When the lightning flashed and illuminated the nighttime street, with its black cars and swaying black trees, it seemed as if heaven and earth were joined by a moving membrane of water. Caitlin and Betty stood at the bay window and watched the rain, and when Betty told Caitlin that she would have to spend the night her words were drowned out by an explosion of thunder that sounded like a sledgehammer against a tin roof.

And when she said it again Caitlin turned to face her and was quiet for a moment, though this was far too solemn, and so she smiled, but this made her feel exposed, a little silly, as if she were making too much of it, or taking it somehow in the wrong way.

"It's nice of you to offer," Caitlin said, in a formal, almost stiff tone of voice.

Betty furrowed her brow; her smile was puzzled. "Are you all right?" she asked.

"I'm fine," said Caitlin. She cleared her throat.

Despite the storm it was too hot for nightclothes, but they could not sleep in the same bed without them and so Betty loaned Caitlin a light blue cotton nightgown and she herself wore a pair of peach silk pajamas.

Caitlin washed her teeth using her forefinger instead of a toothbrush and looked at herself in the mirror of Betty's bathroom. Her face looked so plain to her, so practical, so sensible. She brushed her hair back with her open hands and then breathed out deeply. Betty's nightgown had puffed shoulders and the short sleeves were edged with lace.

When she slipped into bed next to Betty the lights were already out. Betty didn't say a word or make a sound. Was she trying to make Caitlin believe she was already asleep?

Caitlin was on her back, her arms at her side. She took no more room in bed than the width of her body. She was an Egyptian wrapped in rags, closed into the sarcophagus of her own reserve. Yet she was certain Betty could feel the life in her, which was now transformed into sheer desire, certain that it radiated out of her like heat from a stove, the sound of a radio playing in the next room. Care to dance?

"Oh, I forgot to tell you," Betty said, whispering, as if they were children who were meant to be asleep. "I started *War and Peace.*"

Caitlin closed her eyes. A feeling of joy went through her. Betty's following her suggestion was a benediction.

"I was reluctant. Fourteen hundred pages. But you were right. It's wonderful."

"It gets even better as you go along," said Caitlin. She opened her eyes, let out a breath. Headlights from a passing car reflected in the window, casting a rain-spotted light across the ceiling. She felt the bed shift as Betty rolled over on her side.

"Thanks for recommending it," Betty said, touching Caitlin's shoulder.

Caitlin felt her skin come alive. She pulsated. It was as if in order to live an orderly life her body had to be anesthetized, but now the ether of the everyday was gone and she felt everything—her pores, the down on her arms, the knit of flesh along the insides of her thighs, the slight irregularities where her scalp had been stretched across her skull like a sock around a marble darning egg, the tips of her breasts, the cumbersome weight of her tongue as it sulked within her mouth like a tortoise in its shell, her vagina, her pubic hair grazing against the nightgown, the coldness of her pale, parched palms. Every part of her body wanted to be felt, heard.

Caitlin rolled on her side. She faced Betty.

She was used to the darkness now. She could see Betty with perfect clarity.

Betty moved closer, waited. She seemed to be testing, to see if Caitlin would move away. They both understood that the first gestures would all have within them an element of the accidental, that they would have to be able to say, Oh sorry, or Excuse me, at any point, and then withdraw, and that the fiction that they were only friends could then be preserved.

"You smell all tooth powdery," Betty said, smiling.

"I used my finger," said Caitlin. She withdrew her arm from beneath the warm white sheet and raised one finger, her index finger, though it wasn't the one she had used. She had used her right hand, but she didn't dare move that arm because it was next to Betty, and if she were to try and withdraw it then Betty would have to shift away from her, if only an inch or two.

"Ah," said Betty. "Afraid of my germs?" She clasped Caitlin's finger and then turned it around and around like a wooden spoon in a bowl of batter.

"Oh no," said Caitlin. "It wasn't that."

She wanted to put her arm around Betty. It was as if the heat of desire had brought to life a heretofore hidden self, who was now stretching within her and with its first breaths issuing drastic, unprecedented orders. Touch her, just touch her, the voice intoned. And then it said, She wants you to, can't you see that?

Caitlin did not think: But this is a woman who lies beside me. She did not think: Then I will be a homosexual, a lesbian. She did not think about going to hell, or living with it for the rest of her life, or even of tomorrow. All of that seemed completely beside the point. They were just ideas—not even ideas: they were words.

Betty released Caitlin's finger, but rather than let her hand drop to the mattress Caitlin gently placed it on Betty's shoulder. The feel of those silk pajamas was like putting your hand into a cool pond, the hum of water against your skin. Caitlin felt the bone in Betty's shoulder, and then she felt the seam in the pajamas, where the sleeve was joined.

"Mmmm," Betty said, and moved closer to Caitlin. "That feels nice." She tucked her chin in and pressed her forehead against Caitlin's forehead.

They were quiet and perfectly still. Caitlin's hand remained motionless on Betty's shoulder. They were Siamese twins joined at the brow.

"That Russian frightened me so badly yesterday," Caitlin whispered.

"I know, I know. I'm so sorry." Then, after a silence: "Was he touching you?"

"Yes. I just didn't want to make a scene. I thought everyone would blame me."

"Why would anyone blame you, Caitlin? It was him doing it. God, I'd like to kill him. Where was he touching you?"

"I always think of myself as the one who gets blamed."

"I know the feeling," Betty whispered. "The feeling there's something within you and no one must ever find out."

"Yes," said Caitlin. "That."

And Caitlin would never know how many moments passed before Betty lifted her chin and then parted her lips and kissed Caitlin softly on the mouth.

Caitlin thought of a diagram of the body she had seen in school, with the network of arteries and veins, yet now, in her, the traffic was not blood but desire. She wrapped her arms around Betty and returned the kiss with a fervency that held within it eagerness, loneliness, and even something rapacious. She opened her mouth to the kiss and then opened it wider;

she wanted to taste her friend, she wanted, really, to swallow her whole.

She felt Betty's hand press hard against her breastbone, ignoring the breasts themselves. It moved Caitlin, made her grateful. It was more personal somehow to press the sternum than to fondle the breasts. And then as the kiss continued Betty's hand slid down to Caitlin's belly and rested there for a few moments, letting the heat radiate into Caitlin, until it moved lower still, pausing for just a heartbeat and then gliding into that nest at Caitlin's center.

Caitlin made a noise of pleasure and surprise directly into Betty's mouth.

"Caitlin," Betty said. "Caitlin."

Caitlin clutched a handful of the cotton nightgown she wore and pulled it up, and when the nightgown was hitched up to her breasts she took Betty's hand and laid it solemnly against her again, this time so Betty's fingers closed like a door against her opening. A noise like a sob came out of Betty. Caitlin kept her hand on Betty's hand and pressed it harder against her and moved her own hips up to increase the pressure.

"I knew it," whispered Betty. "I knew it from the moment I first saw you."

A jolt of shame went through Caitlin as she realized her body was writhing, moving, it seemed, of its own accord. But Betty's breath touched her, calmed her; there was a smell, left over from the wine they had drunk, a smell of slightly overripe apricot and then Caitlin opened her legs wider and Betty's finger was inside her and the shame was gone, leaving in its wake the merest hesitation of shyness, which Caitlin now escaped by draping her leg over Betty's hips.

She rolled on top of her best friend in the world. "Is it OK if I'm on top?" Caitlin asked and Betty by way of an answer kissed her with liquid enormity. The cuckoo clock knocked its beak against the little locked door in the next room as they began to make love.

AUGUST 26, 1941

Joe Rose now lived in a small apartment in Greenwich Village, on Barrow Street. He had rented it under the name he now used, Fred Hollander. He had taken the false name and a leave of absence from *Fortune* six months ago. With the help of Gordon Jaffrey he had gotten a job working for Metropolitan of New York, something clerical. The life-insurance business was starting to boom just then. The war news, the pictures of bombed cities, the sudden phalanx of bombers you saw over bright banks of cumulus cloud in the Movietone News made people who might otherwise ignore the issue of their own mortality want to take certain precautions. It might have been acceptable work for Fred Hollander, or at least credible employment for a young man with two years of college and a meek demeanor, but for Joe, with a degree from Haverford College and a sense of himself that involved being near the center of this historical moment, the job at Metropolitan was the most dispiriting, difficult, and, really, annoying experience of his life. He and the hundreds who surrounded him seemed to be doing nothing but pushing paper around their desks, while the large, sonorous clock overhead ticked out the seconds of the slowly dying day.

Yet if Fred Hollander was to have a convincing reality, a reality that went beyond a name on a library card, thirteen letters inked onto a piece of masking tape on his mailbox, then employment, a simple run-of-the-mill job, was necessary. How much easier it would make it to be Fred Hollander of Metropolitan of New York. The familiarity of the company would compensate for the unfamiliarity of the person when he introduced himself. Rather than people wondering where he had come from they would immediately be able to picture the Metropolitan building, the swarms of people who lock-stepped in and out of it. The benign, banal occupation would be a palliative, something to soothe any suspicions Joe might arouse when he came into a Yorkville storefront or a midtown gun club and let it be known that he was ready to devote his time, energy, heart, and soul to keeping America out of the war with Germany.

His hair was no longer wavy. Again, aided by Gordon, he had gone to a place in Harlem called The Lenox, where a yellow-skinned man with a pencil mustache and peppermint breath straightened Joe's hair, using a mixture of creams and chemicals he refused to identify but which smelled to Joe suspiciously of lye. He still did not have the silky, fly-away hair he thought Fred Hollander would have, but rather a thatch of coarse, straight hair that felt like the end of a whisk broom. Gordon had gone to The Lenox too, taking pictures of Joe in the barber chair, Joe with the chemical-soaked rag wrapped around his head, for they had both felt that these might be historical documents. Yet when the barber said, "Now we gonna give it a kinda color like a shellac," and then bit down hard on his sucking candy, Gordon suddenly lost his sense of humor about the disguise and watched with a pale, sick, profoundly regretful stare as Joe's black hair was first peroxided dirty whitish silver and then dyed with a color that came out of a bottle simply labeled BROWN.

Joe worked days and went to rallies and meetings at night. He attended mass meetings of the Christian Mobilizers as well as more intimate kaffeeklatsches, in which arcane matters of politics were discussed under topic headings, such as "Why the International Financiers Want War" or "Whither the Balkans?" He was careful not to be too noticeable. When he had confided his plan to penetrate the pro-Hitler movement to Sumner Welles over cocktails, when the under secretary's slight decrease in formality seemed to Joe an invitation to intimacy, Welles's advice had been, "Go slowly, remember. Like a good fisherman. Don't jerk the bait around. Patience, my boy, patience."

And it had been advice worth following. After a meeting of the America First Committee held at the Manhattan Center Opera House, Joe had stood and cheered along with eight thousand other New Yorkers, all waving flags. It had been a long evening of speeches that had alternated between the naïvely patriotic, in which America was portrayed as a strapping youngster wanting to enjoy itself without being dragged down by its hopeless elders, and the terrifyingly hateful, in which Jews were portrayed as maggots equipped with sinister intelligence. The speeches swung between these two notions with such relentlessness that soon there developed a kind of spider's-web connection between them.

After the meeting, the speakers filed off the flag-festooned stage—George Boian, of the Rumanian Iron Guard, Leonora Schuyler, recently of the Daughters of the American Revolution, who seemed in her remarks convinced that Pope Pius was a Jew, Donald B. Hillcrest of Park Avenue, who did not seem to mind being called "The Gentleman Fascist," Gustav Elmer of the German-American Bund, and Charles Lindbergh, who had been the featured speaker. The brass band hired for the occasion continued to play Sousa marches, as well as simple tunes of boundless good spirits, such as "Hail, Hail, the Gang's All Here," and a few members of the audience, including Joe, lingered in the aisles, as if unable to leave the site of such fervor.

He was, as always, alone, and then suddenly a man named Joseph McWilliams touched Joe on the elbow and said, "Remember me?"

McWilliams was about forty years old, with the air of a self-reliant bachelor, used to living within limited means but fully prepared to enjoy whatever transitory luxuries life might bring his way. He had a laborer's useful-looking body. He had been born poor on an Oklahoma Indian reservation, and when he smiled he showed teeth that were strong but discolored. His eyes were dark blue; his eyebrows were so pale it looked as if they had been burned off.

"We met at the Midtown Sporting Club and then again at the reception for Fritz Kuhn," McWilliams said. "Some friends are having a late supper up on Eighty-sixth Street and I wonder, if you're free, if you'd care to join us. I think you might be fascinated by the mixture—the salt of the earth and the cream of the crop." McWilliams had smiled at the very small jest and then shrugged, as if to indicate he wished he lived in a world, a time, in which it might be acceptable to indulge his talent for humor.

It was that night when McWilliams asked Fred Hollander to join the Christian Mobilizers. A month later the Mobilizers' five-cent weekly newspaper, which had been edited by McWilliams, now said it was published by Joseph Mc-Williams, with Fred Hollander as its editor. Soon after that, McWilliams asked his new editor to quit working at Metropolitan and become a paid staff member of the Christian Mobilizers.

From that point on, the velocity of Joe's new life increased daily and his immersion into his false identity became more complete. He felt lost, with the darkness closing in around him and his point of entry a dim memory. Once, while working on a feature about the coal industry for *Fortune*, he had gone into an anthracite mine in Pennsylvania. He had sat backward in the small, rattling coal car that brought him and the miners into the cold, inky cave, and he had stared at the shimmering smear of light at the opening of the mine. But as the car shuttled to the left, then to the right, and then this way and that way, Joe had no idea where he could run if there was an emergency, a cave-in, an explosion, or if it simply became impossible for him to take a real breath, for already panic filled his lungs like wet concrete. As Fred Hollander he often felt that same sense of exile and peril.

He had his notes on his daily activities, which were a path to his real self, but merely recording the particulars of his daily work, the conversations, the meetings, the street demonstrations, the finances, the sporadic contact with probable German agents, seemed deficient. After closing his log and hiding it in the clothes hamper in his bathroom (he wouldn't have been surprised if some suspicious Christian Mobilizer might ransack the apartment), Joe was still aware that he had not really spoken to anyone.

And so he began to keep a diary, for the first time in his life. At first, his entries were sporadic, sparse, tending toward the exclamatory, but as they went on, his journal entries became longer, more detailed, confessional, free-associative. He even wrote poetry into it. Now, he sometimes wrote for an hour in his journal, often before he wrote his day's activities into his log, a reversal of priorities he would have found indulgent and amateurish a few months before. He kept this diary in a paper bag in the back of his small icebox.

Caitlin hung on to the leather strap of a humid subway car, gritting her teeth against the noise. The strap swung back and forth as the train danced its cacophonous conga through the pitch-dark tunnel.

She was wearing a red-and-white-striped dress, white shoes, and a white straw hat. She carried a large white pocketbook and wore red enamel earrings the size of half dollars. A bead of perspiration rolled slowly down her side; she moved her elbow against her dress to blot it out. She had always perspired heavily, just as her menstrual flow was usually wrenching and prolonged, her sneezes explosive, her rare tears copious—it always felt as if there were something within her passionately eager to come out.

Across from her, sitting in one of the tan wicker seats, a rabbi dressed in a heavy black suit sat reading the newspaper. The front page was folded out and Caitlin read that England and the Soviet Union had joined up in an invasion of Persia. They were after the oil. Caitlin could just imagine how Elias and Betty would take this news: it seemed to validate all they had been saying all along, the Brits and the Communists teaming up for a ruthless expropriation of some quiet land's natural resources. John Coleman had even gone so far as to say that Churchill was in league with the Reds. Someone, somewhere claimed to have photographs of Churchill and Stalin on some Black Sea beach, both in bathing costumes, sharing a bottle of vodka, throwing their heads back in laughter.

She had directions from the subway stop to Joe's apartment. Joe had drawn her a map showing the labyrinth of streets she had to navigate, and he had even sketched in an occasional stick figure of a man, holding on to his hat while his eyes bugged out, the men who would be going mad over Caitlin's beauty as she walked the streets of Greenwich Village.

There were no such men, or she did not notice them. The very idea was really a nightmare to her, though there was something touching in Joe's presuming it to be so.

Joe's apartment on Barrow Street was part of a fifty-unit building begun during the flush years and then hastily completed after the stock market crash in '29. To enter it, Caitlin had to walk from the sidewalk through a brick archway that led to an interior courtyard, which in turn radiated to five separate entrances. It was called Barrow Court and it had all the discomforting qualities of failed elegance.

Joe had just gotten into his trousers, his shirt was unbuttoned, when he opened the door to Caitlin. His chest was smooth, boyish, his nipples like peach-colored dimes.

"Caitlin," he said. His eyes showed relief and uncertainty,

as if he were a prisoner whom someone had finally come to visit.

"Joe," she said. She hadn't fully known how much she had missed him.

He put a finger to his lips and pulled her inside. "Fred," he whispered. "Don't use that other name."

"I'm sorry, I'm so sorry."

Joe made a calm-down gesture with his open hand.

"I just brewed up some coffee," he said.

"I'd love some," said Caitlin. She cleared her throat. She was suddenly very nervous and she wondered why. At first she thought it was the awkwardness of having failed to use Joe's new name, but then she realized it was something more personal and vast: this was the first time she had seen him since moving in with Betty. She wondered if Joe could see the difference in her, sense it, however unconsciously. Did she walk differently, smile in a new and alien way? Was there something in the way she combed her hair, stood, the way she held her hands, cocked her head, breathed, spoke, smiled, smelled, was there something in her eyes, a darkness, a glow, an involuntary evasiveness?

Joe had still been in and out of his sister's huge, sunstruck house when Caitlin had realized she loved Betty, he had still been working in Washington when Caitlin and Betty became lovers, he had heard her voice as it made its way up through the sudden tangle of all that new knowledge, those new layers of self. But in those first weeks of loving Betty it had not yet become entirely real. It was still something her old self was doing, a short detour off the original path, a moment, an interlude, something discontinuous from the overreaching arc of her life, and she could hold it at bay. It was really when she moved into Betty's apartment and began living the most serious secret of her life that she began to wonder how much was left of the girl who had stumbled off the train the year before.

The coffee he served her was black, thick as oil. She sipped it and her nerves jumped.

"So you're on your way home," said Joe. He sat in a camel-colored wing chair. He started to cross his legs but then stretched them out instead.

"It's about time, I guess." She looked around Joe's apartment. On the floor there was an old Persian rug the Flemings would have liked. The furniture was old, covered in heavy, uncomfortable fabrics. Everything looked old and uncomfortable. Unstable shelves, heavy with books, leaned away from the smooth plaster walls. A black Underwood typewriter was set up on a folding table near the casement windows.

"All those books come from used-book stalls on Fourth Avenue," Joe said. "I buy them three cents a pound. My real books are at Gordon's. No one from the . . ." He gestured to indicate the words he didn't want to say, lest someone be listening in. "None of my new friends come to visit me," he said, very softly. "But if they did . . ."

"I don't really understand what you're doing," said Caitlin. She sipped her coffee again. It tasted burned in an agreeable way.

But Joe did not answer her directly. Instead he asked her about her travel plans. She was on her way to Leyden, to visit her parents for the first time since leaving to work in Washington. Her father had written her an imploring letter, strongly suggesting that Annie, who had been having a bad year, would improve and be able to work normally again if Caitlin would spend a little time with them. The train for Leyden left that evening; she had checked her luggage in a locker in Grand Central Station.

"You look more beautiful than ever," Joe said.

"But you look so serious when you say it."

"I am serious."

"Like it was a disease, I mean."

"Well, I suppose it could be," said Joe. "If that's all people saw in you. I think you could start to hate being beautiful."

"I'm ten pounds overweight, my ears stick out, my feet are too big, and this is a ridiculous conversation. Anyhow, it's you we should be talking about. You look so different with your hair like that."

"If they even suspected I was a Jew they'd tear me limb from limb."

"Who would? The people you're trying to find out about?"

"People like Stowe, if you must know. You work for a very bad man, Caitlin."

"I don't know what to believe. Betty says Stowe knows Hitler is just a transitional figure. If we would take some of the war pressure off him, the German people would remove him. But he thrives on war and the threat of war. Really, Joe, he's not such a bad guy."

"Hitler?"

"Stowe. I mean once you know him."

"I do know him. Maybe not the way you do. I don't know how he likes his coffee or what's his favorite joke, but I know who his friends are, where his sympathies lie."

"He's not a Nazi. I'd know it if he was."

"What if I could prove he was using public money to mail German propaganda? It would ruin him, you know."

Caitlin fell silent. She tilted her coffee cup and looked into it. A sludge of dark grounds shifted at the bottom of the cup. "He wants peace," she said.

"Does he know you're coming to see me?"

"No one does." She was going to say, Not even Betty, but it wouldn't have made any sense to Joe—at least she hoped it wouldn't.

"Are you sure?"

"Joe, I really don't like that sort of question."

He pursed his lips, shook his head. "Fred," he said.

She sighed. "OK. Fred." Why did he have to pick an absurd name, she wondered.

He got up, went to the window, and looked down at the courtyard. He bent the Venetian blind down and white summer light covered his mouth and nose like a bandit's bandana. Was he looking to see if she had been followed?

"I'd like for you to come with me," he said. "I'd like my new friends to see me with a beautiful girl."

"I've got to be back at the station at six-fifteen."

"Then you'll come with me?" he said, turning toward her, and she surmised from his ardent tone that no one had made a friendly gesture toward him in a long while. He was lonely, he was frightened, and he was clawing at the reserve and formality that encased their friendship, as if he could tear it open like the foil on a bar of chocolate.

He took her to East Eighty-sixth Street. It was the middle of a Saturday afternoon. Shoppers were thick in the street, shopping for veal, paprika, undershorts, ice, used typewriters, brooms, fabrics, religious statues and books, fish, stationery, shoes. The cars, mostly black, looked particularly dark beneath the bright blue sky, and the bus windows were open: here a man in short sleeves leaned out, looking balefully at the street, there a woman in a large hat held her infant near the window to give it a little fresh air.

And through this weekend crush came Joseph Mc-Williams, leader of the Christian Mobilizers. For the past month, he had become a fixture on East Eighty-sixth Street, addressing the crowds from the back of a covered wagon. The wagon was pulled by two white horses with crosses and swastikas on their bridles, and the horses were driven by a small, oyster-colored man with large ears. The driver routinely tossed lazy handfuls of leaflets into the street urging shoppers to "BUY CHRISTIAN" as McWilliams exhorted the crowd through a megaphone, on one side of which was painted an American flag and on the other a cross.

"Stop the persecution of Christian Americans!" he shouted.

Because it was summer, the canvas of the covered wagon had been taken off, and hanging from the bowed wooden frame were dozens of kerosene lanterns, with blue and gold glass chimneys. When McWilliams worked into the night, the lanterns were lit and made his message all the more stirring.

But it was daylight now and the shoppers were not paying much attention to him. From time to time, he lowered his megaphone and chewed thoughtfully on his lower lip, as if this irritating, inexplicable apathy was something he could turn around with a well-chosen phrase. He turned toward Joe. "It's as if these folks are too scared to listen, Fred."

"It's pretty strong stuff," said Joe. He glanced at Caitlin, who was at his side.

McWilliams smiled. He looked like a child who has been left to fend for himself and has been made a little dangerous. "Do you think so?"

It took Caitlin a moment to realize McWilliams was asking this question of her. She was holding on to the side of the wagon while the horses' heavy, shaggy hooves rang against the pavement and the buckboard swayed from side to side.

"It is," said Caitlin.

Renewed by the faint praise, McWilliams brought the megaphone to his mouth again and bellowed, "Sure as shootin' we need a new deal, Mr. President, but we need a CHRISTIAN new deal! And not for the bankers and the professors, but the man on the street."

"That's right!" shouted a voice from the sidewalk. "Heil Hitler, God bless Germany."

It was a man wearing a heavy gray suit and riding boots, despite the August heat. He carried a small paper bag in one hand, inside of which Caitlin guessed was a bottle of whiskey.

He was unshaven and beneath his sweat-stained homburg soiled bandages were wrapped around his skull.

"Don't even look at him," McWilliams warned Caitlin. "He's mental."

"God bless you, Mr. McWilliams!" the man on the pavement called out. He was leaning against the window of a Buster Brown shoe store and a woman leaving the shop with a sun-suited child in tow gave him a look of disdain.

"Go home, Mr. Spilke," the woman said. "Your family needs you."

McWilliams's driver made a clucking noise, shook the reins, and the horses headed east on Eighty-sixth, lifting their tails to void their bowels as they neared First Avenue.

McWilliams drummed his long spatulate fingers against the megaphone. "Did Fred tell you what kind of crowd we had last week at Innisfail Stadium?" he asked Caitlin.

"Fifteen thousand people," said Joe, quickly, seeming to Caitlin a little worried that she might ask, Who's Fred?

"It was a beautiful sight to behold," said McWilliams. He noticed how tightly Caitlin was holding on to the side of the wagon. "Fred told me you were a country girl. Surely this isn't your first time in a good old American horse and wagon."

"I think I'm just wearing the wrong kind of shoes," said Caitlin.

"Whereabout in the country were you raised up?"

"Leyden."

"Oh, up in Windsor County. A lot of fine people up there. Quite a few subscribers. What about you? Do anything special with yourself up there in Leyden?"

Caitlin was silent for a moment. She felt McWilliams's curiosity moving toward her with a kind of brutal nonchalance, an eel under ice. She heard the telegraphy of the horses' hooves against the street; she saw from the corner of her eye a boy in a red shirt running along the sidewalk, weaving in and out of the slow-moving crowd.

"Mostly wait for Fred to come up and marry me," she said, smiling.

McWilliams laughed. It seemed somehow a genuine laugh but he was so used to artificial gestures that even his spontaneity was compromised by guile. He pushed Joe playfully. "Glad to hear it," he said. "To tell you the truth, I was a little worried about Fred here. Fellow his age, living alone. You can't help but wonder." He looked Joe up and down and then nodded, with what certainly looked like approval.

"OK, Freddie my lad, give me a line or two and let's get something going here."

"Let's try asking them if they want their sons and lovers to be killed in another useless war," said Joe.

McWilliams chewed on his lip for a moment. "Well, how about we say loved ones and keep it clean. OK?"

The man at the reins had just thrown another batch of BUY CHRISTIAN leaflets into the air. There was no breeze to carry them and they fell in a clump onto the street. Though his back was to McWilliams, he stopped the cart as soon as McWilliams brought the megaphone up to his mouth.

"How'd you like seeing your sons and husbands, your brothers and friends bleeding to death?" he fairly crooned into the megaphone. A woman wearing a wrinkled white linen dress, with slack yellow hair and dark circles under her eyes, stopped and looked up at McWilliams. She was carrying a string bag filled with canned food; her hand was red from the weight of her groceries. She nodded her head thoughtfully, and as these things so often seemed to go, in Joe's experience, all it took was one person to break the rhythm, to jam the slowly moving gears of life. In a moment the wan woman with the string bag was joined by a furious-looking man in overalls, who seemed to have been trudging home from a dirty job he despised, and they were joined by a slight fellow carrying a doctor's bag, with a mustache and pale, abrupt eyes, and then by a couple of what used to be called husky young men, wearing V-necked undershirts, summer trousers, and sandals, and before long McWilliams had what he had been counting on—an audience. McWilliams was thinking of running for president and, in the summer of 1941, it seemed to some that anything was possible.

Joe brought Caitlin back to his apartment on Barrow Street. She was trembling and it was his version of solicitousness to pretend not to notice.

"What time does your train leave?" he asked her.

"Soon." She had barely spoken for the long ride downtown and during the walk from the subway, and she showed no signs of being capable of real conversation now.

"Would you like some coffee?" Joe asked.

"I can make some," she said.

"It's OK," said Joe. "It'll just take a minute." Yet he made no move toward the kitchen. He stood next to the chair in which she had thrown herself and glanced down at her. Then he touched her hair.

"Oh, Joe," she said. "Those men. How can you stand it?"

"I don't know. I'm not sure that I can."

"What if they found out about you?"

"They won't." He looked at her, smiled. His uncertainty flickered across his eyes; it was like the sudden change of light on the river when the sun is devoured by a cloud. His bravery was, in fact, a kind of retreat—not from his mission, but from the moment. His bravery was a way of not speaking to Caitlin.

"But if they did," she said, insisting. She wanted him close, she wanted after a day of repulsive fantasy to hear only the truth.

"Then it would all be up to you," he said.

"What would?"

"I'm just kidding."

"Joe, I don't think you should be doing this."

"I'm going to write a book, Caitlin. I'm going to drag these night crawlers into the sun. I'm going to—" He stopped himself. It made him feel corny to be beating his breast in front of her. The less said the better. "I'm going to make coffee for us, is what I'm really going to do. Wait here."

He went into the kitchen and left her alone, where she listened to the ruminative noises of his apartment—the creak of the floors, the elevator rattling its chains like Marley's ghost, the exhausted, loveless argument of a man and a woman in another apartment—as well as the sounds from the street below, the trucks on Hudson Street, the boys playing in the courtyard below.

Stacked on an easy chair was a pile of the *Christian Mobilizer*. Caitlin picked one up and began paging through it. One headline said "MOBILIZE AGAINST WAR," with the subhead reading "Lindbergh Appeals to America." Another headline said "AMERICA AND GERMANY—HOPE OF THE CHRISTIAN WORLD." Below this headline was an article written by Frederick Hollander and below that, over an article initialed F. H., was a headline that asked "IS ROOSEVELT A JEW?"

"Oh, Joe," Caitlin said softly to herself.

She got up and joined him in the kitchen. He was sitting in a folding chair, watching the coffee as it percolated on the little two-burner gas stove. She rested her hands on his shoulders and he leaned his head back until it touched her breasts.

"I wish I was in an army," said Joe. "I wish I was marching across a battlefield with a thousand other men and we all knew each other by our first names."

Caitlin breathed shallowly. She didn't want her chest to heave for fear Joe would then move his head off her.

"Or nicknames," she said. "Everyone would have a nickname."

"I never had a nickname," said Joe. "I don't think anyone's ever known me well enough to give me one."

"Joe's a nickname," said Caitlin.

"Not really. It's just short for Joseph. It doesn't mean anything more."

Looking over the crest of his brown hair, his high, rounded brow, she saw his eyes close. The barber had neglected to dye Joe's eyelashes: they were obsidian.

"I feel so alone," said Joe.

"It's this job, it's what you're doing."

"I've disappeared," he said, in a whisper.

Then, a little stiffly, as if the breath it took to utter an intimate word held within it an element that made him heavy, awkward, Joe got up from his chair and took the coffeepot off the stove. He poured a cup for Caitlin and handed it to her.

"Are you in love with somebody?" he asked.

She was silent. It seemed impossible not to tell him the truth. She felt his eyes, his loneliness, and the life he was living pulling it out of her.

"I'm with someone I work with, in the office." She held her expression steady but felt her eyes go indistinct. Joe handed the coffee cup to her but she put it immediately onto the table, afraid that she would rattle cup and saucer with her trembling hand.

"You don't have to tell me who," Joe said. "Not if you don't want to."

"I haven't told anyone. It's hard for me even to tell myself."

"There's nothing to be done about it, is there? The heart's a dog, can't be trained." He slowly filled his coffee cup and then placed the pot onto the stove, turned off the gas.

"It's Betty Sinclair, Joe. I never thought this would ever happen to me."

"I know, Caitlin. I think I've known it for a long time."

"Does it make you feel strange around me, knowing?"

"It makes me feel just fine. It makes me feel I can say anything to you, that you could really know me, too. Does that sound too selfish?"

"No. Not at all." She looked at him closely, waited for him to tell her something hidden in himself, to match her nakedness with a nakedness of his own.

He walked over to the Hotpoint refrigerator. The motor on top of it rasped; the small kitchen was filled with the hot, lurid light of the sinking sun. Joe opened the refrigerator door and reached in for a quart bottle of milk.

"You want milk with your coffee, don't you?" he asked. He passed the bottle back to her without turning around. He was reaching into the back of the icebox and when he turned around again he held a brown paper bag, folded three or four times on top.

"I want you to take this home with you, Caitlin. Read it and then get rid of it."

"What is it?"

"I don't know. A diary, I guess. I'm not as good at just saying what's in my heart as you are. So I wrote it down."

"Your diary?"

"I know, like a high school girl."

"That's not what I mean." She moved away from him.

"Take it, please. I want you to have it. I can't keep it here anyhow. If anyone ever found it, everything I'm doing would be discredited." He opened the bag and took the journal out of it. It was bound in black cloth, with black leather at the corners. "Maybe when all this is over you can give it back to me." He stepped toward her, clasped her wrist, and placed the book in her hand.

"I won't read it," said Caitlin. "I won't even open it."

"But I want you to," said Joe. "I'm in a balloon and I'm drifting away. Your having this and knowing me, it's like ballast, it gives me the weight, makes me think one day I can come back to earth."

"I can't even live with my own secrets, Joe."

"Well, now you've got mine to keep them company." He smiled and then leaned toward her, with a hesitant, formal bow from the waist, and kissed her ceremoniously on her tender, burning cheek.

EIGHT

A rumor lurking just out of view could terrorize Washington just as reports of an escaped madman could immolate inner peace in Leyden, and for the past week in Washington the rumor taking shape was that a reporter had gotten hold of proof that dozens of senators and House members had been using their offices to mail out German propaganda.

There were politicians who knew full well that if this story was to become prominent news then they would be implicated. And there were others who wondered if perhaps, through the influence of a staff member or through their own practical desire to be useful, they had used their congressional franking privileges to send out something that would turn out to be, upon closer inspection, Nazi in nature. Of course, on a certain level, it would be a survivable crisis in the lives of most of the politicians. The propaganda in question was not terribly overt, contained no cries for a master race. Primarily, it was about keeping America out of the war, the dangers of Communism and atheism (now and again called "anti-Christian thought"), as well as the joys of the outdoors, the immorality of vivisection, and the historic roots of German-American kinship. Yet there was the sticking point of misappropriated funds, and it was this issue, the issue of using American money to send out non-American material, that seemed potentially most troublesome.

Joe already had proof that Stowe had sent out documents prepared by German propaganda officers to his constituents in Windsor County. Under headlines such as "GERMAN CHRISTIANS PRAY FOR PEACE" and "PATRIOTISM, OUTDOOR LIVING, AND THE NEW GERMANY" and "WHO PAYS FOR AMERICA'S WAR DEBTS?" Windsor County Republicans had been reading material written by George Viereck, of Scotch Plains, New Jersey, who was known variously as George F. Corners, James Burr Hamilton, Donald Furtherman Wicketts, and Dr. Claudius Murchison, and whom Joe could prove was a Nazi intelligence officer.

What Joe could not prove was whether or not Stowe knew that the literature he was franking was German propaganda in pedigree as well as markings. He had asked Caitlin to supply some evidence—an overheard conversation, a shred of correspondence—but Caitlin, without exactly refusing, failed to do it. It was not that she couldn't see her way through what was at issue: she wanted Joe to have his proof, she wanted to stop and even hurt the congressmen who were sending out the German material, all of them. And it wasn't that she couldn't betray Stowe. The favor of the job he had given her hadn't been a favor to her but to those who would humiliate her. And Stowe had never treated her with anything more than idle curiosity—she was just a girl at a desk. No, what prevented Caitlin from supplying Joe with the extra dollop of proof was her loyalty to Betty.

It was hard to fully understand loyalty just then. It was hard to counterbalance the weight of the one you loved resting trustingly in your arms and the other, unseen weight—palpable at times, merely notional at others—of the world beyond. To Caitlin, the very *word* "loyalty" held within it nobility, reverence, and a sort of stinging, throat-constricting pride. You were loyal. You protected the ones you loved, just as Caitlin had protected her parents from the condescending assumptions of others, at least in the grim, gladiatorial arena of her own heart. She had been loyal. She believed her mother was more beautiful than Mary Fleming and that her father was far more clever than Fulton. Her parents had raised and protected her and she had owed them her allegiance. The flag that drooped in the corner of her classroom deserved it, too, and she pronounced every syllable of the pledge each morning with her hand on her breast.

Yet Caitlin could not fail to ask herself how much of the loyalty she felt toward Betty consisted of the pleasure Betty gave her, in which case the loyalty would have been to her own blinking and bewildered self, now as it pecked itself out of the shell of its long incubation, now as it basked in the sweet, steady light of another's regard. If Betty had given her less, then Caitlin's loyalty would have seemed purer, more on the level with her loyalty to her parents, who gave her almost nothing of what she had really desired—no status, no formal education, no style to speak of—or her loyalty to her country, which was really only a persistent, persuasive abstraction. Yet these loyalties were more august, and certainly unimpeachable, precisely because they carried within them no pleasures or rewards: they were abject, like all true passions. You did not, after all, take Communion out of keenness for the taste of the Eucharist.

Her loyalty to Betty was finally inextricable from passion, from the moments they shared, the fetal curl of the recess Betty's body left in the bed when she slipped away each morning, the smell of perfume and tooth powder when she returned ten minutes later, with coffee and the newspaper.

Betty adored her. Indeed, there were times when Betty's

ardor seemed a kind of madness, times when she would fall to her knees in front of Caitlin and wrap her arms around Caitlin's waist, times when she repeated, You are so beautiful, over and over until it was an incantation and her hands trembled as they hovered over Caitlin's face, times when she would force Caitlin through a recitation of every remotely sexual moment of her life, over and over, like a coach forcing a lazy miler around and around the black, crunching cinder track. Indeed, in declaring her love for Caitlin, Betty had awakened in her own character a quality of obsessiveness that she had not realized was hers before. She arranged lunches together, devised office work that would keep them together, and once they were back at their apartment, it was impossible for Caitlin to read, write letters, bathe, or even pee without Betty at her side or at least nearby.

It was a wonder, really, that Betty's relations with Stowe did not deteriorate. But Stowe continued to rely on her. She had a massively retentive memory, not only for names and for the principal facts, but for all of the smaller moments that precede and succeed significant events. She could remember not only what was said but what was expected to have been said and yet was not.

Stowe relied on Betty's judgment, too. He had gone through two marriages, heedlessly, and his view of women was that they were creatures you chased after, captured, installed in your house, and hid your drinking from. He had never had a conversation with a woman that did not either involve seduction or concealment, yet with Betty, Stowe could discuss politics, strategy, philosophy.

He could take her anywhere. She waved away the cigar smoke and said what was on her mind. And if he said something impolitic, she had a way of correcting him that seemed more clarification than contradiction. She did it with humor, with great tact, yet with a frankness that told others that

Stowe was secure and that, somehow, the young lady at his side basically adored him. Once, at a meeting between Stowe and three representatives of the paper industry, Stowe had thrown back a couple of whiskeys too many and his conversation became garrulous, absurd. Betty literally put Stowe's hat on his head, hoisted him up by the arm, and walked him out of the Commander's Club, and as far as Stowe could tell the overall effect had been rather charming.

Today, Betty was going to Windsor County with Stowe, and as Caitlin and Betty got out of bed together the atmosphere between them was strained. Betty became gloomy at the smallest separation, whereas Caitlin, perhaps in some subtle way less in love than Betty but more overwhelmed by the love she felt, needed their infrequent separations to maintain any sense of self. What made this particular separation different from the other day trips and junkets Stowe and Betty took was that this one was in response to something Caitlin had said.

Caitlin had told Betty two nights before that Joe might soon be releasing the names of politicians who were using public money to mail German propaganda. She hadn't told Betty that Joe had asked her to help him prove his case against Stowe. Betty would only have wanted to know how Joe could have even imagined that Caitlin would do such a thing. But Caitlin made it clear that Joe knew enough about the whole business of the illegal franking to make quite a mess.

"Can you stop him?" Betty had asked. And when Caitlin shook her head No, Betty said, "It's what I hate about this war hysteria. People get so narrow-minded. Something is written by a German and then suddenly we can't touch it. I mean, what does that say about us?"

"It's wrong, Betty," Caitlin had said, her voice calm but a vein throbbing at her temple. "Hitler is evil."

"Because he looks strange on the newsreels? Anyhow, what is evil?"

"Killing."

"Well, isn't that what Elias is saying? Let's stop the killing and keep out of the war."

They had left it at that. There were too many other things to talk about, too many other things to feel. They were still in that part of their love affair in which biographies are presented—childhood, parents, first loves, and ambitions. Yet Betty did not forget what Caitlin had told her, and in fact she had heeded it as a warning and now, this morning, as they stood next to each other in the kitchen, Betty measuring out the coffee, Caitlin slicing the oranges, Betty said to her, "Elias will be cutting some cords, ending certain relationships, but he owes it to friends back in your beloved Windsor County to talk first with them. He's going to be very discreet, naming no names. Just wants to cut his losses, and who can blame him for that?"

"Did you tell him about Joe?"

"About Joe? No. But he's heard the rumors anyhow."

Betty struck a wooden match and lit the front burner of the stove.

"Is he changing his mind?" asked Caitlin.

"Stowe? About the war? I don't know. He's a politician. He doesn't want to get caught on the wrong side of things. And Roosevelt just seems to get more and more popular."

"I voted for the President, you know that, don't you?" Caitlin felt herself wanting to lower her eyes but she kept her gaze level with Betty's.

"Sweetie Pie," said Betty, "I'm only happy you didn't vote for Earl Browder. Really, anything to the right of the Communists I'm considering a personal triumph."

The coffee percolated. They set the table in the sunny middle room, in their robes, looking rather chaste. If anyone were to suddenly come in, they would have looked like roommates. They ate the oranges and buttered toast and drank coffee.

Betty asked Caitlin with her eyes if she wanted some more coffee and Caitlin shook her head No.

"You sure?" Betty asked.

"Well, you can maybe just warm my cup a little."

"I have to ask you everything twice," said Betty. She licked some butter off her fingers and then poured coffee into Caitlin's cup, pushed the creamer across the table. It crossed a bright bar of sunlight that hovered in the air between them.

Caitlin looked at her great friend with some sternness. She wanted it well understood that she was past the time when she needed or would even accept instruction. Her thoughts, her ways of doing things were her own, not part of a soft, unformed mass she needed others to somehow shape. She was not, nor would she ever be, one of those fortunate yet often deluded individuals who can proudly declare: I know who I am. Yet there were emotions, if not insights, she called her own, beads of feeling she could touch in the blindness of her inner self—anger, pride, loyalty, hope, envy, shame, all of them now strung together on a new ribbon of belief: that she in some small way would make the world a better place.

"Don't give me that look," said Betty. "Thanks to you, I've talked Elias into risking his political future and I'm a nervous wreck over it."

"Thanks to me? I thought this was a practical decision."

"That's how I've put it to Elias, but let's face it . . ." Betty shrugged. She looked momentarily lost, as if she had forgotten what she wanted to say. But in fact she was overtaken by a sudden reluctance to sound maudlin. There were between them trust, passion, and ardent friendship, but there were certain matters that Betty hadn't ever spoken of except in a joking, offhand way, matters of politics, and the war. In fact, everything that had to do with the work in the office and with Stowe was kept within ironic quotation marks, a ripple of humor in the voice formed a border, a kind of cartoony outline, that put it all into a faintly comic relief. "Let's face it," Betty said. "You've managed to change my mind about a few things."

She smiled at Caitlin and it looked for a moment as if her tooth, her left front tooth, was cracked, from top to bottom.

Wordlessly, Caitlin reached across the breakfast table and touched the cracked tooth with her fingertip. It wasn't a fissure after all; it was a pubic hair.

Caitlin looked at it, curled now on the tip of her finger.

"I'll take that," said Betty, removing it from the whorls of Caitlin's fingerprint. She tweezered it off with her long fingernails and put it into the pocket of her satin dressing gown.

It surprised Caitlin that this did not make her shy. She and Betty lived in a kind of inviolate privacy, protected not only from the curiosity of others but from the judgments of former, more tentative selves. If anyone else had touched her pubic hair, or if, say, her body had made a strange liquid noise in another's presence, she would have felt it like an arrow in the back, but now she felt only love, acceptance: with Betty, desire was not only recognized but it was welcomed, satisfied.

"I don't think it's too late, do you?" Caitlin said.

"Too late to go back to bed?" Betty asked, looking at the nailed-shut cuckoo clock.

"With the Lend-Lease Bill passed," Caitlin said, "I'm sure that we'll be helping England defend itself, and maybe even supplying the Free French."

"Oh yes, I'm sure," said Betty, checking her fingernails for chips in their dark red polish. "And we'll be sending Haile Selassie fried chicken and a dozen white virgins, too, while we're at it."

"And the Selective Service Act passed, too," said Caitlin, holding her ground. "We'll be fighting soon."

"I think we already are," Betty said, gesturing to Caitlin and then to herself.

"Come on, I mean it. Anyhow, I think Mr. Stowe is doing the right thing, I really do."

"Look, sweetie, this country has no interest in getting involved in a European war. Mr. Gallup's polls still put about seventy percent of the people against our getting involved. Even the Communists are out there singing 'The Yanks Aren't Coming.' When people cast their votes for Rosey, they weren't voting to invade Germany. They were simply voting for the President of the United States. It was a sense of duty, like going home for Sunday dinner because your father asked you to. And they were also voting for all the welfare programs and afraid the Republicans would cause another Depression. They were voting for Social Security and unemployment insurance.

"Look, I haven't nagged Elias into breaking with his goose-stepping friends—and, Christ, most of them are not really as bad as you might think, more like duck steppers, if anything—because I'm worried that America's going to suddenly mount a holy crusade against Hitler and Elias is going to get caught on the wrong side. It's a lot more complicated than that." Suddenly, a flush of color raced over Betty's face, a fox over a field of snow, and she lowered her eyes, cleared her throat. "I just don't want any trouble between you and me. And I can't believe Elias would deliberately get involved with German military intelligence. It's an oxymoron, isn't it?"

Soon Robert, Stowe's driver, was at the door to collect Betty. He was a tall man, with large, soft ears placed unevenly on the sides of his long, sorrowful face; he smelled of coffee and roses.

"Congressman Stowe says to tell you we are late, Miss Sinclair," he said, taking her leather valise.

"Come down to the car," Betty said to Caitlin, taking her hand.

Robert looked at them. His funereal eyes seemed to be saying, Hurry.

Caitlin put on her new brown overcoat and followed Betty down the stairs. A black Cadillac was parked in front of the building. Stowe rolled the back window down when he saw Betty.

"Let's get going," he said. It was a humid day; the deep grooves on either side of Stowe's mouth glistened.

Caitlin noticed that John Coleman was sitting in the back seat, too.

"Caitlin's never been in an airplane, Elias," Betty said, leaning in through the window. "What do you say she just takes the ride and has a peek?"

Stowe looked balefully at Betty. He did not look as if he had had a restful night. He was, after all, on his way home to try to salvage what threatened to be a very bad situation. He didn't say anything more. He rolled the window up; a reflection of an oak tree rose into place.

"Maybe you'd better sit in front," Betty said.

"I don't think I—"

"No, no, please, you have to." Betty's eyes flashed with urgency and she clutched at Caitlin's hand in a heartfelt way that made Caitlin think of Natasha in *War and Peace*.

Caitlin sat in the front seat next to Robert, while Betty was in the back, with Stowe and Coleman. They drove through the gray, foggy streets. Above, a distant dawn moon floated through a rushing river of clouds. They passed row after row of steep porch stoops, each one, it seemed, crowned by a newspaper and two bottles of milk. Robert was humming "Begin the Beguine" and tapping his ring against the ivory steering wheel in a tricky rhythm. In back, Coleman was speaking to Stowe in an urgent whisper, which now and then seemed to rise in anger.

"I've made my decision, John," Stowe said sharply, and for a few moments Coleman was silent and Caitlin listened to Robert humming, his ring finger tapping, and the sibilance of rubber on concrete.

"You're supposed to advise, Mr. Coleman, not instruct," said Betty.

"I think I've done a lot more for the congressman than give advice, Betty," said Coleman. From his tone, Caitlin was certain that Coleman's thin-lipped, crowded mouth was pulled back in an unnerving arrogant gargoyle's grin.

"I've made my mind up," said Stowe. "The game's over and the chips can fall where they may. I'm not going to lose my seat over some foreign-policy matter, for Christ's sake."

"I can't tell you how disappointed I am to hear you speak like this," said Coleman, after a long pause.

"Oh, John," said Betty. "Spare us the dramatics."

There were no more arguments. They drove along the Potomac. Morning light broke through the clouds in long silvery spears that plunged into the river. A nun was walking a large Airedale along the river. Caitlin had never seen a nun with a dog before. The black and white of the nun's habit and the rust color of the dog's curling coat all looked particularly vivid in the chalky overcast light of the day.

They arrived at Gravelly Point Airport, which FDR and the Works Progress Administration had been building for the past three years. There were eight runways, with levees of sand and gravel running alongside them. The terminal building was four stories high, made of stone, and with a hopeful, modern design, like a flying wing, or an immense petrified boomerang.

Robert left them out at the traffic circle and they entered a two-story waiting room, where the ticket and information counter was, as well as the telegraph office. Through the glass wall, Caitlin saw a Pennsylvania-Central Airlines plane coming in for a landing. The front wheels hit the tarmac, bounced, and hit again, and then the rear wheels made contact. Unconsciously, Caitlin held on to Betty's hand.

Inside the terminal, there was a smell as if someone had recently thrown up on the tan linoleum floor. Robert carried the suitcases; he walked in front of Coleman and Stowe, who were beginning their conversation again, and Betty and Caitlin walked at the rear.

"You can come onto the plane with us," Betty said.

"Do you really think so? I've always wanted to see the inside of one."

"I wish you were coming with us. I'd like you to show me where you were born, where you lived, tell me the rest of your secrets."

"You're the rest of my secrets," said Caitlin.

They were walking past the ticket area, down a corridor, and out toward an open door, through which the warm, wet wind was blowing.

"I hate to be away from you," Betty said, in a whisper, pressing her lips into Caitlin's hair. Her voice was full of breath. "I'm so afraid you'll decide this was all a huge mistake and fall in love with someone else."

They walked across the field toward the American Airlines DC-3. The tarmac's surface was cracked; brown, heat-scorched grass grew in clumps through the fissures. The propellers were spinning, and beneath the thick overcast sky they looked to be the color of milkweed. The dimpled steel stairway that led to the entrance was bright silver.

Robert handed the suitcases to an airline employee, who wore green overalls and a leather jacket, and he, in turn, passed them on to a young man on a metal ladder, who was carrying them into the belly of the plane. The man on the ladder looked down and Caitlin would remember two things for the rest of her life: the man on the ladder had eyes the color of bright blue egg tempera paint and dark eyebrows that slanted straight up toward the point in his widow's peak, and, second, that he looked at Coleman.

Coleman shook hands with Stowe and then Stowe called to Betty over the noise of the engines. She went to his side and asked him something. Stowe shook his head No and then

Betty said something else and Stowe shook his head again, more emphatically this time.

"Elias doesn't think it's a good idea for you to come on," Betty said to Caitlin. She needed to shout over the sound of the engines. "We'll be taking off soon."

"OK," said Caitlin. Once rebuffed, she withdrew, as is the rule with people who feel they've worked themselves into positions they do not deserve, where they do not belong.

Betty and Caitlin stood in silence for a few moments. They were trying somehow to calculate what demonstration of affection would be permissible in this context. There was no one, they were quite certain, who suspected they were lovers, but if they were to embrace now it would have been too risky.

In a way, it made them feel more fatally and desperately bound to just stand there, with the wind whipping at their hair and the pitch of the DC-3 going up the scale as the propellers turned faster and faster. Stowe was halfway up the stairs. A stewardess stood at the opened hatch, holding on to her cap while her skirt blew around her knees.

"See you in a few days then," Betty said.

"I'm glad Elias is doing the right thing," Caitlin said. She looked up. Stowe had turned to call for Betty before going into the plane. His small, etched face looked peevish, rather helpless: he knew his voice wasn't carrying.

Impulsively, Betty put her arms around Caitlin, brought her close in an embrace and whispered into her ear. "See what you've done to me? I'm actually doing a good thing and I can barely recognize myself."

Betty turned to leave. She grasped the rail to the staircase.

"Betty?" Caitlin called out.

Betty turned, said Yes with her eyes.

"What's an oxymoron?"

Betty laughed. She liked it when Caitlin asked questions of her.

"A contradiction in terms, sweetie," Betty called, as she backed up the stairs. "Like jumbo shrimp, or nice guy."

Caitlin stood on the runway and watched Betty go up the stairs and disappear into the plane. She thought Betty would turn around again, make a final wave, but that was the last she saw of her. That was that.

"Robert will drive us back," she heard Coleman say. She turned around and he was standing directly behind her. His face was very white, with dark hollows beneath his eyes. Though it was windy, his hair remained in place, as if it had been painted on.

For the ride back to town, Caitlin sat in the back seat with Coleman. He rested his hands in his lap. He did not look at her; he stared through his own reflection as they sped along Mount Vernon Highway.

"Do you know how many men there are on earth?" he asked Caitlin, without turning. His voice was dry, barely inflected, as if he were talking in his sleep. "A few hundred," he said, before she could answer. "That's all, a few hundred. The rest mark time, take out the trash."

"And are you among the few hundred, John?"

"I am making every effort," he said. He turned toward her, smiled. "I am engaged in the painful, mysterious act of becoming."

They heard a deep, resonant boom from the sky, a thud with a slight echo, a single roar from a sheet-metal lion. Caitlin glanced up and saw a dull orange flash somewhere in the sky. Its origin was obscure, as was its importance.

The reverberation of the explosion shook the car windows in their frames. They seemed loose for a moment, they heaved in and out like diaphragms.

"What was that?" asked Caitlin.

"Do you remember that time in the Four Feathers restaurant when we ate lunch with Anastase Vonsiatsky?" asked Coleman. "You showed a great deal of spirit then, Caitlin. I meant to tell you that, and now, as is so often the case, I'm telling you at the same time we are saying goodbye for the last time."

"Are you going somewhere?"

"Yes. I've resigned." He laughed softly, shook his head.

"Where are you going now?" she asked.

They were downtown already, heading toward the Capitol. A light rain was starting to fall. It fell on the early-morning pedestrians, on the windshield, on the darkening trees, and on the bits of flaming wreckage that spread out over a Virginia horse farm after the bomb had exploded in the belly of the American DC-3. Betty, Stowe, eighteen other passengers, and a crew of four were already dead, but Caitlin would not know this for another hour. She would be sitting at her desk, going through Stowe's correspondence, separating it into categories—letters to be answered, letters to be filed, letters to be forwarded—when Mrs. Donnely, the typist, would come in to tell her the news and the two women would just stand there, facing each other, absorbing the news in silence, until Caitlin felt her body go cold and the room began to recede as if all reality were just a piece of scenery that was being pulled back and back and back by a clumsy workman.

But that was still before her, that lurid moment in the future was still curled within the spool of unexposed time. For now, all there was was the rain and John Coleman in the car next to her, explaining himself.

"I don't know where I'll go," he was saying. "Someplace where my point of view is a little more appreciated." His nostrils flared as he took a deep breath. He leaned forward and rapped his knuckles against the glass partition.

"Robert, stop here. I'm getting out."

Robert pulled up next to the curb and Coleman made a final, formal nod at Caitlin. With his hand on the door, he said, "Take good care of yourself, Caitlin. And try to be discreet. It was always very obvious to me what was going on between you and Miss Sinclair."

He opened the door and got out quickly.

The rain started to fall with more force. It was a hard, lashing rain. Robert pulled the car into traffic again and Caitlin had an idle thought: that noise could not have been thunder. There was no such thing as a storm with but one peal of thunder. It must have been something else.

She had sixty more minutes in her life to not be in mourning.

SEPTEMBER 1, 1943

"You don't want to be late for your own party," Caitlin said to Joe.

It was publication day for Joe's book and Caitlin had come in from Leyden, where she was back working at the George Washington Inn. She no longer lived on the Flemings' estate but shared a little house in town with a local girl named Jeanette, whose husband was in the Army—his presence was everywhere in the airless ex-tavern of a stone house, in the flag that hung above the low doorway, the pictures on the wormy pine mantelpiece, in the sounds of Jeanette's sobs as she worried herself to sleep each night.

"It's not a party for me," Joe said. "It's for my book." They were walking on Fourth Avenue and he was holding on to her arm in a way that seemed to lack not only romance but romance's faintest possibility.

His face was sunken; his eyes were pale, evasive. He was no longer coloring his hair, but the life seemed to have gone out of it. His walk was rapid but tentative, an animal scurrying over ice. Caitlin hadn't seen him in six months but their reunion was oblique, his responses unpredictable. He had seemed glad to see her at first, had offered her coffee, fussed over her, told her how beautiful she looked, even asked her what kind of perfume she was wearing. But it was as if those first responses had been learned, rehearsed. Once he had gone through them his conversation was sporadic, his mood phlegmatic, his mannerisms jerky and strange. Caitlin assumed his awkwardness was connected to the party his publisher was throwing in his honor. And it was months after that before she realized this was only a small part of it and that Joe had suffered what is commonly called a nervous collapse. The price inevitably extracted by a long time in an assumed identity was being paid day by day now. And a new terror now replaced the fear of discovery—with his book's publication, he could now fear reprisal.

They stopped at a used-book store. Joe did not want to go inside but browsed instead through the dusty bins of used books outside. Caitlin just could not see why someone would want to buy a book, or anything else, that had been owned once by somebody else—unless, of course, they were so terribly poor they had no choice. As for herself, she would rather have had something cheap and poorly made, new, than something stately and old.

Joe found a British edition of *In Our Time* and paid an old man who looked as if he had been carved out of ivory. Then Joe touched Caitlin on the elbow, using just his fingertip, as if to make as little fleshly contact as possible. He gestured furtively with his eyes. "That's Dwight Macdonald over there, looking at the old maps," he whispered. "He used to work at *Fortune*, too."

"Oh," said Caitlin, making her voice encouraging. It was the first time all day Joe had spoken of anything remotely in the past. His nervousness had kept him chained to the moment like a dog to a fence.

"Then he became a Trotskyist and then he fell out with

Trotsky himself and now he's an anarcho-pacifist. He pub-
lishes his own magazine called *Politics*."

"Maybe he'll be at your publisher's house then," said Caitlin. It was the task to which she had assigned herself: get Joe
to the party.

"Look at the way he's looking at you," Joe said, turning
his back on Macdonald and placing Caitlin so she could see.
She saw a barrel-chested man with wavy brown hair, wearing
a white shirt, high-waisted tan trousers, and summery shoes
with perforations around the toe. He was frowning at an old
illustrated map of Europe.

"He's looking at a map," said Caitlin. "That's all."

"Oh, you never think people are looking at you, or even
notice you," said Joe. For a moment, Caitlin smiled, as if all
Joe were accusing her of was an excess of modesty, but then
she realized there was real annoyance in his voice.

They crossed the street. The light that fell through the
trees was bright, dusty. Shop windows, emptier this year,
glared in the sunlight. The streets were quieter this year with
gasoline rationed and suddenly expensive. And most of the
passersby were either women or very young or old: so many
of the young men were gone.

They came to a white building with thick glass-brick windows. The sign above the doorway read SPORTSMAN'S CLUB—
PRIVATE. In the days when he was Fred Hollander, Joe had
marched in this building, had saluted the swastika, and shot
old Winchesters at tin cups upon which someone had crudely
painted yellow Stars of David. The Sportsman's Club was an
adjunct of the Iron Guard, whose leader was a cracked-
voiced, gesticulating fellow named Herman Schmidt, who always seemed to have carnations of spittle blooming in the
corners of his mouth. Schmidt was himself living out a certain
genealogical fantasy, Joe was to learn: his real name was James
Banahan. What Joe remembered most vividly about Banahan

was his penchant for holding a bayonet over his copy of a well-perforated Bible and then ramming it through with a blood-curdling scream.

Now the Sportsman's Club had a VACANCY sign on the door, and a padlock and chain went through the two handles. The deserted door stoop was a haven for stray cats, for whom some kind soul had left scraps in a little red bowl.

"It's closed now," Caitlin said. She felt she knew exactly what it had looked like inside, just from reading Joe's book—the wobbly wooden folding chairs, the portraits of Hitler, Jesus, the landscapes of the Danube, Niagara Falls, the stench of tobacco, the vaulted brick ceiling, the steel shutters, the little table filled with refreshments such as lemonade, apple slices, and pale green sucking candy.

"I know," said Joe. He was staring at the chained door. His hands were trembling but he seemed not to notice.

"Thanks to you."

"I had nothing to do with it. Hirohito closed it. If Pearl Harbor hadn't been bombed we wouldn't be fighting in this war and you know it. You know it as well as I."

They continued uptown on Fourth Avenue. Caitlin noticed a bank clock. It was five-twenty; the party began at five. The idea of being late made her feel slightly ill; she had always been punctual, even to places she didn't want to go. Betty used to say that punctuality came from a fear of not belonging, but it was one of those insights that, even if it was true, didn't fully matter—being late still made Caitlin's stomach turn.

"You wrote a great book, Joe," she said, quickening their pace.

"It's not even finished," he said, half mumbling. He allowed her to pull him back onto the curb as a street-cleaning truck went by.

"What do you mean?"

"Well, I never found John Coleman, did I? I never even

proved it was he who killed Stowe and Betty Sinclair. I let you down, Caitlin. I really let you down."

"No matter what we do, we can't bring them back," she said.

And then, to her immense surprise (and in this sense of surprise there was a measure of horror and in that horror was a small but undeniable tremor of disdain), Joe made a kind of strangulated cough and began to cry. People were everywhere but no one looked at Joe. It was as if a curtain had been drawn around him, the way a nurse will in a hospital when a patient's condition will demoralize his roommate.

"I never could have written this book without you," he said, still crying, not quite seeming to realize that he was.

"You were writing your book all along. You were born to write it, really you were," said Caitlin. They crossed Fourteenth Street. Joe's publisher's house was on Gramercy Park; they'd be there in ten minutes and she hoped Joe would have composed himself by then.

"Not only because you took the chance and gave me those files from Stowe's office."

"I'm a good thief," said Caitlin.

"But that wasn't all. Just knowing you were out there, in the real world, and that you . . . knew."

"Knew?"

"Me." He stopped and took Caitlin by the shoulders. He gazed at her with a look of panic and departure, as if over the bow of a ship that was taking him far away. "I'm sorry," he whispered.

"You're exhausted, Joe," she said, hoping it would reassure him.

"I'm supposed to go all over the country, speaking you know, selling my book. Philadelphia, D.C., Baltimore, St. Louis." He named each city as if it were a nail in his coffin.

"I'm going to miss you," she said.

"I couldn't have written it without you, Caitlin. Without

you and Sumner Welles. I keep having this feeling he'll be at the party today."

"That would be nice," said Caitlin, coolly. When she had read in Joe's diary that he loved Welles she had felt bonded to Joe—even though the nature of his love for Welles seemed vague, disguised in the writing, disguised, perhaps, even from himself. She knew some small amount about how the heart can chase after the most remarkable creatures in some frightening steeplechase of desire, and it was a comfort to know that this was a secret she shared with Joe. But now she was alone, and hearing of Welles, even hearing his name, caused in Caitlin a feeling that is one of the saddest by-products of grief—she was jealous.

Soon they were in front of the townhouse on Gramercy Park where Erroll Tate, Joe's publisher, lived. Joe had kept his composure over the past several blocks but now he seemed rattled again. He looked up at the three-story red-brick building, with the reflections of sycamores in its tall windows.

"Is this the house?" asked Caitlin.

"Yes," said Joe, very quietly.

"Are you going to be all right, Joe?"

"Let's go," he said, taking her arm.

They were let in by a maid wearing a black uniform and a frilly white apron that was more a matter of symbol than function. Caitlin wondered if there was something in her own bearing that would tell the maid that Caitlin was the daughter of a servant, or perhaps even a servant herself. There were ways of telling; Annie could tell which of the Flemings' guests had the wealth or position to back up their stratospheric airs. The ones who didn't hold their sherry glasses too tightly or look at everything in the room as if they were taking a kind of inventory.

The maid led Caitlin and Joe through the small black-and-white entrance foyer and up a narrow staircase. The walls along the way were lined with framed dust jackets of Highland Press books, most of them geared toward outdoorsmen, books about fly fishing and preparation of wild-game casseroles, along with an occasional murder mystery. Joe's book was called *Home Front*, though Caitlin would always think of it as *American Reich*, the original title, which Tate had persuaded Joe to change, saying it was too aggressive, too finger-pointing.

As they ascended the staircase, Caitlin could hear the noise of the party. A woman's high looping laugh rode herd over the general merriment like a clarinet over a Dixieland band. Caitlin walked behind Joe; she wondered what his face looked like at that moment. And then he reached back to take her hand—to give it, she imagined, a comradely, conspiratorial squeeze—but before their fingers touched Joe was on the top stair, in full view of the guests.

Joe was almost as much a stranger at this party as was Caitlin. Even when he had worked at *Fortune* his contact with other writers and editors had been sporadic, and now coming off two years as Fred Hollander he felt even more out of place. Caitlin could sense him looking for a familiar face.

Erroll Tate came to greet Joe. Tate was in his fifties, portly, contented-looking, with silver hair and a smoking jacket. He had a drinker's regretful good humor. "So there you are," he said, putting his arm around Joe. "Thought maybe you'd gone underground again."

He steered Joe into the party and Caitlin was left behind. Joe turned to look at her and Caitlin saw in his eyes that he was feeling three things at once—resistance to being taken over by Tate, a sudden rush of happiness over being the guest of honor, and regret over leaving Caitlin to fend for herself, and she knew as well as this last feeling was the faintest of the three but the one he chose to concentrate on, the one he felt best about experiencing.

Caitlin looked out across the room and tried to appear absorbed. She hoped she didn't seem like one of those pathetic people who stand around waiting for someone to rescue them from social starvation with a scrap of conversation. The room was salmon-colored, narrow, and filled with people. At the far end was a wall of windows beyond which a willow stood like an apparition in the fading light. The languid branches of the tree, with its feathery, silvery leaves, shuddered in the breeze for a moment, and Caitlin was suddenly plunged into an indistinct haze of memories of Betty Sinclair: twilight, a summer theater, the taste of butterscotch candy, the smell of Evening in Paris talcum powder. And then the memories were swallowed back into the vast interior darkness from which they had momentarily emerged and Caitlin was struck squarely by the moment she was actually living, struck squarely in the face as if she had been walking around in a daze and stepped on a rake.

And it was then, just then, that she saw Gordon Jaffrey. He was looking across the room at her with a look of pure unadulterated friendliness on his large face, so delighted to see her that he called out her name.

Caitlin was glad, even relieved, to see Gordon, but her happiness *was* adulterated. She had wondered to herself if Gordon would be at Joe's party and had decided in all likelihood he would not. Joe and Gordon hadn't spoken since Erroll Tate had insisted that Gordon's photographs not be included in *Home Front*. In fact, Joe had tried to change Tate's mind but he had failed and it wasn't clear to Caitlin if Gordon knew Joe had argued strenuously in the photos' behalf. "They are all so damn corny," Tate had said. "Everyone has shadows going across their eyes to make them look evil. Anyhow, I don't see why we need photographs in the first place."

Gordon looked flushed, exhausted, not quite organized within himself. He came bounding across the room toward Caitlin.

"Oh, Gordon," said Caitlin. "I'm so glad you're here."

"Catey," he said. Her hand disappeared inside of his. He

was breathing heavily; there was a dotted line of perspiration above his rosy lips. He had put on weight and he looked just a little silly in his shiny blue suit and red tie. "You're the most beautiful woman in New York." He looked away as soon as he said this, to make certain she wouldn't mistake it for a flirtation.

"Have you said hello to Joe yet?"

"Well," said Gordon. He looked back at her. "He's occupied at the moment."

"Joe was hoping, really hoping, you'd be here."

"Really?" asked Gordon, not with any particular skepticism. He turned to look in Joe's direction. Joe was being led by Tate toward a tall, elegant woman wearing a wide, white hat pulled down so it touched her right eyebrow. She extended her hand toward Joe in a pantomime of pleasure and humility.

"He seems good, Caitlin. I hope he doesn't think I'm sore about the pictures. It was an education working with him. And that book doesn't need any pictures. Tate was dead right about that, he really was." He put his hand on Caitlin's shoulder. "Will you tell him that for me, please?"

"No, I won't," said Caitlin. "Joe would never forgive me if I let you leave without saying hello." She felt she was way out of line here: Joe hadn't shared any hope whatsoever that Gordon would be at this party and he might be, for all Caitlin knew, relieved if Gordon just slipped out unnoticed.

Gordon smiled. He lowered his square jaw, with its patina of coppery razor stubble, and looked at Caitlin through the tops of his eyes. "I wonder if I should butt in while he's meeting all these people." He looked at Joe and rubbed his massive hands together, as if to prepare them for the moment they would touch his great good friend.

Joe and Tate were talking to the woman with the white hat. A small circle had formed around them, and whatever the woman was saying to Joe captivated them all. She was enumerating conversational points on her long fingers. Joe was nodding but Caitlin couldn't see his face.

Then Gordon tapped Joe's shoulder, and when Joe turned his expression was startled, evasive. But Gordon's own emotional state was a stone rolling down a hill, crushing everything small in its path. Joe's embarrassment and its aftershock of annoyance disappeared inside Gordon's embrace.

"Will you look at this guy?" Gordon said, as he pounded Joe on the back.

Caitlin cringed within herself. It was painful hearing the false heartiness and the implied need in Gordon's voice. In the most fundamental, unconscious, and selfless ways, Gordon was attached to Joe, and Caitlin had an inkling that, in all probability, Joe would never find anyone who would love him as much as Gordon.

"Is that the author over there?" a voice asked her.

She turned to see a small man in his thirties, with a dark birthmark at the corner of his mouth. He wore a wool suit and looked resigned to his discomfort in this crowded summer room.

"Yes," she said.

"The dark-haired one?" the man asked. He took a handkerchief out of his pocket but did not mop his perspiring brow. Caitlin didn't answer, which the man took for assent. He leaned forward and seemed to be taking Joe's measure.

"Do you know him?" he asked Caitlin. He had a dingy pallor and an overall sense of dishevelment about him, except for his brown hair, which was as carefully combed as a child's on the first day of school.

"Yes. Very well."

"Russian-Polish Jewish, I'd say. Am I right?"

"I don't believe we've met before," said Caitlin. She said her name and put out her hand.

"Ah, Dutch and Irish. Am I right? Henry Lehman." He took her hand. His grip was fierce. "I work with the Combined Emergency European Relief Committee. Have you heard of us?"

"I'm afraid I haven't." She glanced toward the center of the room. Tate was leading Joe toward the piano, where a knot of people seemed to be awaiting him. Gordon walked uncertainly behind.

"Well, don't feel bad about that. We're a nickel-and-dime outfit, no money for publicity. I read your friend's book, by the way. Hell of a job. I mean, you know, as far as it goes. Who you here with, by the way?"

"I happen to be here with Joe Rose."

"Then tell him he forgot to talk about the most important way this country's in league with the Nazis."

"We're at war with them now, anyhow."

"Sure. Thank God, too. But all through the last decade and up till now what the hell were we doing about people trying to escape Nazism? Not a goddamned thing, is what. No one knows how many Jews have already been killed by Hitler. Thousands, at least. Maybe we'll never know. It could be more, it could be hundreds of thousands. Think of it. The mind boggles. And we do nothing. We say there's no room. It's like sitting in your room with the door locked while someone is pounding at the door to get in and someone else is stabbing that person in the back, over and over. What do you do? Have a drink, turn up the radio? It's a disgrace, is what it is, and something we're going to have to live with for the rest of our lives."

Suddenly Erroll Tate's voice rose like a balloon from the front of the room. "If I could just have your attention for a moment, mesdames et monsieurs."

"Gentlemen dilettantes shouldn't own publishing companies," Henry Lehman muttered to Caitlin. But she was looking for Joe and she refused to acknowledge the remark.

"I want to thank you all for coming to my home," said Tate, rubbing his hands together, "and helping to celebrate the publication of what we think will be a truly important book. *Home Front* is by Joseph Rose, a former writer for *Fortune*, who went underground and now has come back to us to tell about the really quite alarming activities of groups who operate outside the law and often in direct opposition to American interests. I'm referring to various Nazi groups here at home, and the story of their recruitment techniques and their outmoded beliefs is detailed with chilling authenticity in Joe's fine book.

"I've twisted Joe's arm and gotten him to agree to say a few words to us, but before I bring him up here may I please remind you that Highland Press is going to be making these intimate, by-invitation-only publication parties a kind of tradition. With the newspapers and airwaves increasingly dominated by war news, it's gotten more and more difficult to bring quality books to the public's attention. As a way of combatting this frustrating situation . . ." Tate paused and fished in his pocket for a slip of paper. The branches of the willow tree blew close to the window and the leaves scratched across the pane. "Next month we'll be introducing Miss Cynthia MacGregor, who has written a charming book called *Summer in Calgary* and we hope to see you here on October third, which is a Monday. And now, everybody, let's say hello to Joe Rose."

"Well? Do you? Do you know anything about the Combined Emergency European Relief Committee?" Lehman was asking Caitlin, as if Tate's words and Joe's coming to speak next meant nothing.

"It's not only Jews we're trying to get out of Europe," Lehman was saying. "Anyone who's in Hitler's path. Anyone."

"Please," Caitlin said, tensing with impatience—his voice was like someone stepping on your heel on a crowded street. "I'd like to hear."

Caitlin moved away from him, closer to the center of the room, closer to Joe. There was a ripple of welcoming applause, and she pressed her hands together and kept them clasped, like a girl in a fresco.

"We'll talk later," he whispered, retreating.

Joe began his speech with a few pleasantries, thanking the Highland Press, Mr. Tate, the guests. His manner, to Caitlin's astonishment, was polished, glib. His voice, which all day had been porous and unsteady, was now firm, round, just so. He barely gestured as he spoke and his lips were turned up in a small, rather melancholy smile that made him look mysterious and dashing.

"One day this war will be over," Joe was saying, "and Hitler and the Axis powers will have been crushed." A few of the guests cheered this sentiment, and Joe was silent for a moment, as if waiting for the noise of a train to pass. "But can any army defeat the forces from which Hitlerism emerged and upon which Hitler feeds? I spent two years of my life as a man named Frederick Hollander, and as Mr. Hollander I got to know many of our own fellow Americans, some of whom would have liked to see a swastika flying in front of the White House, and others who would have been content with a Nazi–U.S. alliance, as we swept through the world and butchered Jews, Communists, Gypsies, and anyone else who did not fit in with the master plan."

Caitlin had never heard Joe so eloquent, so assured. She was one of those women from the recent past who could have her heart moved by oratory. Her face flushed. It felt as if she were allergic to joy, that the happiness had harvested up from the hive of her secret self some nectar that was too sweet for her to digest. She wanted to move closer to Joe but doubted her legs' ability to carry her gracefully, so she contented herself with looking around the room to see how the others were hearing Joe's speech.

"Because of paper rationing," Joe was saying, "I was dissuaded from putting in an introduction to *Home Front*. But I want to take this opportunity to point out that I had the help of my good friend Gordon Jaffrey, who was with me on some of the more ticklish assignments, and I also want to acknowledge my friend Caitlin Van Fleet, who kept her faith in this book and helped me keep mine, and who herself had an inside look at some of the pro-Nazi elements my book describes."

Caitlin felt her face burn. This brief recognition from Joe in public scalded her, she felt weak from it. She felt someone touch her arm and she turned to her side and there was Henry Lehman, nodding at her, smiling.

And then Joe said, "But I most particularly want to thank Mr. Sumner Welles. The Under Secretary of State was helpful and generous to me from the very beginning. And as he waged his fight against the appeasers and isolationists inside the government, he always had time not only to encourage me but to guide me, and most importantly, for me, to remind me that the defense of American democracy is truly a fight worth fighting. If it was not for Mr. Welles—"

"Does he know what he's saying?" Henry Lehman demanded of Caitlin in a completely frantic whisper. She looked at him. Lehman's face was tense, incredulous, and he thrust it at her like a fist. "My God in heaven, doesn't your friend know what's happened to Mr. Welles? The man was caught having sex with a porter, both of them in the President's private train. Welles is ruined, utterly discredited. Finished. *Kaput*. By this time tomorrow Sumner Welles will be out of the government, completely out."

SEPTEMBER 1, 1967

"My own son treats me as if I were an inquisitor, and I end up feeling that maybe he does have something to feel guilty about, something I ought to know." Caitlin stood at her office's protractor-shaped window and looked down at the police barricades, loitering cops, and knots of patient citizens waiting for the Labor Day parade, which was still fifty blocks north.

"What kid worth his salt doesn't have something to hide?" said Gordon.

She turned around to look at him. His ample stomach rested in his fishnet tee shirt like a watermelon in a hammock. He wore a white sailing cap, blue slacks, tennis shoes.

"You've got to be kidding," Caitlin said, gesturing at Gordon's tee shirt.

He looked down at it, as if someone else had dressed him. "No like?" he asked. His smile was missing a left bicuspid.

"Hate," said Caitlin.

Gordon gestured to a Pan Am flight bag at his feet. "Well, I'm not surprised. I packed an extra, just in case." He picked up the blue plastic bag, slung it over his shoulder. "In fact, I think I'll change right now, and then if I can tear you away from your work we can hit the road."

Gordon changed in the men's room, and then he and Caitlin walked through the shadowy, deserted offices of the World Refugee Alliance. She had been the only one in. The others were either in their apartments, or at inexpensive places on Long Island like Westhampton or Port Jefferson.

As for Caitlin and Gordon, they were going to drive to Windsor County. Gordon had brought himself a used Fairlane. Unlike most New Yorkers, Gordon always had a car; he was willing to exert the ceaseless vigilance needed to keep up with the alternate-side-of-the-street parking rules and even paid the shocking fines he sometimes incurred when he overslept fifteen minutes.

"Easy parking today," he said, escorting Caitlin to his car. There was a smell of burnt coffee in the air; the sky was a pale, cheesy yellow. Caitlin was going through her purse; she had of late developed a nagging fear that she had forgotten something. She poked around a box of Sen-Sen, a packet of

Stim-U-Dents, her ring of keys, a compact, an old, half-corroded tube of red lipstick, and then she quickly opened her wallet—thirty dollars in fives, a new Master Charge card, a library card, a membership in the ACLU. She finally had a driver's license. Five years ago, Gordon had taught her to drive an old Pontiac GTO, which was eventually stolen from in front of his apartment on West Ninety-ninth Street. It was the only car Caitlin had ever driven.

When Caitlin looked up from the inventory of her purse, she saw her son sitting in the back of Gordon's car. He was wearing an Oxford-cloth blue shirt, which had evidently been thrown in the wash with bleach: it had white streaks down the front. His hair was thick and the longer he grew it the more it raged away from his head, forming a veritable shelf of tangled locks above his ears, a mantelpiece of infrequently shampooed curls. He smiled at his mother, shrugging his shoulders. He seemed to be apologizing for his presence in the car.

"He *wanted* to come along," said Gordon, opening the back door for Caitlin and smiling happily, as if the boy's being there was some sort of triumph.

"And what are you supposed to do?" asked Caitlin. "Sit by yourself in the front like a chauffeur." She cringed at her tone of voice. She sounded lonely, accusatory; she didn't sound like a person she herself would much like to know.

"You know that's not such a bad-paying job, these days," said Gordon. He touched her elbow as she slid onto the back seat and then he closed the door with a flourish. Gordon's judgment about the worthiness of a car was based in part on the sound of the back door's closing, and he seemed satisfied with this one.

"How are you?" she asked Skip, as soon as she was in the car. He'd been working as a messenger for a small film-production company near the UN and living with a girl named Janet Gorman. But the relationship had ended—as far as Caitlin could make out, it had concluded abruptly—and then one night about a week ago he had called her in the middle of the night and wept copiously, unashamedly over the phone. Somewhere between sobs was a half-expressed notion that he wanted to kill himself. "I'm no one and everybody sees right through me," he'd said. It had been enough to put Caitlin in a taxi at three in the morning and send her up the steep, fluorescent-struck stairs in his Turtle Bay tenement and stand pounding his steel-enforced door with her umbrella handle until he finally let her in.

"Merry Labor Day, Mom," said the boy. He moved next to Caitlin and patted her hand.

"You know he had an invitation to spend the weekend with Janet's family," said Gordon. In his tone was an admonishment to Caitlin: he *chose* to be here.

"Oh, they hate my guts," he said, quite airily. "Come on, now. And I mean it." He made his voice hearty and sincere, the voice of the thickest camp counselor on the planet. "Let's everybody get together, OK? And make this the *best* darn Labor Day we've *ever* had!"

He charmed her. She didn't like to admit it; she didn't quite believe in charm. She put charm in a category with hypnosis—something for which you needed a willing subject.

"Janet Gorman's father is a career naval officer," Gordon said, glancing up. Caitlin saw his sad, eager eyes in the rearview mirror.

"And he's never really appreciated me swabbing his daughter's deck," said the boy.

"He'd just like to see her on the arm of some seaman first class," said Gordon.

"Rather than mixed up with my first-class semen."

"Will you two stop it?" said Caitlin. "I mean, really. What do you spend your time doing? Working out comedy routines?" She looked at them both, hesitated. "I wasn't aware you two spent so much time together."

"We don't, Mom. We're psychic. It's strictly neuronal."

"Yeah," said Gordon. "Neuronal."

The piers along the West Side Highway, once the site of such passionate arrivals, were now for the most part empty, rotting away. Around Thirty-eighth Street a cruise ship under Greek registry was docked. Elderly people in straw hats and bright pastel clothing milled around. That was what was left.

"Do you smell a burning smell?" Gordon asked. He tapped his temperature gauge with his blunt index finger, as if trying to intimidate it into confessing some concealed truth about the engine's heat.

Caitlin sniffed. "I don't."

"Me neither."

"It's probably coming over from Newark," said Caitlin. Less than two months ago, a thousand people had been arrested, more than a thousand injured, and twenty-six killed when blacks in Newark took to the streets, fighting police, burning out the shopkeepers. In Harlem, the mayor of New York demonstrated his courage by simply walking down the street.

Gordon drove them north. Riverside Park was full of poor Harlem families with picnic baskets, radios. Caitlin looked at her son and thought about Janet Gorman. She knew it was not altogether wholesome to let fantasy or speculation intrude on your own son's sexual privacy, but Caitlin could not help it and wondered if any mother could. The boy was so joky and evasive it was hard to imagine his face startled by passion. This boy whom she had borne and cuddled, a man now, with a hastily shaved face, a powerful jaw, unkempt fingernails, and massive, square knees poking through his frayed white bell-bottom trousers, was someone's lover now.

"So I assume you and Janet have more or less patched things up," said Caitlin.

"I don't know. I don't think you want to know about it."

"It's up to you."

"I've got sex problems, Mom."

Caitlin was silent. She felt that far too much depended on what she said next.

"The whole concept of sex is a problem," said Gordon. She saw his fervent eyes appear in the rear-view mirror. In some vague but instinctual way he was trying to rescue her. "Once we got beyond the simple idea of mating, procreation, survival of the species, it got all mixed up," he was saying.

"You can talk to somebody about it, if you have problems," Caitlin said. "It doesn't have to be me. You can see someone, a counselor, a doctor, there's nothing wrong in that, you know that, don't you?"

"I can talk to you and Gordon about it," he said. "I mean, if I can't talk to you guys, who can I?"

"All I'm saying is you don't have to." Shut up and let him talk, for God's sake, she thought.

"It's just that I have this, you know, penis, and Janet thinks that's what I'm about, you know, that that's the main thing about me. It's like a girl with big breasts, I guess. I don't know."

"People pay good money for this kind of problem, Skip," said Gordon.

"Well, it's just that . . . I don't know. Screwing is not what I'm mainly into. I like to hold her and have her hold me, but that makes her angry. She says I'm incredibly selfish."

Caitlin looked out the window. Gordon was really making time, weaving from lane to lane, passing cars on the right and the left: it was strange how these little pieces of male vanity persisted, like roots from old trees in a field improperly cleared.

"I don't think I can be of any help in this, Skip," Caitlin said. "It sounds more like Janet's problem."

"And, Mom?" he said. He took her hand again. His own hand was warm, soft. He gazed at her and she noted that despite everything he could disarm you with the trust in his eyes. Maybe that's exactly what Janet and the considerable string of girls who had preceded her had found so attractive in him, before further considerations had interfered. What was he trying to tell her, she wondered. That he was incapable of love? Impotent? Scared to death?

"I don't think I want you to call me Skip anymore, or Skippy. Especially not Skippy."

"I never call you Skippy."

"Gee, maybe I do sometimes," said Gordon, with a you-know-me sort of wave.

"What do you want to be called?" asked Caitlin. "I mean, we've always called you Skip. On the posters for your play your name was Skip."

"I'm too old for it now. Anyhow, my friends call me Monk."

"Monk?" said Caitlin, her voice a blend of amusement and alarm.

"Not after Thelonius Monk or anything," he was quick to say.

"I don't know who Thelonius Monk *is*," said Caitlin.

"It's after Monk Eastman. One of the great Jewish gangsters from the old days on the Lower East Side. He was a real terror. He put so many people into the hospital that at Bellevue they called the emergency room the Monk Eastman Ward. We were reading about him in this incredible book by John Asbury called *The Gangs of New York*."

At "Monk's" urging, Gordon had the radio on. A group called the Byrds were singing lyrics made up of advice from the Old Testament. Their voices were sweet, harmonious, though static kept sweeping across the station like sudden tropical storms. Caitlin leaned back, closed her eyes. It was warm in the car; she felt a trickle of sweat begin in the hollow of her throat and roll down her chest, between her breasts. She had not been held, caressed, truly comforted in over a year. It no longer made her anxious so much as it embarrassed her, as if she had been excluded from some great universal ritual.

"I don't like when the office is closed," she announced.

"We know that," said Gordon. "That's why we've spirited you away. We're operating on the theory that enough is enough."

"It's not as if I'm selling gumdrops up there, you know," said Caitlin. "What I do is very important."

"We know that, Mom. That's not—"

"People all over the world are being destroyed. In one day, we were working on cases in Argentina, Vietnam, the Soviet Union. You weren't alive, but you know that this country turned its back on the Jews and all kinds of other people in Europe when Hitler was *murdering* them. That's a shame on us all. And we work *damn hard* to make certain it never happens again."

Her voice was sharp, and she knew it was not how you spoke to people you loved. They were silent. She listened to the sound of the tires on the parkway: it sounded as if the tires needed air or the treads were somehow coming loose.

They were on their way to Leyden. The last time Caitlin had been up to see her old house was ten years before, again with Gordon and the boy. They had been taking Annie back for a look at her old house. The poor old woman had sat in the back seat, bundled up in two overcoats and a woolen scarf, moving her mouth up and down, and staring silently out the window—she had given absolutely no indication that she recognized anything or that the entire ordeal held the slightest meaning to her. Yet when they finally arrived on the estate— empty that autumn and the lawns thick with crimson maple leaves—Annie had been agitated and refused to get out of the car. It was not until they were halfway back to the Woodlawn Convalescent Home, where Annie would die six days later, that she finally said her one sentence of the day: "They treated me badly." And then she nodded to herself, stopped moving her mouth, as if she had finally chewed what needed to be chewed, and that was that.

As they reached Leyden, Caitlin began pointing out the landmarks, both public and personal, to her son. "That's where the Cohen brothers had their fruit stand," she said, indicating where there was now a small playground, with a slide, a monkey puzzler, and a teeter-totter. "During the Depression, when the price of apples went way down, someone set it on fire. It was the most beautiful stand, all slatted wood and carvings of different fruits. Travelers used to stop there. But people blamed the Cohens because farmers weren't making money on their crops. And over there, across the stream, that small blue-and-yellow house, that used to be where my father's friend Junior Winters lived. Winters had a small orchard outside of town, and there were some people who thought it was either Junior or his brother Wade who set the fire." She glanced at her son, primarily to make certain he was paying attention. She remembered what it was like to be twenty, how the stories of old people seemed so irrelevant. She remembered how her own mind would glaze over with inattention when Joe's sister Hilda would talk about the wine-importing business, or her memories of Austria, or even of her fears for her family left back in Vienna.

He *was* paying attention. He was listening to every word, as if collecting clues for a hunt he would undertake at some future time. He was staring into her eyes; he was memorizing not only every word, but each gesture, the fall of her brown hair, the sheen of her light red lipstick, the arc of her eyebrows, the enduring nobility of her bones, the smell of her cologne, the whisper of cotton as she shifted in her seat, moved and a little embarrassed by the avidity of his concentration.

"I'm really glad I came for this," he said. "You never tell me anything about yourself, your life, or anything."

"That's not true," said Caitlin, too quickly.

"I sometimes think that's why I, I don't know, have my problems. I sure don't know my father and you're kind of hidden, too. I've had to make myself up, is what I think. Nothing gets passed along, and it's like having to reinvent the wheel. It's been all this unnecessary work and I don't think it's fair."

"There's a time in everyone's life," Caitlin said, her voice cooling, "when he thinks that what he must know is the truth about his parents. But that time will pass."

"I really want to know," he said.

"Well, if you look out the window right here you'll see Pell's Pond. That's where poor Michael Burnett fell through the ice and drowned, when we were in high school. He was a tall, graceful boy, vain about his hair, without much on his mind. I could never tell why, but it was widely assumed we were sweethearts—"

"Sweethearts," said Gordon. "Now there's a lovely word from the past."

"I never felt I really knew him," said Caitlin. "I went to the funeral. The whole school did. And all the girls in the class, you know the girls who embodied the spirit of the place, the morality, the social cliques and arrangements—it was all very tribal, when I think back on it—they all approached me after the burial. And they made this terrible ceremony, giving me poor Michael Burnett's school sweater, his football, and his school notebook. My name was written on it. But not by Michael, you understand. One of those girls did it. Not to fool anyone, but because they decided it was what Michael would have wanted, what he would have done himself if I'd only been more encouraging."

"I'll bet he loved you," said Gordon.

"Then you'd lose the bet. What they really wanted was someone to play that role, the part of the grieving girlfriend. They insisted on it and I was too . . . I don't know what I was, but I didn't resist. I stood there at his graveside, clutch-

ing his gray-and-gold sweater. Weeping. Weeping. Just absolutely weeping."

Caitlin paused for a moment. Gordon had stopped at the
town's light. To the left was the George Washington Inn,
newly painted white, with middle-sized poplars on the front
lawn where the gigantic elms had once grown. To the right
Central Smoking Supply had a window display of curved
English pipes and checked woolen Sherlock Holmes caps.

"We're early for our succulent country dinner," said Gordon. He had reserved a table for them for two o'clock, certain
that Caitlin would feel some sort of triumph being served in
the place where she once had worked. He had planned their
arrival in Leyden so they would have time to look around the
town before they ate.

"Maybe we'll see some of your old friends from when you
used to live here," said the boy. "You never told me even what
their names used to be."

"I didn't have one friend in this town," Caitlin said. "Not
even anyone to talk to. No one wanted anything out of life
more complicated than a soda and a date. I just felt completely
alone."

"Sometimes it seems you still think you're alone," the boy
said, his tongue suddenly thick.

"Isn't this where we met when you took Joe and me to
that Nazi summer camp?" asked Gordon, pointing to a street
corner where there now stood a Texaco gas station. "There
used to be a diner here or something. Am I right?"

"It was a butcher shop," said Caitlin.

"Did your mother ever tell you about our visit to . . .
what was it called? Camp Sunrise?" he asked the boy through
the rearview mirror.

"I think so," he said. "I'm not sure." He turned to his
mother. "Did you?"

"Yes," said Caitlin. "I guess you had other things on your

mind at the time." She leaned forward. "Turn left at the next intersection," she said.

Single-family houses where shopkeepers had once lived were now broken up into two or four apartments. Open fields had been seeded over with lawn, clover-leafed with driveways, and filled with new pastel ranch houses. Swimming holes were choked with cattails and ablaze with the commerce of the red-winged blackbirds. Barns had either been razed or turned into garages or workshops, where a new generation pursued what it called hobbies, and where the phrase "do-it-yourself" was suddenly current, as if it were a daring decision to glue together your own broken chairs.

Yet, when Gordon steered the car onto River Road, thirty years disappeared before the turn signal clicked off. Most of the river families were no longer in their mansions, but the walls and gates remained, the fields were still tended, still full of cattle and sheep, and even the purple asters and the chicory that grew wild at the side of the road seemed cultivated.

"Where's your house, Mom?" asked Caitlin's son. He hadn't been in Leyden in ten years, but he remembered the mansions on the road where his mother had once lived. He gave things like that too much thought, in Caitlin's opinion. His impulses were archival. Nostalgia was tough to take in the old; it was simply unacceptable to her in the young.

"We certainly have time to pay it a visit," said Gordon, looking at his watch, pretending to come to the decision spontaneously.

"Just around this turn," said Caitlin. "There's a white oak, the largest oak tree in New York. And then the main gate is right after. It'll probably be locked." Her voice was light, hollowed out. She was leaning forward, her arms resting on the back of Gordon's seat.

They came to the iron gate. It was wide open, and where the No Trespassing sign had once been there was a placard that said WELCOME TO OUR LABOR DAY PICNIC! It was a hand-drawn sign with pictures of frankfurters and balloons on it.

"Oh, let's go in," said Gordon. "I'd like to see where you grew up."

"Is this your way of getting out of taking us to lunch?" asked Caitlin. She'd meant it to be a tease and was again surprised to hear how stern her voice sounded.

"Yeah," said her son. "Let's check it out. Please."

"I can't tell you how many lousy memories I have of this place."

"But you always said it was so beautiful," said her son. He was still at the age when he pounced on contradictions, as if they were a kind of betrayal.

"Plantations are beautiful, too," said Caitlin. "But the freed slaves didn't come back sightseeing."

"Aw, come on," said Gordon. "We've come this far."

They were silent. Caitlin felt as if her blood had momentarily stopped flowing and then it began again, with a lurch. Her eyes stung and she realized she could no more turn away from Twin Ponds now than she could fail to greet an old friend on the street.

"I guess I knew all along we'd be coming here," she said.

The driveway was no longer packed dirt but bright white pebbles. The stones crunched beneath their tires as they entered Twin Ponds. To the left were the ponds that had given the estate its name: one right next to the other, forming a gleaming aquatic 8 in the sunlight. A tractor came into view, a new blue Ford. But it wielded no thresher, no harrow; instead it pulled a slatted wagon that was full of elderly people wearing straw hats.

It had been eight years since a Fleming had lived at Twin Ponds. After Fulton and Mary were gone, Jamey and his wife, Consuela, had tried to live there, but the inheritance of property had exceeded the inheritance of cash, and as Jamey had put it in an interview in *Fortune* (an article called "The

Land-Poor Gentry"), "It was like owning the sky but not having an airplane—what good does it do?" Jamey had sold the
house and the three hundred acres in a down market to the
Baptist Charitable Trust, which then turned Twin Ponds into
a convalescent home.

Gordon steered the Fairlane along the gravel drive. Red
reflectors on steel rods stood between the trees. To save on
taxes, Jamey and Consuela had razed some of the outbuild-
ings. The ice house was gone, a couple of the large, more
unstable barns, the converted root cellar where Shorty Russel
and his family used to live—gone now except for the slab of
concrete foundation still stuck into the side of the hill.

Yet the yellow-and-white Victorian where Peter and Annie and Caitlin had lived was still there. It was painted brown
now; its gingerbread trim had been removed and it seemed
like a very ordinary house indeed. A Plymouth station wagon
was parked in front. Peter's compulsively proper plantings
were nowhere in sight. The blueberry bushes that came ripe
in regular waves, the cascades of baby carnations, the hedge
of laurel—uprooted, or expired from neglect. All that was
around the house was flat lawn that looked badly in need of
fertilizer and water. There was a rusting metal swing set along
the side of the house. Two small boys in crisp trousers and
striped tee shirts swung back and forth, their faces composed,
their hair wet and combed precisely.

"Here's where we lived," said Caitlin and then lurched forward as Gordon applied the brakes.

Dust seeped through the gravel and rose into the warm,
still air like smoke.

"It doesn't look like the pictures," said her son.

"Are you going to get out and look around?" asked
Gordon.

"No, it's OK." She tilted her head, trying to get a view of
what had once been her bedroom window. "I always had a
Mason jar of fresh violets on the windowsill," she said. "Back

then, most all the violets grown in America came out of Leyden, winter and summer."

"I don't think anyone grows violets anymore," said Gordon. He shifted the car into Park and then put his hand in the back of his shirt to scratch an itch near his spine.

"I think we should get out," said the boy. "We may never come here again for the rest of our lives."

"Would you really like to see it?" asked Caitlin.

"Me? Sure."

She thought for a moment. "I think we'd be intruding. It's not as if this was a national monument."

Just then, a man in his thirties wearing a tan short-sleeved shirt came out of the house. He had a small, curious face, blue eyes, practically nonexistent eyebrows. He stood on the porch, looking at their car.

"The picnic's up by the main facility," he called out.

Gordon lowered his window and smiled at the man on the porch. Years of working as a photographer had given Gordon the idea that it was easy for him to charm and manipulate that mass of strangers he called The Public. "Howdy," he said. Coming from the Midwest, he thought that his common touch was as indelible as a thumbprint.

"What?" the man on the porch said, cupping his ear.

"My friend back here was raised in your house and we were wondering if we could have a look around," said Gordon.

"Gordon, please," said Caitlin, softly. Her heart jumped like a dog that's been kicked.

"Unless it's any trouble," Gordon added, with the bountiful spirit of someone assured of cooperation.

The man from the porch stared into the back seat of the car. He nodded formally to Caitlin and then addressed himself to Gordon.

"My wife and I are physical therapists; we work up at the main facility," he said.

Gordon nodded enthusiastically. "Well, that's fine," he said. "Just fine."

"Today's our day off and my wife's cleaning the house," the man said. His voice was sharpening itself like a knife against a whetstone. "Afraid she just couldn't have any visitors right now."

"You see," said Gordon, "it would just be for a minute." His smile was starting to droop and he forced the corners of his mouth up again. "We've had, well, you know, quite a long drive."

"Sorry," the man said.

"Gordon, will you please drive away from here?" Caitlin said. She half rose from her seat and spoke to the man through Gordon's open window. "Thank you anyhow. It was just a passing thought."

Gordon turned. "Don't you want to see your old house?"

"I see it."

"I mean the inside."

"Gordon, if you don't drive away from here right now I'm going to bite you."

"I have this friend in Chaucer class who everyone calls The Biter," said her son.

"Well, thanks anyhow," Gordon said to the man, who nodded, and stepped back toward the porch as Gordon put the car into gear and gently pressed the accelerator. Caitlin looked back at the house and the space its sloping roof wedged out of the deep blue sky and the children going back and forth on their swings like two out-of-synch pendulums, and then without quite knowing why she reached over and took her son's hand.

At what was once the Flemings' house what passed for Labor Day festivities were under way. Except for the ramps that led into the various entrances, no obvious changes had been made in the mansion. Yet it looked as transformed as the Van Fleets' stripped-down Victorian. Its shabby edges had been shored up, the stone-pointers had been at it, the siding salesmen had made a killing, the painters had been busy, and the overall effect was somehow sad, even upsetting: it was like seeing an elegant old woman dressed in a bright polyester pants suit.

The Baptist Home had hoped to attract townspeople to this Labor Day celebration, but all who were there were inmates of the home and family members who had come to spend the day. In clusters of three and four, they wandered around the lawns holding picnic baskets and blankets, choosing places to sit that afforded the best views of the river.

Caitlin, Gordon, and Monk stood in front of the house, looking up at it as if it were a ship that had just docked.

"I don't think anyone would mind if we walked in and looked around in there," Gordon said.

"My mother scrubbed every room in this house. That was her life's work. And now . . ." Caitlin shrugged.

"And now they're dusty again," said her son.

"Monk," Gordon said, in a faintly admonishing tone.

"I don't want to go in there," Caitlin said, taking Gordon's arm.

He placed his hand on top of hers.

"Then we don't have to," he said.

Yet without a plan to see the rooms in which Caitlin's past had unfolded and with no one at the home to visit, they were suddenly without anything to do, any reason to be there, and this lack of purpose struck each of them with its own eerie power. And so, like frightened tourists, they attempted to assert not only their right to be there but their very reality by shopping for something to buy.

Folding tables filled with foods, crafts, semi-antiques, and old books had been set up near the house, and Caitlin, her son, and Gordon inspected the baked goods and bought a mince pie and a dozen apple-spice cupcakes. Then they compared a blue afghan with an orange-and-white one. The woman who was selling the knitted goods assured them that each piece had been hand-fashioned by a resident of the home, and she immediately quoted the price of whatever one of them touched.

The sun was suddenly very warm. A drone of bees. The far-off singing of the old people in the tractor-drawn wagon. Everywhere the smell of the trees and shrubs her father had planted.

Caitlin turned away from the house, to face the hill from which Jamey used to say there was the best view of the river and its valley, the place where you could see no other house, no evidence at all of civilization, a crypt of beauty that time could not penetrate. It's time that makes us human, Caitlin thought. She heard the sound of the tractor motor and she thought of her father, riding high in the steel bucket seat of the old International Harvester. How he had begged the Flemings to buy another tractor, but they were not interested in machinery: it made no sense to them; they didn't care for it. And if it saved labor, what did they care? They didn't do the work and they barely paid the men who did. It was more picturesque and somehow more comforting to have most of the work done by hand or animal.

Caitlin, her son, and Gordon drifted along from table to table. Gordon bought some old daguerreotypes at the knick-knack table and Monk bought a pretty beaded purse for Janet, paying for it with sweaty, crumpled dollars from his front pocket. Caitlin watched the old woman's long, rouged face as she smoothed out the boy's money and laid it to rest in the gray tin money box.

Finally, they came to the table where the used books were sold. Monk was happy to find a copy of *Farewell My Lovely* in paperback and Gordon bought an old Howard Fast novel about Thomas Paine. Some of the books were discarded from the library, others had been donated by people in town, or by the families of the home's residents—there seemed to be a general divestment of Pearl Buck and A. J. Cronin in process—and some of the books had been left behind by the Flemings when they sold Twin Ponds. Caitlin recognized some of the leather-bound decorative volumes that had been in their library—*Captain Horatio Hornblower, De Profundis, The Selected Essays of Edmund Burke.*

And then, as she browsed through the cartons of books, Caitlin saw *Home Front* by Joseph Rose, its jacket still intact, showing the American flag with the stars replaced by swastikas. She turned slightly, not wanting either Gordon or the boy to see what she had found, at least not yet. She opened the book.

"If it's not marked, it's a quarter," said the man behind the table. He had an egg-shaped, bald head, long-sleeved tee shirt, suspenders. He looked at Caitlin with unnerving intensity, as if he were trying to read her thoughts.

Caitlin looked down at *Home Front.* A bookplate had been glued onto the end paper. The bookplate showed a drawing of the mansion and beneath it said "From the Library of James Fleming."

She remembered wondering once, long ago, if Jamey had ever read Joe's book. She turned the pages and saw that not only had Jamey read it but he'd annotated it as well, and had even debated it in the margins here and there.

"Look what I found," Caitlin said, showing the book to Gordon.

"Oh my God," Gordon said. "Will you look at that."

"Now, there's a blast from the past," said Monk. "We've got to buy it."

"Well, we can't very well leave it here," said Gordon.

"I'll take it home with me," said Caitlin.

"Hey, look at this," said her son. "This book has your father's name in it." He was holding a falling-to-pieces copy of *Great Expectations*. The red top stain had faded; it was practically white. He showed the inscription to his mother. It said: "Peter Van Fleet, Twin Ponds, New York. 1919."

"This is the copy he read aloud to me," said Caitlin.

"It's only fifty cents," said her son.

"This is amazing," said Gordon.

"Thank you," Caitlin said, softly, taking the book in her hands. She had a brief fear that it would just crumble to dust at her touch, like Miss Havisham's wedding cake, but it felt heavy, solid. It was the first thing of her father's that she had touched since his death. And after she bought it, it would be the only thing of Peter's she would own.

"Oh, hey, now look at this," said Gordon. He was going through a box of books rather quickly, feeling a little competitive now that both Caitlin and the boy had discovered treasures. "A really beautiful edition of *War and Peace*."

"Maybe it's yours, Mom."

Caitlin looked at the book in Gordon's hand. It was a thick brown book with black lettering on the spine. "L. Tolstoy" it said, just as her copy had.

"Maybe it is," she said. She felt the sudden pressure of tears in her eyes. Of course, she had a copy of *War and Peace* back in her apartment, but to find the pages through which she had first devised her vast picture of the world, to find *her* Napoleon, *her* Natasha, *her* beloved Rostov.

She placed *Home Front* and *Great Expectations* on the card table.

"Do you want these?" the man behind the table asked.

But she did not answer. She solemnly accepted *War and Peace* from Gordon and opened the cover.

Yet she did not find her own name inscribed on the end paper.

She found the name of Michael Burnett, poor Michael

Burnett, whose body was swallowed into that broken maw of ice more than thirty years before and at whose funeral she had wept such copious tears.

Caitlin held the book before her, as if waiting for someone to take it from her and relieve her of the burden. "I never knew him," she said, covering her eyes. "We could have been such friends."

Gordon reached out as Michael Burnett's book slipped from Caitlin's grasp, and he caught it gracefully with his large, steady hands before it hit the lawn.

NINE

Somewhere in gray, trembling Tokyo Bay, General MacArthur had just accepted the official Japanese surrender, and in New York the police were out in numbers, hoping to contain the celebration they felt would surely come. But the joy that greeted this, the official end of the war, was quiet, contained—nothing like the night of delirium in August, when the Japanese first raised the flag of surrender. Today was a Monday, it was the end of the Labor Day holiday, the first three-day holiday in America since the beginning of the war. As if there were a collective desire to escape the waking nightmare of history, there seemed to be more people celebrating Labor Day than the final victory over Japan.

Victory over Japan scarcely mattered to Caitlin. As far as she was concerned, the real war had been over for months. First Mussolini and his fatuous whore were shot in April, then Hitler and his blue-eyed whore were dead a few days later, and then on May Day that grotesque puppet Goebbels deprived the Allies of the catharsis of revenge by killing himself, and a week later Europe was at least nominally free.

As for the Japanese, they had been driven out of the Philippines in July and then in August Hiroshima and Nagasaki were yanked like teeth from the jaws of the earth, leaving behind two molten, steaming pits.

Even the first wave of celebration, in August, had gone right past Caitlin like hometown hoopla when the Yankees win the pennant.

She was still working at the Combined Emergency European Relief Committee. This was nearly eight years before the committee was suspected of left-wing ties and, as Caitlin herself would put it, all the financial angels turned into chickens. There were six people working with Caitlin then, and like her they would put in twelve to fourteen hours a day in that loft on Fourth Avenue, with the gouges on the floor where the old industrial sewing machines had once been bolted. Caitlin worked closely with Henry Lehman, whom she had met at Joe's publication party, and for the past several months, though she had not allowed herself to say it, she had been working away at a cause she believed was already lost.

The Jews were dead. No one had come to their aid, no home was found, just a handful of heroes arose and that was not enough. Europe was a graveyard, a hideous horizon of black chimneys smoking against gray sky. Europe was a pile of skulls, truckloads of empty shoes. Lehman counseled her that the great task of gathering the survivors still remained. Yet remains were all that existed: remains of villages, shards of history, pieces of bone, shadows of former selves.

And so Caitlin refused to celebrate V-J Day because with millions dead and a million more still wandering, what was the use of clicking beer mugs with strangers and waving flags?

And Caitlin did not want to celebrate the war's end because she had succumbed to bitterness. The dancing in the streets seemed an affront to the dead. And the hypocrisy made her tremble with shame: everyone exonerated, everyone a hero. In a sickening embrace, America was gathering itself close to its own breast. Coughlin forgiven, Vonsiatsky forgotten, the rallies, the torch-lit parades, the hate wagon making its way through Yorkville with the tinkle of hanging kerosene lamps like the laughter of glass children, the singing marchers in lederhosen in Camp Sunrise—fading now and fading fast. It was as if it had never happened, never mattered, and Caitlin was appointed by the forgetfulness of others to guard the true and shameful history of her time.

Today, the offices were closed and Caitlin slept late. When she awakened, she drank a glass of water, ate an apple, and listened to the sound of her neighbor's radio. Sousa marches, on and on. Greenwich Village, she thought. Her internal self had taken on a caustic voice now, and since she had assumed it—at first as a pose, an alternative to her former, more pliant and hopeful inner voice—she could not speak to herself in any other tone.

Joe had given her his apartment, but the neighbors that went with it were less than desirable. She had expected opera singers, sculptors, a French Communist, perhaps, or at least a dizzy, promiscuous girl with wild hair and cherry-red lips. But those she lived with were just ordinary men who carried lunch pails and their cross-looking wives whispering among themselves on the way to the grocer.

She'd been living on Barrow Street for nearly three years and no neighbor had asked her in for tea or even said hello to her. A Mrs. Ernst once appeared at Caitlin's door holding a scabrous ginger cat and asked if Caitlin would mind the animal while she, Mrs. Ernst, visited relatives in Harrisburg. Caitlin had declined and Mrs. Ernst had squinted at her and said, "Oh, a movie star, with a beautiful face. Excuse me for asking," delivering the line as if she were starring in some comedy on the radio.

Caitlin had friends in New York, friends from work, and Gordon, of course. Gordon was in the Communist party now, and going out with a tall woman with a slight mustache who did not understand Gordon's attachment to Caitlin—though if she were to have understood that he loved Caitlin partly as a way of abiding with his vanished friend Joe, it would not necessarily have made things any easier.

Caitlin went out on Saturdays with a man named Tom Lawson, who taught anatomy at the Art Students League—a sexually avid man of forty-four. Lawson was rather skeletal himself, as if he did not want any extra flesh to interfere with the intricacy of his bone structure. Like so many men, his idea of intimacy was sharing his plans for the future with the pliant woman of his choice, and what made this particularly trying was that Lawson had irritating plans for the future. They had a far-flung Jamey Fleming quality and seemed mostly to concern finding a spot in the world where civilization had not encroached and where Lawson and his beloved—he was never very specific about who might be cast in the role of the beloved—might live on breadfruit and fresh fish and he himself could become the Gauguin of bones.

Caitlin kept the curtains drawn against the heat of the day. She was wearing blue-and-white man's-style pajamas, bought years ago in Washington on a shopping trip with Betty. She walked into the bathroom with its tiny black-and-white tiles and the boiler pipe pushing up through the floor and disappearing into the ceiling like a cast-iron beanstalk. She looked at herself in the mirror. She had been up until two reading *Brideshead Revisited*, which she had found snobbish, though the pastoral nostalgia moved her in ways she could scarcely admit even to herself. Her face no longer absorbed those long nights like a deep river; now the restlessness left its bruises and hollows. She was glad to look slightly a wreck. She had always felt that something hurt and dissipated was her true face. She was bored and even antagonized by what was pretty and wholesome in her face; it was annoying to be thought beautiful, or so she thought in 1945, when her beauty was in perfect balance with her intelligence and her melancholy and she was more beautiful than ever before, or ever after.

She dressed in the bathroom, as if there were people in the house and she needed to be modest. She put on a pale green skirt and a matching, wide-shouldered jacket. She had no green shoes to match but she had gray ones and she had chosen a grayish blouse to go under her jacket. There was somewhere in all this an anticipation of a moment, a personal drama, in which she would take off her jacket and some unknown person would notice that her blouse matched her shoes.

The Combined Emergency European Relief Committee was on the second floor of a cast-iron building filled with commercial tenants who were willing to sacrifice charm and even tidiness for a reasonable rent. When Caitlin arrived that morning at eleven it was quiet; sunlight drifted through the small gray and beige lobby, caught in a net of silence. Her footsteps resonated as she walked up to the second floor; a single fly buzzed around the enormous glass globe that lit the way. Upstairs, the tiled corridor was in shadows—the only light came from beneath the door to the Wo Trading Company, where a tall Chinese businessman seemed always to be talking loudly over the telephone to people who, judging from his tone of voice, either didn't understand him or had willfully betrayed him.

Caitlin walked slowly to Room 208, where the CEERC had its offices. The corridor, the doors, the cool, drab light, the sound of Mr. Wo's plaintive warble, all seemed part of a world separate from the merriment outside, a place that had been tucked away and then forgotten, like one of those towns on a country road that slowly die when a new highway carries all the traffic ten miles to the west of them.

The frosted glass of the door to Room 208 was dark and the door itself was locked. She had just assumed that at least Lehman would come in. She stood there, feeling a little foolish, and a little self-righteous as well, and then she tried the door again.

Footsteps. A clatter of mop and bucket. Caitlin turned to see Mrs. Oberman, the building's cleaning woman, limping past the darkened offices of Dr. Marcus, the dentist, and then Rosenberg Ceramics, coming toward her with a broken gait that seemed more the expression of a deep melancholy than a lameness in any limb.

"Everybody's closed, Mrs. Oberman. It's a holiday."

"Closed except for Wo," Mrs. Oberman said. She was a small woman with protruding eyes, a small chin, a cringe that was slowly curving her spine. She wore a black dress and black high-top shoes without laces. She gripped her mop handle as if it were her staff. "For the end of the war?"

"I think for Labor Day, Mrs. Oberman."

"The dirt doesn't know the war is *kaput*."

"You should be home. Enjoying yourself, relaxing."

"Me?" Mrs. Oberman was sixty; her hair was colorless, unkempt, and Caitlin had assumed that madness roared inside of the old woman like a furnace, burning away sense, humor, hope, leaving only instinct, fear. But then she shrugged and moved her fingers as if to grasp something delicate, something tangible only under the most extraordinary of circumstances, and there was an unexpected grace in the gesture that made Caitlin wonder if once perhaps Mrs. Oberman had been a student, or danced, or painted, or sat alone on some distant hill and watched the sun slowly set, sending up flares of color like the final chords in an organ sonata.

"For me this war has taken everything," Mrs. Oberman said, moving close to Caitlin, touching her wrist with one hand while holding tightly to her mop with the other. "Everything and everyone. A mother and a father and my little sister, all from Sofia. Also nine cousins, and my aunt Rosie, God rest her soul. She was always my favorite, she treated me so good. My whole family rubbed out like you take an eraser on a mistake. Except for me, who comes here to America, and my husband, and my uncle Isaac. That's all. For the whole war we say, One day the Nazis will get it in the neck and we'll dance in the streets. But now . . ." She stoppped, shook her head. "Maybe I got too old for dancing."

Caitlin reached out to hold Mrs. Oberman, who merely allowed herself to be held. She was no more responsive than a doll upon which a distraught child unleashes a fit of sorrow.

"Really, really," Caitlin said, "if there's anything I can do, anything. If you need anything. You know, already in Europe there are committees looking for survivors. I could put you in touch with some. I'll go with you."

Finally, Mrs. Oberman lifted one arm and patted Caitlin softly on her back. "Shh, that's all, that's all."

Caitlin bowed and rested her forehead on Mrs. Oberman's oddly childlike shoulder; it seemed hard as a darning egg beneath her coarse black dress. The old woman's touch filled the chambers of Caitlin's heart as a summer tide seethes within an empty conch shell—but in an instant the tide shifted and she felt empty again.

Mrs. Oberman stuck her mop into her bucket and stood for a moment in front of Caitlin, assuming an aspect that was a mixture of cool appraisal and waiting to be dismissed. Then she turned her back and walked down the hall, with her back to Caitlin, at first moving slowly, and then briskly, and by the time she was fifty feet away Mrs. Oberman was practically running. The mop smacked against the sides of the bucket like a crude clapper inside an even cruder bell.

Caitlin turned away from the door to Room 208 and headed for the stairwell. She was halfway to the lobby when she heard the doors to the street open. A roar of traffic and human excitement came in and then was muffled as the door closed again. Whoever had just come in made his way to the directory on the north wall. Caitlin spied over the banister; a man with black hair, wearing a tan summer suit.

She proceeded to the lobby and the man who had been scanning the building directory turned toward the sound of her feet on the stairs and it was Joe. She could barely believe it was happening, but it was true, it was he, Joe, looking a little surprised to see her, reacting with a certain drawing back, a certain defensive glaze over the eyes, but, on the whole, looking just as he had the first time she'd met him at his sister's house five years before, dark, with a hidden male sultriness, a stubborn delicacy.

"Caitlin," he said, his voice falling a little bit short of the task of animating all the silent air between them. He reached out toward her and then closed his hand. "I was just now coming to see you."

"We're closed. Everything's closed."

"Caitlin?" he said. He made a gesture that said, Are you going to stay on the stairs?

She descended toward him. His suit was wrinkled; his shoes were scuffed. He looked as if he had slept sitting up the night before—on a train, or a bus, one of those men trying to maintain a certain appearance but overwhelmed by exhaustion.

He waited for her at the foot of the stairs. Then he stepped back and they stood in the lobby with a few inches between them. Neither of them said a word; there was no language for what they felt. Everything would have been wrong. Then, finally, Caitlin extended her hand and Joe shook it briskly, making matters a little worse. Now they had something to overcome.

"Where have you been?" Caitlin asked.

"Uncle Sam discharged me three weeks ago and then . . ." He gestured vaguely. "I was worried I wouldn't be able to find you. I had this terrible feeling that everything would be someplace else when I got back."

He reached out for her, took her in his arms. It felt as if he were holding on to her while he died. He breathed slowly and nuzzled the side of her face and pressed his forehead against hers.

"I've never been so glad to see anyone in my whole life," he said.

He gathered her closer and the silence between them was soft wind.

"I knew it was just a matter of time," said Caitlin. "I think about you all the time. I know you're not supposed to tell someone that."

"Let's go next door," said Joe. "I noticed they're open and I could use a drink."

They left the building, walking close to each other but not touching. The sunlight was bright, assaultive. And it was hot, the heat came from the air, the pavement, from the buildings and the cars, it radiated everywhere. A plane droned overhead and the passersby stopped to look up.

Caitlin and Joe walked into the Amsterdam Bar and Grill. It was dark inside, full of noise and smoke and the slightly skunky smell of beer. The men's faces were golden and moist; their eyes receded in the darkness, leaving only dark holes in their faces. Reflexively, Caitlin stood closer to Joe. She had been working next door to this bar for over two years and had never walked in. She had pictured it just as it was, a place for men who were alone, alone in their drinking, alone in their beds, unclean men, unshaved, sour-looking, the sort of men who even in this time of lonely women felt bitter and rejected.

The bartender was sallow, with wiry hair, and something truncated and incomplete about him. The victory celebration seemed to be faring slightly better in this saloon than in other parts of the city, but he himself remained dour. When he asked Caitlin and Joe what they would have he immediately got a worried look, as if expecting them to order something he no longer had.

"Four Roses and a glass of water," said Joe, describing a small glass with his thumb and forefinger. Caitlin wondered if this meant he wanted a small amount of whiskey or a small amount of water.

"I'll have the same," said Caitlin. "Except for the water."

Joe smiled at her. "Sure?"

"Oh, I may as well."

They waited for the bartender to bring their drinks. The silence between them was encased in the noise of the bar. A small, dapperly turned out but utterly plastered old gent in a plaid suit and bowler hat stood on a table and hoisted his beer mug up toward the lilac galaxy of cigar smoke that hovered between him and the tin ceiling. "My nephews are coming home!" he bellowed. His voice was surprisingly deep, resonant, as if he had come by it on the sly, a black-market voice.

The beery men over whom he now unstably loomed cheered the old man and his bowler.

"Did he say nephews?" Joe asked. He moved his fingers on his whiskey glass, rotating it in his palm. All the time that he had been gone was somehow captured in that gesture, that display of some new nocturnal elegance. His fingers had lost some of their taper and his bottom teeth were discolored.

"I thought only Donald Duck talked about nephews," said Caitlin. She lifted her glass, clicked it against Joe's, watched to see how much of his he drank in one swallow, but could not match him.

He took a small sip of water; he seemed to have made a bit of a science out of the procedure. Then he smiled at Caitlin. "Donald Duck," he said. He touched her elbow and then looked away. "Well," he said, "I missed you. I certainly missed you. At least we've ascertained that. I don't see you, I miss you. Fact."

"We've also ascertained that you don't see me, you don't write me," said Caitlin. "Fact." She took the water glass out of his hand and sipped from it. Water served with whiskey seemed colder than ordinary ice water; the glass itself seemed narrower, denser, ceremonial.

"I wrote to you," said Joe. He gestured to the bartender. "I wrote to you right after I enlisted, I wrote you from basic, and then I got assigned to *Stars and Stripes* and I wrote you from there. The only time I stopped writing you was when I got that goddamned fucking intestinal disease and my whole life was just shit in a pot."

"Then what happened to all those letters, Joe?"

"I don't know. I just threw them away as I wrote them. I seem to be living that kind of life, just a long letter never sent." He laughed—and it was a rather awful laugh, full of scorn, and mystery, and aloneness.

The bartender brought their refills. Caitlin had only half finished her first and she placed the second one to her left, as if it had been ordered for somebody else.

"I was in France," said Joe. "Now that was something. So much of my time was spent flying a desk, but I was in France, I guess I'll never forget it. I was there when the Free French took the city back from the Germans. The Nazis fought like complete cowards and then De Gaulle came marching down the Champs-Elysées and the city went mad."

"Oh, God, I wish I could have seen it," said Caitlin. "I saw the pictures and the newsreels, but to be there, really be there . . ." She sipped her drink and added, "I've never been anywhere," and then quickly put the tumbler down again, as if it were making her foolish.

"Do you know who I met in Paris?" Joe asked. He scooped the ice out of his second drink and dumped it into the empty glass that had held his first.

Caitlin watched him. He needed a shave, a hot bath, a long rest.

"I don't know," she said.

"Welles," said Joe, in a murmur. He turned toward her, offering up his dark sorrowful eyes.

"They ruined Sumner Welles," Joe said. "That incident on the President's train was a setup. But he's landed on his feet. He's an aristocrat. God, if something like that happened to me, I guess I'd put a bullet in my head."

"How did you happen to run into him?"

"Luck. Blind luck. I was sitting in a café with another soldier and Sumner saw me, came right up, put his hand on my shoulder, and that was it."

"It must have been amazing, I mean since it was Paris and all."

"His hair was combed straight back, he was wearing a seersucker suit, carrying a cane. He was tan. He told me he liked my book and that I should go home and write another one. I'll probably never see him again."

"Who knows? If the last few years have taught us anything it's that anything can happen."

Joe shrugged, looked away for a moment.

"I think about you all the time, Joe," she said, retrieving him.

"It makes sense, you working to get people across borders. I mean, you've crossed these frontiers inside of yourself, those borders we all have set up to keep us in one place. Telling someone, You can go here but you can't go there, is a kind of fascism, isn't it? But it's not only how most of us treat the people around us, we treat ourselves like that, too. You crossed the border, Caitlin. You erased the boundary lines. So it's no wonder you want to help others cross the borders, too."

He took her hand, turned it over as if to study the lines on her palm. And it was then that Caitlin's heart, so long in hibernation, flew from the cave of her body toward Joe.

In love, it seemed, the heart was not filled but stolen. She felt love for Joe not as a swelling in the chest but a sudden, eerie emptiness, as in one of those dreams where we think we are falling, falling out of bed, out of time, out of the universe, and where once the great solidity of sleep filled us there is now a vibrant hollow, a vivid void.

They left the Amsterdam Bar and Grill, walked out into the dusty sunlight and the heat and noise. They walked to Greenwich Village, where they went to Caitlin's favorite market and spent Caitlin's remaining ration tickets on oranges, French bread, olives, a small chicken, a little sack of coffee, and a can of condensed milk. Caitlin adored sweet milk, considered it a luxury item.

They walked south on Sixth Avenue and then west on Waverly. Car horns blared—some out of anger at the traffic, some out of end-of-the-war high spirits, and a few as a simple response to hearing others make noise. Some boys in their teens were pushing an Oriental man in his twenties against the green tin of a newspaper kiosk. The Oriental man was saying, "I am Chinaman, please. Not Japan. Chinaman." When Joe and Caitlin stopped, the boys suddenly left the man and Caitlin used the moment to link her arm through Joe's.

Even on Barrow Street, Joe seemed unmoved, seeing the houses and trees he had once known so well. There was something labored in his gait, and once he stopped in the middle of the block and took a deep breath.

When they reached her building, Caitlin pointed to it and said, "Feel like home?" He looked up at it, nodded vaguely at the stolid brown building, plain as home-baked bread. The windows that faced the street were open today. Mrs. Nicholas as usual leaned out from her perch on the top floor, the cement sill digging into her fleshy forearms as she stared down at the street, frowning. The window to the Clarks' apartment was open, and their leggy geranium, with its pale red flowers and its leaves fringed with decay, had been put out to sun. Mrs. Ernst's eternal cat paced around the potted flowers, twitching its tail.

"Look at that old cat up there," said Joe.

"That old cat can go to hell," replied Caitlin. "It's been nothing but trouble. Well, come on up." They walked up the five cement steps to the front door—heavily varnished mahogany and leaded glass that held the sunlight like little points of flame.

And by the time she let him into the apartment, Caitlin's

heart was beating so fiercely she could barely keep her balance. She wanted him, wanted to embrace everything about him that she knew and discover everything she did not know. She wanted to kiss him, make love. Desire was going through her like a wave of sickness. She dropped the sack of groceries onto the plain kitchen table and they thudded so loudly that Joe looked at her, wondering if she had perhaps lost her temper.

"Do you want to eat now?" she asked.

"Isn't it a little early?"

Someone was listening to patriotic music on the radio. The sound was oppressive though its origin was indistinct. It was marching-band melodies, with tubas and whistles and crashing cymbals, all played at a furious clip.

"The happiness is incredibly contagious," said Joe, sitting at the table, resting his head in his hands.

"Why do I feel as if the war was lost as much as won?" she asked, sitting across from him.

"I wonder where John Coleman is today," said Joe. "Probably marching in a parade or making patriotic toasts in a bar somewhere."

They were silent and it was not a difficult silence at all. It was fine just to sit together and breathe.

"Do you mind if I say something about you and Betty?" Joe said, after a few moments.

"I don't have anyone else in the world to remember her with."

"It's just that—well, if you look at things in a certain way, if you hadn't known her and then if she hadn't been on the plane with Stowe, then you and I probably wouldn't have had much to do with each other."

"I think about her," said Caitlin. She lowered her eyes. She had placed her hands on the edge of the table and the sun came into the kitchen and touched the tips of her fingers.

She brought Joe into the front room. Sitting in a kitchen

seemed to Caitlin something for people who lived on farms. They brought the oranges and a large blue enamel bowl for the peels and they sat close on the red velvet sofa. They were not courting. They were two people eating oranges while the rest of the world listened to martial music on the radio.

"It's as if we don't belong here," Joe said, after a time, and there was in his voice a simplicity that made her take his hand.

"Where do we belong?"

He answered her with a kiss. It was simple, unforced, he was not trying to capture her or stake any claim. His hand touched the side of her face as he kissed her and it was not a kiss to end a movie or even a night on the town. It was not sexual, it did not burn, it did not move through her. Yet it overwhelmed her. It was solemn and as serious as a vow.

"Caitlin," he said, his voice low, suddenly not afraid. Low and calm, the way it was when she first knew him.

They held each other in the heat of that apartment. Beyond the walls were the radio announcers and the awful music and the truckdrivers honking their horns and the foghorns in the harbor and kids throwing firecrackers and cherry bombs in the echoing air shafts.

Joe kissed the top of Caitlin's head and she placed his hand between her thighs.

And then they brought each other to her bed and collapsed together and stayed poised for a moment, entwined, until Caitlin put a little pressure on his hips and Joe rolled languidly onto his back and let Caitlin crawl on top of him.

She made love to him and it was as if she were making love to the entirety of her life. He held her firmly, moved when she did, and cried out softly when he came, yet even then did not let her go, did not want her to stop. And later she lay beside him, touching the sweat on his chest, and knowing in some deep and frightening animal way that she was pregnant.

TEN

"I don't give a hoot about being lost since everything is so beautiful," said Caitlin, turning up the collar of her bright red wool coat. "Lost in Holland," she said, with satisfaction.

The temperature in Amsterdam was a few degrees warmer than it was back in New York, but the air was dead and damp. They were walking along a canal; the water gave up its dark, ancient aroma, an odor at once domestic and alarming, like dishwater from a century ago. The houses along the canal were dark brown with white trim. Here and there a door was painted royal blue or scarlet. Notices for rock concerts and protest rallies were posted on the ancient trees, and their edges shuddered in the clammy breeze.

"I can't believe our hotel gives us peanut butter and chocolate for breakfast," her son said. His matted curls shook slowly in the wind. Unshaven, his chin looked as if he had pressed it down into a mound of black pepper.

"I thought it was delicious," said Caitlin. "And I love the hotel. Don't you?"

"I'm still so tired."

Even on the KLM flight over, the boy kept on talking

about needing to crash—an odd choice of idiom, it seemed to Caitlin, who could rarely even see an airplane without thinking of that DC-3 whose wreckage still burned in her memory.

Some students came out of a small basement café. They were carrying books, smoking cigarettes, all of them talking at once. Before the door closed, Caitlin caught a glimpse of the coffeeshop. A stack of cups and saucers, a rack of sweet rolls, the chrome of an espresso machine, a blue-and-white poster with Russian lettering. A pang of loneliness went through her, as resonant as the hum of a tuning fork. She felt that odd nostalgia we sometimes feel for all that we never knew. The life of a student . . . She glanced at her son. His eyes were cast down; he was waiting for the students to cross the street. He's ashamed to be seen walking around with his mother, thought Caitlin.

"OK," she said. "Let's see if we can figure this out." She opened the street guide to Amsterdam. Her hands were tired, fingers clumsy. The wind tried to tear the map away. "Oh-oh. I think we've been walking in the wrong direction. The Prinsengracht seems to run like this." She traced a curl of canal on the map. "See?"

Caitlin was in Amsterdam to attend a three-day conference called "The Rise of the Extreme Right in Europe and the Americas." She was a representative of the World Refugee Alliance, and Gordon, at the last moment, gave her son the money to take the trip, too. (Gordon had just been given the account to take all the class pictures at the Walden School and he was feeling flush.) The conference would convene at the Anne Frank House in two days; they had deliberately come early to see a bit of Amsterdam. After a lifetime of dreaming of travel, this was Caitlin's first trip abroad.

She had risen at dawn, and while the boy had snored lightly in the bed beside hers, his hands thrown over his head, his chest bare, hairless, the blanket kicked off during the night and the sheet clinging to his lean shape like a shroud, she had dressed quietly and left the hotel. In her purse she had an aerogram from Joe, the last word from him, received months ago. He was living in Amsterdam, at least he had been at the time of the letter, where he was working on his tenth book. None of them sold very many copies; he was far from being a rich man, he was not even comfortable, but whatever money he made combined well with his sense of determination and he kept at it, book after book. The one he worked on now was about the United States's role in helping certain key Nazi intelligence officers escape from Europe. His letter had mentioned that he would be going to East Germany soon, where a certain Professor Heinemann would give him access to his files. And so in the chill of the first light, Caitlin had taken a taxi through the Vondel Park to 38 Von Eghenstraat, asked the driver of the old Mercedes to wait, and then mounted the steps of the tall, narrow rooming house with its scarlet shutters and matching door. Drizzle wafted past the street lamps, the ducks in the park were beginning to squawk. She had no intention of awakening this house at such an hour; she was not certain if she even wanted to see Joe. Yet even if she were to see him, it would not be like this, not as a surprise. She would leave him a note and let him decide. Her heels clattered against the stone steps as she approached the door. A mailbox was affixed to a column next to the door and the names of the tenants were written on masking tape. Syversten. Holder. Westervelt. This last name seemed to be more vivid than the others, and Caitlin lifted the tape up to see what was beneath it. Rose. He had already moved on.

Now, the sky was beginning to brighten. The sun edged past a mountain of yellowish clouds and the bright ribbon of gold around the cloud was light's pure nectar.

"It's like a Rembrandt up there," the boy said.

"Maybe we'll have luck with the weather after all," said

Caitlin, taking his arm. She felt an abrupt jolt of sadness, as if she were in a car hitting a hole in the street.

"What's wrong, Mom?"

"Nothing. Why?"

"You . . . I don't know. The look on your face." The observation might have been born of sympathy but it was communicated testily; he experienced the bond between them and rejected it in the same breath.

And Caitlin was suddenly tempted to tell him more of the truth of her life than ever before. What goaded her? Was it the otherworldly edge of electricity around that mammoth cloud? The sudden mutability of time that traveling great distances suggests? Or this sullen, watery city, containing somewhere in its vast mesh the microbes of her ancestry?

"There's just a sadness in life," Caitlin finally said. "When you get to my age, you'll understand." She closed her eyes, wishing she hadn't said it. Hearing these middle-aged platitudes come from her own mouth shocked her more than catching her reflection in the mirror unawares.

But her son let it pass, apparently too bored to be offended.

"What are you going to do if we ever find this place?" he asked her.

"Anne Frank House? Go in, say hello."

"Say hello? Like, hello everybody?"

"Don't be a wise guy. Let them know we've arrived. They probably have a registration period and all kinds of information. And I think I'd like to see the house, too. Her room. Wouldn't you?"

"I've read the book, seen the play, and the movie. I think I've had enough of it."

"Well then, what were you planning to do?"

"I don't know. Wander around and see what happens. Is that OK?"

Caitlin shrugged, patted the boy's hand. An iron railing

bordered the canal; they were just then passing a cluster of houseboats, a floating shantytown. A dark-haired woman wearing trousers and a loose-fitting tank top was throwing water from a blue plastic bucket over the side of a houseboat. There was something about the angularity of her body and the whiteness of her skin and something else, something less definable about the rhythms of her gestures, that evoked Betty for a moment—just a moment, but it plunged in and out of Caitlin's heart like a blade of light.

"I thought we would spend some time together here," she said. She heard her voice as reasonable, kindly.

"We will, of course we will." He smiled. He made it so clear that charm was really a form of evasion. "But my room-mate gave me all these tips, places to go, and I'd like to check some of them out."

"Then where will we meet?"

"And there's a Roy Lichtenstein show at the big museum here, whatever it's called," he went on, ignoring her question, the proposed rendezvous.

He's giving me the shake, thought Caitlin. "The one who makes the cartoon paintings?" she asked.

"'I'd rather drown than call Brad for help,'" her son said in a falsetto, holding up his hand and assuming the look of someone going down for the third time. "Do you know that one?"

Caitlin shrugged. He felt culturally superior to her, but she no more begrudged than believed it.

"If you want, I'll stay with you," her son said.

"No, you have fun," she said, in an exaggerated tragic voice, making fun of mothers who heap guilt upon their children and, in that fissure between the emotion and its bur-lesque, staking her own emotional claim: she wouldn't have minded if he *did* feel a bit of guilt.

"We can meet in this place called the Vondel Bar," he said.

His voice sounded uneasy, a clumsy con man. "It's on the Leidseplein."

"Oh, the Leidseplein. That makes it easy," Caitlin said.

"Well, if I can find it you can, too." He rocked back on his heels, looking plaintive.

"Ah," said Caitlin. "The Prinsengracht. At last."

"Are you sure it's OK? Me not coming along?"

"It's fine, sweetie. Really, I never expected."

Caitlin turned away. Sweetie? She had never called him that, or anyone else. It was Betty's word, her voice, coming through for a moment, the rattle of a train over weedy tracks abandoned for years.

They kissed goodbye. His kiss was boyish, wet, dear. And then he was off. He seemed to know exactly where he was going. She watched him as he walked; he had his father's determined gait, that odd, truculent bounce, the walk of an angry man made a touch ridiculous by broken pavement. He did not once look back.

Caitlin found the Anne Frank House, an ordinary house in this city of ancient domesticity. Near the house, an old man in a blue knee-length jacket and wool cap was painting tar on the trunk of an old bare tree. Caitlin saw her father's dour Dutch expression on the man's face but she suspected she was forcing it, too much has happened, too much lost; she was trying to find her reflection in a mirror over which time had cast an impenetrable shadow.

The Anne Frank House was filled with visitors. There were schoolchildren, excited, pushing the limits of the discipline their well-meaning teachers could enforce. There were a few Africans in robes, immense, obsidian, bejeweled. Japanese, Indonesians, a scruffy Canadian couple with maple leaves embroidered on their backpacks. The heat of all those bodies. Caitlin flexed her fingers, thawed.

There was a long line in front of the ticket window. It cost six guilders to get in, a dollar fifty. She waited with the others, and when she reached the window she told the young dark woman selling tickets that she had come for the conference. Caitlin spoke very slowly, hoping the girl's English was good.

"Then you must go to over there," the woman said, with a smile. She had a gold tooth like a Gypsy. She was pointing across the crowded room, once the living quarters for the extraordinary Dutch family who hid the Franks during the terror and now a white room filled with photographs of Hitler, street rallies, war, the camps.

Caitlin stood on her toes to see over the crowd; there was a door with a sign in Dutch on it.

"There?"

"Yes, you must ask for Margot Spijkers."

Caitlin walked across the lobby. In the next room there were fifty or so people looking at photographs in an exhibition called "The Rise of Extremism Today." The narrow staircase leading up to the rooms where the Frank family hid was jammed with people, holding orange admission tickets, talking to each other.

Caitlin knocked on the door and was let in by a young, large-faced woman with pale, almost denatured frizzy hair the color of fallen leaves. This was Margot Spijkers, sallow, slow-moving, who even if she were standing in a stark, empty room would always seem to be peering out from behind something. They introduced themselves, Caitlin told Margot she had arrived for the conference, Margot welcomed her, and then pointed to a desk upon which a high, unstable stack of papers seemed ready at any moment to slide onto the floor. In the middle of the clutter was a rather foreign-looking telephone— it looked more like an obsolete piece of medical equipment— with the receiver out of the cradle. "I am only just now talking to my boyfriend," explained Margot. She had an odd, delicate voice; she was one of those people who didn't mind not being heard.

The office was small, damp, with a virtuous gray chill in the air. There was a poster from Indonesia, presumably to save on heating costs through the power of suggestion.

Caitlin sat in a swivel chair near a metal desk, which was empty of all papers and had on it only a teacup with delicate blue flowers on the outside and dark amber tea stains on the inside. Margot was, with obvious strain and unhappiness, speaking to her boyfriend. There were occasional bits of English, like *OK*, or *movie, Rolling Stones*, and *collect call*.

Then, quite abruptly, Margot hung up and for a moment just stood there, staring at the phone and composing herself.

"I'm sorry," she said to Caitlin.

"I could have waited outside, you know," Caitlin said. Now that the girl was facing her and she saw the flush in her cheeks, the dark blue eyes, the broad, earnest mouth, Caitlin liked her enormously, and in one of those leaps of feeling that feel for a moment like premonition, she imagined introducing Margot to her son—they fall in love, marry, insist that she spend at least half the year with them in their houseboat on a canal.

"My boyfriend is my great problem of life," said Margot, with no apparent intent to be humorous. "And working here, it makes it seem very small."

"It's none of my business," Caitlin said. It came out sounding wrong; she hadn't meant to express impatience, only benign disinterest. And Margot was, at first, taken aback. She tilted her head to the left as if to see Caitlin from the other side of the barrier between them. But then Caitlin smiled, made a self-deprecating gesture—a small shrug with the hands held near the heart—and Margot relaxed, sensed this middle-aged American lady as a friendly presence.

"Would you care to see the house?" Margot asked. "I can take you up the private staircase and save you the long queue."

At the top of the narrow, dignified house, where on July 6, 1942, Otto Frank and his wife and daughters went into hiding, everything was as it was during the Occupation—all that was missing was the dirt and stench of people living in terror. Today, the chilly bare rooms, with their low ceilings and slanted walls, were filled with both pilgrims and tourists. It seemed, really, there were too many people on the old, bare wooden floors, and the fear went through Caitlin like a gust of leaves that this house was cursed, doomed, and that at any moment the floor might give way and they would all plunge through it, down through the well of the house, drawn faster and faster by the ravenous silt upon which it rested.

Margot showed Caitlin around, giving no evidence of boredom, of having seen these preserved rooms a thousand times before. She brought Caitlin to a window from which they saw an old tree that Margot named in Dutch and that looked to Caitlin to be a pin oak.

"This is the tree Anne looked at," Margot said.

"And over there," Margot continued, "is the church whose bell rang the time every quarter hour. The Westertoren clock. It used to make Anne's parents terribly nervous. They simply did not like it, day and night. But Anne loved it. Did you read the diaries?"

"Yes, I did," said Caitlin. "But some years ago."

"She said she loved the clock most especially in the night," said Margot. "'It is like a faithful friend.'"

And as she said it, the clock in the Westerkerk began to toll. A few of the other visitors turned toward the sound; a nun with a dozen ten-year-olds in tow was reminded that it was time to go, and she began herding the children out of the room.

"I am named Margot in honor of Anne's sister," Margot said to Caitlin, as she led her out of the common family room, into a smaller room where the walls were pocked and cracked and covered with old pictures of movie actors and actresses. "My mother did not want to call me Anne. It would have been impertinent. But her older sister, Margot—that we could do, at least."

"Many times," Caitlin managed to say, though now what had begun as a wordless anxiety was becoming a very specific and demanding dread: You must get out of here, it said to her. "Many times children with committed parents decide to reject all of those things."

"Yes, I have seen that, too," Margot said. "My sister is like that."

Caitlin nodded. She imagined Margot as a girl older than her years, sexually shy, dutiful, somewhat disdainful of her irresponsible, hedonistic contemporaries. She guessed that her own son would prefer the sister.

"This was Anne Frank's room," Caitlin said.

"Yes," said Margot. "It was so bare. She put the postcards and her film-star collection up with paste."

"Yes, I know."

"She wanted always to make things more beautiful," said Margot.

"She was just a child," Caitlin said. She had meant to say it as a way of putting those old, innocent pieces of decoration into some kind of manageable perspective, to somehow denude them of their awful, awful pathos, and she had meant as well to place herself slightly above the experience of being in this room, and to distance herself from what she perceived as Margot's wish to sentimentalize the pictures.

"Just a child," she repeated, driving the point deeper—but her own heart broke like an egg, with a terrible, almost unsavory ooze of emotion. Her throat closed as if to suppress a cry, and Caitlin covered her eyes with her hand. She had not meant to say that, after all, had not meant to allow herself to be invaded by the pity and anger she felt now. This girl, this child: destroyed. Where was the world? Where was justice? Where was God?

"Are you all right?" Margot asked, touching Caitlin's elbow gently.

This act of solicitude was finally too much. Like a stranger who has been stalking her, hiding behind this linden, that pine, Caitlin's grief leapt out, wild-eyed, fatal, and seized her. She felt it clutch at her heart. And her blood, as if in flight from grief's fierce grip, rushed to her face. She was scalding from the inside out. It felt as much like some rapturous humiliation as it did like sorrow. She thought of Anne Frank, of Betty, of her son and his anxiousness to be away from her, of her own life running down like a top someone has sent spinning and then left, and she thought of that house on Von Eghenstraat with the scarlet shutters, the ever-changing names taped to the mailbox.

"Shhh," said Margot. "It's OK, it's *goot.* You are not the first, not the only one." She had her arm around Caitlin. Caitlin wanted to stop crying but she was too tired to control herself entirely, the blow was too sudden, too hard. Those pictures, the sad gray light coming through the annex windows, the calm faces of the tourists, and the ghosts everywhere. There are days when you miss everyone you've ever known, ever loved, ever lost.

Margot led Caitlin down the plunging, vertiginous staircase and back to the offices. Caitlin had stopped crying. Margot sat her down in the swivel chair and poured a cup of coffee. It was tepid but good. "Many come here to weep," Margot said, as she watched Caitlin drink.

"I didn't . . ." Caitlin stopped herself. "I don't know why I came here. I mean here, to Amsterdam. I thought I might see someone."

"Family? You are Dutch, yes?"

"Yes, partly. But I have no family here." She hesitated again, and though her habits of privacy were as much a part of who she was as the scent of her scalp, the timbre of her voice, she felt suddenly that this girl, Margot, was someone in whom she might at least begin to confide. Caitlin had no idea what had brought her to this moment. Was it the large, forgiving, sorrowful eyes of the girl, the weight of the coffee cup in her own hand, or had travel and exhaustion allowed her to slip from the tether of habit?

"For me the war was two people," Caitlin said to Margot. "One of them was murdered. She didn't understand what the war was about, though she was intelligent. She was from a certain time and place. And I cared for her a great deal."

"Oh, I'm sorry," Margot said. Unlike most people her age, Margot seemed to understand that twenty-six years is not very long, the gap between the then and the now can be spanned by just one of sorrow's cold fingers.

"I don't know why I'm going on like this. It's just been on my mind."

"Did they catch the murderer?"

"I looked for him, with a friend. A dear friend. The man was never brought to justice. He was trying to stop a congressman from making certain statements, statements that might have exposed a great deal of German influence in the government at the time."

"In the American government?"

"Yes. The congressman was on a plane to Windsor County—that's where he was from. And my good friend, who was with him, who worked for him, was killed, too. A bomb. There were nineteen others on the plane, all killed."

"What happened to the man, the murderer?"

"Disappeared. And you see, my other friend, the friend that I thought I might see here, he has spent many years looking for this murderer. But of course he will never find him." Caitlin sipped her coffee. It was quite cold now and it had gotten sweeter. "I have to go. I'm traveling with my son and I said I would meet him. What time is it?"

"Almost twelve in the noon," said Margot. She said it without consulting a clock.

"I'm supposed to meet him at a place called the Vondel Bar. Is it far?"

"It's on the Leidseplein."

"Yes, he said that. I like to walk. New York is a walking city. And before . . . I've walked all my life. It helps me think. Is it very far?"

"You could walk but it would take you a long time," said Margot. "It will only be a few guilders in a taxi."

"Do you know this bar?"

"Yes," said Margot, coloring slightly.

"It has a bad reputation, doesn't it."

Margot shrugged. "For now it is for the hippies. But before, during the Occupation, it was a Resistance bar."

Caitlin left soon after, with a packet of information about the conference folded over and stuck into her large black pocketbook. There was a taxi, a tan Mercedes, in front of Anne Frank House, and she got in, told the driver to take her to the Leidseplein and he pulled away without any questions.

She settled back in the cab and watched the houses and the canals go by. The sun was out now and the light mixed with the heavy air to make a color like water in a slightly dirty glass.

She rolled the window down and let the wind blow on her face, let it muss her hair. Holland, she said to herself. And then an ancient voice within her added: I'm free. I'm free.

The Vondel Bar was on a square, with a symphony hall on one side, and bars, Dutch and Indonesian restaurants everywhere else. In the middle, trolley cars were pulling in and out. In the warm months the Vondel Bar put chairs outside but now the patio was bare except for a thick length of rolled-up tarpaulin.

Caitlin opened the door and walked in, feeling, as she had all her life upon entering a new place, that someone might come up to her and challenge her right to be there. She adopted what she had come to think of as her Fuck You walk:

shoulders back, bosom forward, her eyes moving from side to side as if she were searching for someone far more important than the nobodies who might be judging her.

The bar smelled of beer, cognac, cigarettes, and wet wool. It was just the outer edge of afternoon and they were drinking as if it were late evening. The bartender was a large man with hair as pale as Chablis and small blue eyes in a strong, secretive face. He said something to her in Dutch and Caitlin answered, "I'm here to meet my son."

She found a table along the wall, near the billiard table, which at this time was covered with a plank of plywood and a tablecloth and was being used by a large party of friends who were smoking cigarettes and drinking beer. They wore turtleneck sweaters and berets, and many of them had books next to their drinks, though to Caitlin they looked too old to be students.

She saw her son near the back of the café. He sat with an older fellow, dark-haired, bearded, with the look of someone routinely questioned by the police, someone clever enough to keep out of jail but not out of trouble. Also seated with her son was a long-faced woman who was combing her red hair with her fingers. She wore a bright turquoise Chinese jacket and chewed her lip as the bearded man said something to Caitlin's son that made him laugh. They were doing nothing more than that, but the thought that Caitlin had was: This has something to do with drugs.

She thought of her son. She wondered why he took drugs, why he was alone, why he needed a woman to hold him in bed but not to make love to, why he floated above his own life like dust—dust kicked up by a parade that has long since passed. I have failed him, she thought to herself.

And as she had this thought, her son looked across the bar and saw her. His face lit up with surprise and what looked like, at least from a distance, pleasure. He said something to his companions, stood up, and then reached down for his glass of beer, finished it. He shook the man's hand, bowed slightly to the woman, who might very well have been blind for all her reaction, and then he walked quickly across the crowded, smoky, noisy café and joined his mother.

"What did you come to this place for?" she asked him, as soon as he was seated.

"Do you want a Heineken?" he asked. "They make it about a mile away from here." And then, before she could answer, he leaned close to her, took her hand easily, lovingly, in a way that he had not been able to for some years.

"Do you know this place used to be a hangout during the Hitler days, I mean for Resistance people, who'd come here and plot against the Germans?"

"Yes, I heard that," Caitlin said.

"They were telling me . . . " her son said, indicating the table he had just left. "I don't know." He hesitated and his face looked soft, his green eyes not quite so clever, not quite so evasive. "It just made me feel so proud of you, it really did."

She put her hand on his shoulder, brushed her fingers against his heavy, unwashed hair.

"I don't want to take all your time," Caitlin said. "I know you have things you like to do. But while we're here I'd like to talk to you about something."

"Yeah?"

He looked at her questioningly, a little mistrustfully. It did not seem to him that this was necessarily a conversation he would want to have.

Caitlin felt a will to retreat, an impulse to just let it drop. But she forced herself to say it, as best she could.

"It's just you're all I have, you know, and if you're interested I'd like to tell you about my life."

ELEVEN

DECEMBER 5, 1948

"I don't know what the hell you call this dish," Caitlin said, bringing to the table the cast-iron skillet she had inherited from Joe. "It's rice and chopped sirloin and green peppers and I think it smells a lot better than it's going to taste."

It was night and it was cold. The wind shook the icy windows in their frames. Caitlin was serving dinner to Gordon, who came to eat once every two weeks now. For a while he had been telling her that he loved her, that they must marry, but she had worn him out on that subject without hurting his huge mass of unformed feelings.

Gordon waved the rising steam from the skillet toward his face and breathed in deeply. He was wearing a dark blue suit, a white shirt, like a well-mannered cop. He had not gotten soft, but he had thickened in the last year. There were pouches beneath his eyes, broken capillaries on his nose. He'd often said he didn't trust men who did not show their age. He said such men were clearly not paying attention.

"Mmmm," he said.

"It looks disgusting," Caitlin said, serving it up with a spatula.

"Food is the hardest thing to photograph. It's not really all that visual—it's about smell and warmth, and being hungry."

"Well, then, I hope you're hungry."

"Starved—though I really shouldn't say that, not with all the people in the world truly starving to death." He patted his stomach, smiled shyly.

"Do you want some wine with this?" she asked. They ate in the small dining alcove; she was turning off the overhead light, putting a wooden match to the candles.

"No—well, maybe a little."

"Good. This sweet little man gave me a bottle of Chianti at the office today. A shoemaker, in exile from Italy since '32 but so homesick now I think he'll go back." She went to the kitchen, came back with the bottle and a corkscrew, and handed them to Gordon. She always at least tried to make allowances for male vanity.

"A left-winger?" asked Gordon.

"I guess so."

"Well, he must have been pretty disgusted with how few votes Henry Wallace got this election." He pulled the cork out of the Chianti and smiled with some satisfaction. He poured some in Caitlin's glass and then a little in his, and then a little more.

"Yeah," said Caitlin. "It's all he thinks about."

The irony eluded Gordon as he brought the food to his mouth; it was very hot and his eyes glazed with tears, but he tried to hide his reaction, feeling that gluttony had done him in again.

"Can you imagine?" Gordon said. "Truman drops the atomic bomb and all's forgiven. This country. Red scares all around. Strom Thurmond's Dixiecrat party got more votes than Wallace and the whole Progressive party." He shook his head, took another forkful of dinner but was careful to blow on it this time.

"The thing that struck me," Caitlin said, "is they're all, I don't know, *hicks*. The CP might have been for Wallace, but, let's face it, the man was secretary of agriculture and lived with hens and hogs. Truman's from some backward little place in Missouri, and Thurmond's one of these old Southern bourbon-and-branch-water types. And Dewey, too. He's from up where I was raised. I want to vote for someone who lives in a penthouse and has a subscription to the opera."

Gordon laughed, took a swallow of wine, filled his glass again, this time to the very top. "You know who you sound like? Joe." He said the name with a downward thrust of his hands.

"Joe," she said, shaking her head, to warn Gordon away from the subject.

"His cynical sense of humor."

"I never thought of him as cynical."

"I'm sorry," Gordon said, "I didn't mean for you to take offense."

"I'm not taking offense. I just never thought of him as cynical."

Gordon rested his fork against the side of the peach-and-white bowl. "I got a letter from him—"

"I know, Gordon. Six months ago. Postmarked San Francisco, and he's working for the *Chronicle*."

"I forgot I told you."

"Forgot you told me? All we do is talk about Joe. Joe, Joe at the magazine, Joe's book, Joe in the Army, Joe gets a job, Joe loses a job, Joe and the infected hand, Joe gets better. I don't know. Have we gone into Joe gets a haircut?"

"Well," said Gordon, weakly, "he *did* introduce us." But the notion of his and Caitlin's relationship as central and Joe being only fifth business struck them both as absurd, pitiful.

It was Joe's name she had affixed to her own to save herself the public stigma of being an unmarried woman with a bastard child. It was Gordon who was peripheral and he knew it. He was having dinner with Mrs. Caitlin Rose.

She loved that name.

Gordon grabbed the wine glass so quickly a bit of the wine sloshed out on his white cuff.

"How's your mother?" he asked, once he was calm again.

"Lonely. Not doing so well. Waiting to die, I guess."

"How does she like being a grandmother?"

"She seems completely unaware of him. She holds him for a second and then hands him right back to me. And she sniffs when she does, as if he smells bad."

"Well, you know babies."

"He doesn't smell bad. He's not that sort of baby." She knew this sounded silly and she smiled, but maintained the point. "Really. He's not."

"Oh, I'm sure. After all, he must smell like a rose."

Dinner was accomplished; Gordon helped Caitlin clear and then waited in the living room, smoking and thinking and jiggling his leg, while Caitlin washed the dishes.

She came in holding a tray with a percolator full of coffee, a plate of Lorna Doone cookies, and two coffee mugs. She glanced over Gordon, toward the slightly open door to the bedroom where her son slept. She heard a sound, a loose, phlegmy cough, the rattle of the crib's side as he turned in his sleep.

"You like packaged cookies, don't you?" she said, as she sat in the velvet easy chair across from Gordon.

Gordon reached for one, bit it in half, dusted the shortbread crumbs from his lapel.

"I finally got that family out of Greece today," Caitlin said.

But Gordon did not hear her because at the same time he was finally saying something he had been trying to get out for a few months. "I've met someone," he said. "Her name is Arlene Zeiring, she's a schoolteacher. She lives—" He pointed nervously at the iced-over window, behind which the blur of a street lamp hovered like an angel. "Not far from here, actually. On Waverly, with her sister. Her sister is very political, but Arlene isn't. Oh, I mean she wants all the right things, but she isn't what you could call a committed person." He shrugged and looked at Caitlin, giving her permission to criticize this woman.

"I'm sure you're committed enough for two, Gordon," Caitlin said.

He smiled. His face was scarlet but his eyes looked grateful. "That's what I think," he said. He seemed relieved she had seen it his way and deflated that she was so willing to let him go. "Anyhow," he said and then fell silent.

"Would you like some coffee, Gordon?"

He shook his head, shifted in his seat, but did not get up—not yet. "I sort of told her I would drop by for a visit, after we had dinner."

"That's OK, Gordon," said Caitlin. And truly, she was glad. Gordon pined for Joe, longed for him, his real emotional range was as a best friend, not a husband. But he deserved every happiness. "You sure you wouldn't like a cup of coffee to keep you warm for the walk over there? Waverly Place can seem a far distance on a winter night."

"Oh, Caitlin." His eyes blazed with tears.

She smiled warmly at him, but the truth was she was a bit irritated. There was nothing in their relationship, as far as she was concerned, that warranted this sort of emotional farewell. She felt abandoned, brittle, and she knew it was an awful thing to think, but she suspected Gordon was using the occasion of his announcement to give her the baleful looks he would not dare indulge normally, like those men who use the occasion of weddings or funerals to choke you with the slobbering kisses they have the sense, any other time, to keep to themselves.

"You know if I'd had my druthers," he said, standing up—to take her in his arms?

"Gordie," she said, lightly. "Shame on you. I'm a mother."

"He should have married you," Gordon said, solemnly.

"As far as the world is concerned, he did. And I certainly don't intend to give them any more reason to doubt it than they already do, seeing me living alone all these years. As far as my landlord and the people at work are concerned, I am a poor, deserted wife, bravely raising her son alone." She clutched her breast, batted her eyes, like somebody in the worst movie.

"Why don't you come over with me, Catey?" Gordon said. "I'd like you to meet Arlene and she's heard a lot about you."

"Are you crazy or something? You want me to come courting with you? And sit there while you drool over her?" She couldn't believe or understand what she had just blurted out. She covered her mouth with two fingers and whispered. "I have to be careful with the restless one in there. I think he hears everything. I think he's a spy."

When Gordon left for the schoolteacher's house, Caitlin poured his coffee and hers back into the pot and put it on the gas stove to warm up again. She recognized this as one of the habits of solitude, like drinking milk out of the bottle, or carrying her reading glasses in an envelope after the leather case for them was lost, but loneliness seemed no longer to hold any special terrors for her. It turned out that her greatest fear had always been to live and die in Leyden, and now that she was securely out of there, nothing else held any real power over her—not the fear of a thousand nights alone in her bed, nor the fear of poverty, of growing old and sick alone. She was conscious that her most fervent dream had come true, and she accepted that in life, if we are lucky enough to get what we most desire, we must accept that other comforts might not come our way.

The percolator sent up fragrant steam through its spout and Caitlin turned off the gas, poured the hot coffee into her cup. Holding it, she walked into the room where her son was sleeping.

The boy had been born on June 2, 1946, the day the Italians voted to abolish the monarchy, and since the doctor who delivered the child was Italian, Caitlin had been tempted to give her son a sort of Italian name, like Anthony, or perhaps a middle name like Ignazio, after Silone, whose *Bread and Wine* was one of the few novels Joe had ever read. But finally it had seemed too complicated, too fancy, and she settled on something plain. Ever since, however, she had made up for the last-minute conservative impulse—which she now thought of as a kind of degrading deathbed conversion—and the boy had gone through an uninterrupted stream of extravagant nicknames, beginning with Thor, continuing with Juan Domingo, Chou En-lai, Junior, Tennessee, and now Ardo, which was how he pronounced *olive*, his favorite food.

Ardo had thrown his toys out of his crib. Caitlin saw them in the dim light—the child could not sleep in darkness yet—and she picked them up, arranged them around him so they would look entertaining when he awakened and perhaps occupy him for a few extra minutes while Caitlin slept.

She kissed her fingertips and then pressed them to Ardo's head. He sweated when he slept, profusely and coldly; he felt like a rock in a cave.

She walked slowly back to the living room and sat with her coffee, reading through a file she had brought home from work that day. There were still requests for entry coming in from Jews, some of them bearing postmarks from China, India, Cuba, Palestine, though with so few Jews left alive and with so many of the survivors focused on a Jewish state, the bulk of the requests for help came from a new kind of immigrant. In fact, the Combined Emergency European Relief Committee was at war with itself over the would-be immigrants who now held out their beseeching hands from such places as Yugoslavia. It seemed that many of these people had been Nazi sympathizers during the war, and now that their countries had been dealt to the Soviets they feared reprisals. If the committee wanted to stick to the original spirit of their charter, they would help these refugees, too, no matter how unsavory their politics. But Mr. Lehman and most of the others chose instead to more or less ignore their cases. Caitlin was basically in sympathy with this position, but she was the only one who went over those politically questionable requests with any care: you never knew if someone decent might be inadvertently lumped with the collaborationists seeking asylum.

Suddenly, she heard the rattle of what sounded like hailstones against the window. She leaned back in the chair, felt the thick fabric beneath her palm, closed her eyes. The noise against the window repeated, more insistent this time, and she realized it was not hail at all, but someone throwing stones.

She went to the window and pressed her hand against the ice until she could see through.

And there was Joe, standing under the street lamp. He saw the oval of her face through the patch of defrosted glass and he waved his hand over his head, a child at the edge of the train tracks flagging down the enchanted engineer. He wore a black overcoat, a fedora; he had a small mustache.

She hurried down to the entrance to let him in. As she ran down the stairs, she did her best to discover exactly what it was she was feeling at that moment, but all she could find was a kind of frantic, rattled excitement that had as much in common with nervousness as it did with happiness.

Joe was waiting for her. She opened the door to him; the night, like a crowd of panicky refugees, rushed in.

"I don't have a key," he said. He hugged himself and shivered.

"Was that you throwing stones?"

"It's so late. I didn't want to wake . . . the baby." His voice was gentle, shy, rather hurt, the voice of an outsider who accepts the terms of his exile.

She stepped back, looked him over. It had been more than three years since she'd seen him but he seemed to have aged more than that. There was nothing boyish in him. His skin was a little loose and the pallor came from months of indoor work—not even the December night had brought color to his cheeks. The mustache made him older, too. It drew his face down in a kind of sorrowful scowl.

"Joe," she said, "I didn't even know you were in New York."

"I've found John Coleman," he said. "At least I think I have. Can I come up?"

"I was just having some coffee," she said.

As they climbed the stairs, Caitlin resolved to tell Joe he could stop sending money to her—those checks for ten or twenty dollars that arrived now and then, sometimes with a note that said, How is he?, sometimes just folded into a small blank piece of paper, the emptiness amounting to a withering eloquence. Now that he was here, she realized that having the child, or keeping it, was her idea, and so her responsibility. Perhaps even that time in bed on the day the war ended was more her doing than his: she had taken him in hand and placed him directly inside of her, with the sacred deliberation of a farmer planting the last seed.

Joe looked around the apartment. Nothing in his face to betray that these rooms had once been his own. He was a stranger here and perhaps a stranger everywhere. He sat with his overcoat unbuttoned but still on while Caitlin hurried to the kitchen to pour the rest of her coffee back into the pot and reheat it. He peered toward the partially opened bedroom door but didn't get up to look in, nor did he ask after the child who was sleeping there.

"So tell me about John Coleman," Caitlin said, bringing

the coffee in along with a plate of those Lorna Doone cookies. It was perfectly all right for him to talk about John Coleman before even seeing the child, or talking about anything more personal.

"Well," he said, "I think he's in New York. And I think he's a cop now, working on what they call the Red Squad, doing undercover work, spying on radicals, disloyal professors, that sort of thing. He lives in Brooklyn. Married, two kids. And his name now is John Donnelly. Someone has gotten him new identity cards, an honorable discharge, the works."

"Can you prove he put the bomb on the plane?"

"I think I can. And more besides. Train derailment. Passing secrets to the enemy. He's a regular Kate Smith now, of course."

"Fat?"

"Patriotic. God bless America, that sort of thing. But let's not talk about it now. Not now."

"It would be great if you could get him, Joe," Caitlin said.

Joe nodded, relaxed a little, and the slight withdrawal of tension made him seem more exhausted. He took a long drink of his coffee; when he put the cup down, his mustache was dripping like a dog climbing out of a pond.

"Very distinguished," Caitlin said. And when Joe cocked his head as if to say What? she added, "Your mustache. It's new to me."

"Oh, this," he said, wiping it off with his fingers. "I grew it when I went for the job at the *Chronicle*."

"So. How's life in Frisco?"

"They hate it out there when people call it Frisco."

"Sorry."

"It doesn't make any difference to me. Just a point of local pride."

"The first person from San Francisco I ever met was Jamey Fleming's Uncle Roscoe. He had white, white hair, and he was on his way to Europe to see this Hungarian man about a patent for a pen, or something. I can't remember right now. But he had this great braying voice, like a rich donkey, and here's how he described the Hungarian: 'He's as queer as Dick's hatband.'" Caitlin delivered this in a loud, deep voice and then laughed. Yet even as she laughed she wondered why she told this story, if she wanted to prod Joe in some way.

And Joe did seem faintly uncomfortable, though he hid it by smiling and looking puzzled.

A silence settled over the room, but it did not make them nervous. It was a comforting silence; it seemed to tell them they were all right now, that this room wanted to be their shelter.

"It's so good to see you again, Joe," Caitlin finally said. She felt her heart pounding as if she had said much, much more.

"Thank you," he said, and then laughed because it was an odd thing to say.

"Where are you staying. With friends?"

"Midtown, at the Hotel McAlpin," he said.

"In a hotel? Why are you wasting your money? Or is the newspaper paying for you?"

"No, no. I don't work at the *Chronicle* anymore. I didn't much care for San Francisco." He paused. "I wanted to come back to New York. I had the tip about Coleman. And I wanted to see you."

"Are you going to stay here until you find him?"

"I thought I'd go to Europe. Maybe Paris. I liked it in Paris an awful lot. It's not any of that Lost Generation bullshit. I could really work there, is what I think."

"Oh. I could never live away."

"Why not? There's plenty of better places."

"I don't know. This is my home."

"This country?"

"Yes, it's my home."

"Well, it's not mine. This country doesn't want people like me in it."

"What's so bad about you?"

"I'm just not . . ." He made a fist and shook it, like a college boy at the big game.

"You can stay with us, you know," said Caitlin. "It is your apartment, in a way."

"No, it's not," said Joe. His eyes seemed to fill and come forward for a moment, but then they were distant again. "Are you with somebody yet?"

I'm with you, is what she thought, but all she said was "No."

"Kind of a waste, isn't it?"

"How long have you been in New York?" she asked, steeling herself to look neutral no matter what he said, even if he confessed to having been in town for days, weeks, without coming to see her and the child.

"I took the Twentieth Century. Today. I mean I got here today."

"Joe."

"What?"

"Nothing. Just . . . Joe."

Caitlin took his hand and fervently he brought her hand to his lips and kissed it, once, again, and again.

She laughed.

"I'm being ridiculous, aren't I?" he said.

"No. I just never had my hand kissed before. It's strange. Feel." She lifted his hand and bowed over it as if looking for her reflection in a pond. She placed a kiss on the back of his hand. His skin smelled of tobacco and the night. And when she looked up at him he had leaned far back in his chair and had raised his other hand and covered his eyes.

"It feels good to be with you again," he said. His voice was soft, unstable.

Caitlin held on to his hand and leaned forward, to be

closer to him. She felt the way you do in a house when a loose shutter finally stops banging.

"Do you want to see Ardo?" she asked. It made her light-headed with happiness to be finally asking this question of Joe.

"Ardo?"

"That's his nickname. This week anyhow."

"I don't get it."

"It's what he calls olives."

"As in 'What are doze?' "

Caitlin laughed. She hadn't thought of that one. It was the difference between one mind and two. "No," she said. "I don't think so. It's just what he calls them."

They were silent for a few moments and then Joe said, "Does he look like me?"

Caitlin stood up and held her hand out to Joe, the hand he had pressed with his lips. She led him into the bedroom, where the crib was, as well as Caitlin's bed.

The boy was awake. He had thrown all those carefully arranged toys out of the crib and was sitting up, wearing a pair of pale blue pajamas, watching the reflections of the head-lights of the passing cars skitter across the ceiling. When he saw Caitlin and this stranger come in, he scrambled up and held his arms out to her.

She lifted him up. He felt the warmth of her hands through his pajamas. "What are you doing awake?" she asked, but her voice was pleased.

"I don't know," the child said, looking at the man and then at her.

"Do you want to say hello to your father?" she asked, and what a question, but she hadn't spent what time she had to read going over books about child psychology.

"No," the boy said, his voice a nasal croak.

"Oh God," Joe said, almost sobbing it, and reaching out to take him.

The boy looked at his mother as this dark, melancholy man scooped him into his arms.

"I didn't know myself how I've waited to see you hold him," Caitlin said to Joe.

"Let me stay," said Joe. "We understand each other. We need each other. We can be a family."

"I want you to stay."

"I'll never leave. I must have been crazy, all this time."

Caitlin was silent for a moment. She stood next to Joe, pressed her forehead against his shoulder, reached around him to touch their son.

"Maybe you will leave," she said. "But for now—"

"I'll never leave," said Joe.

"We're very different," she said.

"And very alike."

"That's so. Maybe things work out better for people who are only a little bit different and a little bit alike."

"I can't believe I've been missing all this. Look at him!" He touched the child's chin and then withdrew his hand as the boy smiled.

"Joe, it doesn't matter now. Whatever happens after this. I think you can know, actually *know,* when your life is coming together, when you are in the very best part of it—and for us, at least for me, for me, it's now. I don't know if I can say I completely care what happens after. I'll always have *this.*"

"Will you look at him? He's looking at me, as if he knows who I am."

"Talk to him, Joe."

"Hello there, Ardo," Joe Rose said, trying to be hearty. "I'm home."

He held the child above him, the way men like to, high, up toward the ceiling with its moving shafts of light cast up like calls of hello and farewell by the cars on Barrow Street below, and, as he said, he was home, home from his long moment in history, home for just as long as he could manage to stay, but, in a sense, forever, because now he had claimed this woman and this child as his family.

Caitlin touched Joe's shoulder, to caution him, and to caress him, and the child opened his arms because he had never been held like this. He was flying, the room turned on its side this way and that, the blue of his bed receded and then rushed toward him, and though for a moment it seemed possible that he might howl, he looked at his mother and she cooed reassuringly and she had never looked so beautiful, so mysterious, as she did right then.

And so as it happened he did not cry but reached down toward the magic presence who had come to transform this room, to turn the steady frustration of parallel lines into the contagious chaos of a triangle, the child reached down with his small reddish fingers to touch the dark, smiling, yet ineffably sad male face below, and that child, who would live his life in the afterglow of this moment, that child looking down at his father was me.

DECEMBER 5, 1989

Caitlin had me promise that I would not publish the story of her life while she was still alive and I have, of course, remained faithful to my word, as I have tried to remain faithful to the stories and the legacy she left for me. I often attempted to get her to speak into a tape recorder, but she would have no part of it. It wasn't until she had died (in her sleep, peacefully, with the bedside lamp blazing and her thumb holding her place in the middle of *Travels with My Aunt*) that I realized that, except for me, she had left no trace of her story behind. There were no diaries, no notes, and, as far as I have been able to tell, no letters of any consequence, except the following, which she sent to me in 1970, written in her proper, somewhat overdisciplined script, on the parched, pale-blue skin of an aerogram.

My dear son,

Gordon's heart attack threw a scare into me, too, but his health problems—which really are not as desperate as you and your father fear—have nothing to do with our decision to marry in January. I think what Joe says is right. Gordon with a heart problem is like a giraffe with a sore throat.

I have so wanted someone who would know exactly what I was thinking about when I thought about the war and about all those terrible people like Coughlin, who wanted us to sit on our hands while the Nazis tore the world apart like pulling petals off a flower. I wanted somebody who could know what I know, and know me, too, and the strange path I've taken, and after things didn't work out between your father and me I suppose I let that hope die, or just decided that I had had my moment in the sun.

I would prefer you not to discuss this with your father, though I realize that it is your decision—and with you all the way in Denmark, I wouldn't have any idea what you were saying to each other, anyhow.

Don't misunderstand me. I am glad you have found your father. I was worried when you first told me you intended to look him up. I didn't know if you'd be able to find him and I was even more worried about what you would find him to be. Having lived without him all your life, you must have had quite a few dreams, or unrealistic expectations, and like any common garden-variety mother I was concerned that you would have your hopes dashed—or worse. I frankly did not know if your father would be particularly anxious to have you track him down.

I do think, however, that for you to bring your father with you when you come to the wedding is ridiculous. I know there's been a lot of water over the dam (or is it under the bridge?) but nevertheless I am not prepared to suddenly have Joe back in my life. For the first years of his expatriation I continually expected him to come back—if not to me then at least to America. After all, it was Joe who taught me—well, not taught me, that's not true, but helped me to learn, yes, helped me to learn that we must erase or ignore all the borders—between countries, between people, between parts of ourselves, between the public parts and the secret parts, between the parts we have learned to love and the parts we are trying the best we can to accept. It was the feeling I had on this very day twenty-two years ago when he came to see us smelling of the night, his mustache wet with frost, and though there have been times I felt a little gray and cheated that that moment did not last for very long, I still know that it was the best time of my life. My heart was never so huge and never so happy and everything I felt and everything I was made sense, and in so many ways that clarity has lasted.

I love you and I can hardly wait to see you next month. I feel right now that my life has been on the whole a good one. I have loved and I have known love. I have had a wonderful son, whose presence in the world gives me great joy. And most important of all, I have been a part of my time. Darling, I say this to you knowing you will understand.

A NOTE ON THE TYPE

This book was set in a digitized version of Janson. The hot-metal version of Janson was a recutting made direct from type cast from matrices long thought to have been made by the Dutchman Anton Janson, who was a practicing type founder in Leipzig during the years 1668–1687. However, it has been conclusively demonstrated that these types are actually the work of Nicholas Kis (1650–1702), a Hungarian, who most probably learned his trade from the master Dutch type founder Dirk Voskens. The type is an excellent example of the influential and sturdy Dutch types that prevailed in England up to the time William Caslon (1692–1766) developed his own incomparable designs from them.

Composed by Graphic Composition, Inc., Athens, Georgia
Printed and bound by The Haddon Craftsmen, Inc.,
Scranton, Pennsylvania
Designed by Virginia Tan